PENGUIN BOOKS
FINDING US AGAIN

Francois wanted to be an author since he first learned to read. He returned to his childhood dream after leaving a successful corporate career.

Francois has since authored works of children's fiction, young adult fantasy and romantic fiction. His first series of five children's books were published by Speaking Volumes LLC. He has also had a series of children's books published by Indonesian publisher, PT. Kanisius. The series is named *Seri Hewan Unik* and the books in the series are titled *Rahasia Bunglon, Rahasia Badak* and *Rahasia Bekantan. Finding Us Again* is Francois' third romance novel.

He has participated in a number of literary events in Indonesia including the Ubud Writers and Readers Festival in Ubud, Bali.

Francois is South African and lives in Bali, Indonesia. He divides his time between his family and his writing.

T0096263

Finding Us Again

Francois Keyser

PENGUIN BOOKS

An imprint of Penguin Random House

PENGUIN BOOKS

USA | Canada | UK | Ireland | Australia
New Zealand | India | South Africa | China | Southeast Asia

Penguin Books is part of the Penguin Random House group of companies
whose addresses can be found at global.penguinrandomhouse.com

Published by Penguin Random House SEA Pte Ltd
9, Changi South Street 3, Level 08-01,
Singapore 486361

First published in Penguin Books by Penguin Random House SEA 2023
Copyright © Francois Keyser 2023

10 9 8 7 6 5 4 3 2 1

ISBN 9789815144048

Typeset in Garamond by MAP Systems, Bengaluru, India

www.penguin.sg

Present Day

Bryce

I think we all have times in our life that we remember more vividly than others. Times that we remember for one reason or another. There have been many such times in my life but there is one that stands out more than any other.

Events from then would come back to affect my life many years later. I guess it's to be expected when it wasn't so much a moment in my life as it was a whole year.

My last year of school. The year when kids suffer the agony of finding a date for prom—hopefully with the person they want to go with—and then graduation. For me, it was that as well as the year of my first true love and the breakup that followed. Though the breakup was through no fault of my own.

Much of it I remember fondly and much of it I remember with sadness, and there's much of it that I don't think I have let go of, even after all this time.

I'm no one special. At least not in the context of being a celebrity. I'm just another one of the eight billion people on the planet living my life and getting by.

Even so, I love myself just as I am. I think. There are things I'd like to change but is it my life I'd like to change or myself? I'm not sure. Aren't they the same thing?

There is one thing though I don't think I can change even if I want to. That's letting go of the one woman I know I truly loved. My soulmate.

I don't know where she is now. I made her a promise before we were torn apart. A promise that I would write to her often. Only I don't write to her by e-mail or on a blog or social media. I don't write snail mail either.

Maybe writing to her the way I do is a stupid idea. At the time I believed that if we were meant to be together, she would find my writing. I told her where to look for my writing but honestly, the world is full of hotels and hotels are full of art. Finding the messages I left for her must be like looking for a needle in a haystack.

Sounds complicated right? I guess it is. I was a hopeless romantic when I told her. Maybe that's all it'll ever be, a romantic thought and gesture.

But I did write to her, and I made a note of every place I ever wrote, in the order that I wrote them. I must be crazy thinking she'll find the writing in every place I ever wrote to her, much less in the order I wrote it all.

I look at the stack of notebooks against the wall. The history of what I wrote, where I wrote and when I wrote something for her is contained in those notebooks. I've never stopped. Despite the fact that I leave messages for her behind pictures in hotels, there have been other women since her. None have ever lasted. A long time has passed since we parted ways but still, sometimes I find myself wondering if my first love has affected my ability to love anyone else.

If I don't break up with them, I ruin the relationship. It's almost like I have a reset button when things get too intense. Maybe I subconsciously blow it all up when it gets too serious.

I mean, what would I do if I was married, maybe even had kids and *she* found my writing? What if she called me? What if she never married either and has been searching— all across the country—for my writing? I know it sounds crazy, but I can't help but wonder what it would do to her if I married someone else and moved on, while she devoted herself to finding my writing so she could find me again. How would she feel if that happened?

But then she might have moved on anyway, probably *has* moved on, and I am the fool though I don't know it. A fool for love and a fool of life. My life specifically. Wasted. Dreamed away on a stupid, futile, romantic idea.

I sigh as I randomly pick a picture hanging on the hotel wall.

I remove it from the wall and look at it. It's abstract. A reproduction of an artwork. A print. They're the cheapest to decorate hotels with while still looking classy. I look at the nebula of random colours surrounding what appears to be a sun somewhere in the universe. It's the best way I can describe it.

A waiter passes by on his way to deliver room service for a guest and stops. He recognizes me.

'Can I help you sir?' he asks.

'No, everything's fine, thank you, Harry,' I smile. I'm grateful for his name tag which spares me having to ask his name. I always try to make employees feel important and often it's the little things that go a long way, like using their name. I like Harry's attitude. He exudes happiness and confidence. I feel buoyed by his warmth and cheerful countenance.

'This picture is just interesting, and I wanted to take a closer look.'

'Very well, sir. If I can help with anything, please let me know.'

'I most certainly will, thanks, Harry.'

He nods, turns and continues on his way to deliver the room service order he is carrying. It smells delicious. My stomach growls and I decide I will have lunch as soon as I am finished writing on the back of the picture.

I remove the blackboard marker from my pocket, uncap it and flip the picture over. I begin to write.

On days when I feel like a blind man in the black of the darkest night and adrift in the furthest, darkest place in the universe, just the thought of you makes my day brighter than the light of a thousand suns and a nebula of exploding everlasting joy. Thinking of you. 6043 days . . . My number is still the same . . .

I leave my number with every second message and with every message I add the address of the last place I left a message.

I don't leave my name. Not ever. If she finds my writing, she'll know it's me. She'll know my name when and if she calls. I don't want any crackpots calling and pretending they know me just because I left my name.

It will be easy to sift out the hoaxers with a few questions, but I can't be bothered. Some people call out of curiosity and I get rid of them quickly.

I hang the picture back on the wall and make my way to the dining room.

I don't see Harry return from his room service delivery. He stops at the picture and looks at it curiously. Then he looks around and removes it from the wall. He studies it for a moment and then turns it over. His eyes are immediately drawn to my writing. He reads it a few times, eyebrows raised.

He has no idea who it is for but knows that it is a romantic message for someone. He smiles as he thinks just how romantic my gesture is. He notes the address below my message and recognizes it as another property in the group. He thinks he knows why I have added the address and files it away in his mind for some unknown reason.

Then he returns the picture to the wall and heads back to the dining room.

Harry takes over serving my area and I am very impressed with him. I think he will be more of an asset than just a waiter and we strike up a conversation. He is young, a fresh college graduate who is ambitious and intelligent.

I make a mental note to speak with his manager before I leave. I believe in giving credit where it's due and that means promoting staff who deserve it. I don't believe that people have to reach a certain age before they can be promoted. If they have the skill and the talent, that's what matters.

I finish my lunch and settle the bill before heading to the hotel manager's office. Albert is in his office, and I tell him I have finished my audit. I tell him I will send my report and also give him a heads up on Harry. I don't believe in going over people's heads. It just makes people insecure and resentful. Involving them gives them your support, especially when you give them the credit for your decision.

Before I leave, I record the details of my message in my current notebook and then write up the summary of the details for my report.

I get in my car and leave for the airport. I will be home for a change tonight and I am looking forward to it.

On Monday I will be in another city to audit three hotels. I will leave a message in every hotel.

I am the regional quality manager for a large hotel chain, and I spend most of my time on the road doing audits and mystery shopping.

Nothing's changed since I was a child. I'm amazed at how my life has followed in the footprints of my father. Almost to the letter, with a few exceptions.

Exceptions in the departments of love, romance, marriage and family. I won't do to anyone what my father did to us.

Nora

Love really is blind, I think to myself. At least while it lasts that is . . .

'What the hell is wrong with you?' I ask, finally losing my patience.

'What do you mean?' Jenson asks looking at me with that 'what have I done wrong now?' expression.

I know the look. I loathe it and I loathe Jenson, too. I've seen that look a lot lately. I know why. Because I've become a nag. I've had to, but it's pointless.

I can nag, and *nag, and nag*, and all I get is excuse after excuse after excuse from Jenson. I can say nothing, or I can nag. It doesn't matter. The result is the same.

We've been together for more than a year now and I can't do this anymore. I'm the only one working and we're one step away from being evicted from the dump we call an apartment.

'What have you done about finding a job?'

'I searched the internet today. I checked some job sites. There's nothing that I like,' Jenson whines.

I look at his face and wonder what attracted me to him in the first place. Then I remember.

His cute, pretty-boy face, his cheeky smile, his sense of humour and his 'couldn't care less' attitude . . .

Everything I despise about him now.

'You searched the internet? I'm guessing you found games instead. Why don't you try looking for professional gamer jobs? Oh, wait. I know. Because there *aren't* any!' I say angrily.

'Well actually there are pro gamers who make a lot of money,' Jenson says.

'And you're not one of them. All you do is play games all day, every day. Maybe that's your life but it's not mine. I can't live like this anymore. We are one step away from eviction. Where do we go from here? Do you have *any* idea? Do you even *care*?'

I leave him in the living room holding his gaming console. I'm beginning to think that it's glued to his hands or gradually becoming an appendage of his body.

I enter our bedroom and open the wardrobe. I reach into it and pull out a suitcase. *This ought to do,* I think as I place it on the bed. I unzip it, flip the lid open and begin tossing Jenson's clothes into it.

Jenson enters the bedroom and sees the mess.

'What are you doing?' he asks, sounding offended.

'What does it look like? I'm packing your things,' I reply. 'It's time for you to get out. It's the only way you'll ever learn to stand on your own.'

'Oh, c'mon babe,' Jenson says in his whiny, pleading voice. 'We can work this out. I promise I'll do better.'

'Do better? At what? Your high score?' I ask sarcastically.

'No. I'll really look for a job. I promise.'

'So, in other words, you haven't been looking for a job all this time? You didn't look for one today?'

Jenson realizes his mistake and turns red in the face at being caught in his lie.

'That's exactly my point. I can't live with a liar anymore,' I say. 'Get your shit and get out. Take the TV too if you have to for your games. I don't care.'

'I won't leave,' Jenson says obstinately. 'Just calm down and we'll talk this through. We always do.'

I am about to scream at him when I hear my phone ring. I leave the room and remove it from my bag before it stops ringing. It's my boss, Sherlyn. *Why is she calling me this late?* I wonder.

'Viviane?' she says in her educated accent when I answer. My first name is Nora and my second name is Viviane. After I finished school, I decided to use Viviane instead of Nora. It just sounds so much better to me. That, and the way my name was abused when I was at school, influenced my decision to use Viviane.

'Yes, Sherlyn. Is everything okay?' I ask.

'Everything is just fine. I have some good news for you. It's about the position you applied for as head of housekeeping.'

'Yes?' I reply. My voice trembles with hope and fear simultaneously. I remember applying for the position. It was a while ago though and, having not received a response, I had assumed I was not successful. I cross my fingers and send a quick, silent prayer that Sherlyn has good news for me.

'You didn't get it,' she says.

'Oh . . . okay.' A flood of emotion rises. My heart sinks and I wonder why not getting the job would be good news. It would have been my ticket out of this hell. I look to the bedroom door. I can hear Jenson unpacking the suitcase.

My anger and despair turn on Sherlyn and I wonder why Sherlyn would bother to call me so late on a Friday night to tell me I didn't get the job. In the next instant, she gives me the answer I'm looking for.

'There is another opening that management feels you are better suited for. It's a promotion as well.'

'Really?' I choke out hoping I don't sound distraught. I close my eyes and begin praying. *Anything. Please just get me out of here.*

'It's a regional housekeeping trainer position. It means you will travel a lot and you will train housekeeping staff for the group and ensure that the quality stays above the required standards.'

'That sounds fantastic,' I say. I notice that the sounds of Jenson's movement in the bedroom have ceased. I am sure he is eavesdropping, wondering who I am talking to and about what.

'I take it you're interested then?' Sherlyn says.

'I am. I'll take it,' I say.

Sherlyn seems a bit taken aback considering she hasn't shared all the details yet. 'There is a catch though. They need you to start Monday and they want you on a flight tonight or tomorrow to Chicago. You'll be based there for the foreseeable future. Can you do it? Do you still want the job?'

'I'll be packed and ready by tomorrow morning. Please just send me the ticket and the details,' I tell Sherlyn.

'Okay,' Sherlyn says sounding as if she thinks I am mad to take a job without knowing all the details or even the salary. I'm sure she would understand if she knew my predicament. *Walk a mile in my shoes,* I think before I thank Sherlyn profusely and end the call.

Jenson appears in the doorway of the bedroom. He says nothing but it's obvious he is waiting for me to tell him who I spoke with and why I am over the moon.

I ignore him. My frustration at hearing him unpack his things is gone. I don't need him to leave. I am leaving.

I take in the dingy apartment I have worked so hard to keep for us. Pride, sadness and guilt all hit me at the same time. I know I have done well to keep this place and I am sad to leave, in a way. But I'm happy because I know there is something better for me. My mind shifts into gear, and I think of what needs doing. First things first. I leave the apartment and descend the stairs two at a time to reach the landlord's apartment.

I tell him that I am giving immediate notice of termination of my lease on his apartment. I tell him I am leaving tomorrow, and that Jenson can spend the rest of the month in the apartment since I have already paid, but after that I am not responsible for the rental anymore.

I head back to the apartment where I find Jenson is on the sofa again, game console in hand. When I enter, he drops the console as if it has suddenly become scorching hot and follows me into the kitchen.

'Where did you go?' he asks.

'To speak to the landlord. I gave notice on the apartment. You can stay here for the rest of the month since it's already paid for but after that you're out unless you pay your own way.'

'Wait, what?' Jenson asks, worried.

I prepare sandwiches for us and don't answer immediately as I concentrate on finishing them. Then, I push his sandwich across the counter to him.

'I'm leaving.' I meet his gaze and see the panic in his face.

'You can't leave.' Jenson says as if he really believes I can't go.

'I can, and I am,' I reply. 'I just got a promotion and I have to leave tomorrow. I'm not coming back.'

'Where are you going? I can come with you . . .' He trails off as I hold up my hand and shake my head. I finish chewing before I answer him.

'None of your business and no way in hell.' I finish my sandwich and the milk I poured myself before brushing past him on my way to the bedroom. Jenson unpacked all his clothes but left the suitcase on the bed. Typical. It's okay though since I'll be packing my things now.

Jenson follows me.

'I'm sorry. Please let's talk about this.' I know by the tone in his voice, he senses a finality to our relationship. We have been at this point many times before and somehow, I have always given in and stayed.

'There's nothing to talk about,' I say as I fill the suitcase with my clothes.

'We've been here before many times. We will get through this. Please, think about it. Think about us.'

I finally pause my packing. Breathe in. Breathe out. He always does this. Gets under my skin with one of his remarks and then my resolve unravels. I close my eyes. Breathe in. Breathe out.

My resolve isn't unravelling this time, but his comment has made me angry. I don't want to reply but can't help it.

'Think about us?' I ask scornfully. 'I suppose you're thinking of us when you're playing your blasted video games! Have any high scores helped us? I can't love high scores. I also can't eat them or bank them. I don't even know you anymore!'

'Look, please don't go,' Jenson says. He is pleading, almost begging. 'We can work this out. We always have.'

'Yes, we always have because you've always promised to change but you haven't. You've never tried. All I am to you is a free ride,' I say, meeting his gaze.

'I will change. I promise!' he insists.

I'm done. I can't go on believing that he can or wants to change, even. It's been so long that he has done nothing about finding work. He just plays all day. This time won't be any different.

I shake my head. 'No. We are done. I have already accepted the new position and there's no going back now. If I have to call them and tell them I changed my mind, I may as well join you on the sofa. If I have to be really honest with you and myself, I'm doing this because I want a career, and this is a step up. I also don't plan to live like this for the rest of my life and there really isn't an "us" anymore. I just don't feel the way about you and us the way I used to. We're dead. Accept it.'

As he looks at me, I can't say I see disappointment or sadness. I see fear. Fear of having to take responsibility for himself after I'm gone. He hasn't taken any responsibility for so long that I don't think he even knows where to begin.

'Tell me where you're going. I'll finish the lease here, and I'll get the money to come to you and we can start over. Things will be different . . .'

I continue packing my clothes. I need a distraction. I don't want to listen to this. 'Things are different. We are finished. Don't you get it? We've started over already. Tonight. Separately. Go play your games, do whatever you want. I have to pack.'

Maybe he recognizes the futility of his pleading. He gives up and leaves the room leaving me to finish. After my clothes are packed, I move through the apartment collecting some personal belongings.

As I grab my favourite books from a shelf in the living room, something falls from inside one of them. I bend and pick it up.

It's an old photo. The colours are faded. I do a quick calculation and realize the photo is about fifteen years old. It's a photo of me and a boy. At least he was a boy then. I wonder what's happened to him as a sense of longing rises in me, even after all this time. My boyfriend from my last year of high school.

Bryce.

I look at Jenson and back at the photo. *If only I had someone like Bryce now.*

It's an irrational thought, I know. Even so, I wonder what happened to Bryce. For all I know, he went off the rails and ended up like Jenson. *Be careful what you wish for,* I tell myself.

A memory stirs somewhere in the recesses of my mind. I remember Bryce's promise to me. I wonder if he kept his promise or forgot it the moment he left town. I guess it was the latter. I sigh and put the photo in my wallet before I pack the books in my bag.

When I'm finished packing, I shower and get into bed. I lay awake, excited about what lays ahead and afraid I'll miss my flight if I fall asleep. What lies before me feels like the adventure of a lifetime. It's only a new job but it's freedom.

Jenson sleeps on the sofa for our last night together. He even pleads to have sex one last time which I decline. Loser.

I wake up early the next morning, make breakfast and call a cab. I say a brief goodbye to Jenson. The moment I am on the way to the airport, I feel like the weight of the world has been lifted off my shoulders.

Bryce

I've completed my audits for the week and am relieved to be back in my hometown. I'm looking forward to a weekend of relaxation.

I exit the airport shortly after 3 p.m. My phone rings and a glance at the screen tells me it's my assistant, Lisa. She seems to have a knack for calling me at the exact right moment, such as right now when I'm leaving the airport, and I wonder for the hundredth time if she somehow knows exactly where I am at any given time. I suppose in a way she does know, at least during work hours. She is my assistant and a very efficient one at that. I sigh and answer her call. I have to admit, I enjoy speaking with her although I was hoping to go straight home from the airport. I am guessing her call means I probably need to go to the office. 'Bryce, did you have a nice flight?'

'I did indeed,' I reply. Her voice, her manner, her tone, everything is pure professionalism. I'm glad she is my assistant while I am on the road. I need strong support because I am hardly ever in the office. She is great and I don't know what I would do without her.

'That's great. I'm glad I caught you. I just wanted to let you know there is a celebration at the office after work.

The group has had another fantastic quarter and there will be drinks in the bar after work. There are rumours about the head of hospitality's position going vacant and a restructure. You might want to show your face. You know what they say. Out of sight, out of mind.'

I drop my head. The last thing I feel like doing is going into the office today. It's Friday. But if I can get the head of hospitality job and get off the road, it'll be worth it. I'm tired of the travel and want some stability.

'Okay. Thanks for the heads up,' I reply and add. 'I'll be there. I'll finally get to meet my very efficient assistant who I can't live without.'

'I'll have to disappoint you there,' she says when she's finished chuckling. 'I have an appointment after work that I can't miss. And unlike you, I'm not a corporate climber. I'm happy with my job so I don't need to network. I'm glad to help you any way I can though.'

'Well, maybe I'll get to have a drink with my very efficient assistant next time then,' I say. I thank her again and we end the call.

I flag a cab and give the driver the address for the office.

Traffic is better than expected. I guess it must be the school holidays. I don't have a family, so I don't know. I should know though because school holidays affect our business. The holidays vary across states, so I normally have a general idea of the period but in my home city, I seem to have missed the boat.

I make it to the office around 4.20 p.m.

I reach our floor and step off the escalator.

'You're back!' I hear someone say loudly. I recognize the owner of the voice immediately.

'Harris!' I call back. 'Good to see you. I'll come and see you just now. You are staying for a drink, aren't you?'

'Wouldn't miss it for the world,' Harris calls back as he disappears from view on the downward escalator.

As I turn back to look in front of me, I collide with someone. They bounce off me, stumble back and fall, landing hard on their butt on the floor. It's a woman. Her bag drops and papers scatter everywhere.

I'm frozen for a moment in shock. I just walked into a woman and knocked her off her feet.

She is beautiful. Her hair is on fire. It looks that way anyway. It's orange and tied up in a ponytail. Her eyes are blue, and she looks young but not too young. She is dressed in a grey jacket and matching skirt. Her face is red. Whether it's red from anger or embarrassment I can't say.

'I am so sorry,' I say to her. 'I should have looked where I was going. Please forgive me.'

I don't wait for her response but bend and start gathering the papers scattered over the floor. She says nothing but gets to her knees and gathers some of the papers. She takes the ones I have collected without a word.

'I'm truly sorry,' I say again. 'I hope you can forgive me. Perhaps I can buy you a drink to make up for it?'

She rolls her eyes as if to say, 'First he knocks me over, and then he tries to hit on me.' Then, looking me squarely in the eyes she says, 'I don't drink with strangers. If you want to make it up to me, look where the hell you're going.'

She steps past me, and I catch the scent of her perfume. It suits her. It is her. Fresh, floral and powerful.

I watch her as she heads for the escalator. Her back is straight, and her posture is perfect. I want to run after her and ask her for her name, but I decide not to.

I watch her until she is gone from sight and then enter the office. checking my watch as I go. It's not four-thirty yet

Finding Us Again

and I hope to catch the assistant I've never met. The office is open plan and I crane my neck to see our department from as far away as possible. I spot her desk. It's empty. I walk faster and then slower as I near, and finally reach her desk.

It's tidy.

Too tidy.

She's gone.

I'm sure of it.

My hope sinks . . .

'Hey, Bryce,' I hear another familiar voice.

I turn and smile. 'Geoff, how are you?'

'I'm good. I haven't seen you in ages. I'm glad you could make it.'

'Yeah, Lisa told me about the celebration otherwise I would have missed it. I just got back into town.'

'That's great. Come on, let's go and have a drink,' Geoff says, and I follow him to the staff bar area used for celebrations where the party is almost in full swing.

I meet co-workers I have not seen in months, and I enjoy myself far more than I expected I would.

The general manager of our department calls for silence and makes an announcement none of us expected. The new head of hospitality has been appointed. It isn't me.

In hindsight, I wonder why I thought I might be in the running at all. If I was in the running, the general manager would have called me in to discuss it. That never happened.

Well, I guess I'll be hitting the road again come Monday.

Nora

The company does its best to help me settle into my new role. I am met at the airport and driven to the hotel where I am welcomed by colleagues, allocated a room in the quarters that the company maintains for staff and generally made to feel as welcome as possible.

I struggle to contain my excitement when I enter the quarters I have been allocated. It's not five-star but compared to the apartment I shared less than twenty-four hours ago with Jenson, I'd rate it a galaxy of stars.

After the bellboy leaves, I flitter from room to room like Goldilocks in the three bears' house. Thankfully, this is my place and no bears will be coming home any time soon. I test the sofas. They're good to sit on and lie on. I turn on the television and flip through the channels, satisfied that there are some good programmes to watch. I leave it on and head to the kitchen. I am very pleased. All the utensils I think I'll need are there and then some. The spare bedroom is next. Then the bathrooms. I test the water. It warms quickly and soon steam is billowing from the shower. I turn off the water and enter the main bedroom. The bed looks so inviting but I resist the temptation, as if saving it as a reward. I open every cupboard and look inside. There's more than enough room for my belongings.

I sigh blissfully and finally collapse on the bed and close my eyes. My head sinks into the plump, full pillows and I inhale their freshly laundered scent. I feel as if I am on holiday. The mattress is firm, and I know immediately that I will sleep like a baby.

I close my eyes and quickly drift into a short, dreamless sleep.

When I wake it's still bright outside the windows. It's Saturday afternoon and my first day in Chicago. I decide to explore the city. After consulting the in-room materials on the desk, I head to the lobby where I ask the staff for their suggestions.

When I finally head out on my own, I feel brave and adventurous. I'm excited to explore this new city and learn what I can. One of my stops is the BYOB Spray Paint 'n' Sip at Studio W.I.P. I sit through the workshop and listen to the guide as he explains the different ways to paint. When the lecture is over, I'm handed a canvas and I try my luck at painting. My effort is amateur but then a lot of graffiti art is anyway. I'm proud of it and I take it with me. I'll find somewhere to hang it in my accommodation.

I make my way to the Art Institute of Chicago. I'm no art genius or connoisseur but I do enjoy seeing beautiful art. I am particularly struck by the Hartwell Memorial Window which is displayed in the institute. It is massive but so vibrant and colourful. I marvel at the sixty-eight Thorne miniature rooms and enjoy some of the other works on display.

After the museum, I jump on the Big Bus for a Hop-On Hop-Off tour. They have an audio recording that explains much of the history of Chicago. I learn that it is called the Windy City because of the cool breeze from Lake Michigan that blows through the city and also because of a tornado that blew through the city many years ago. Other people call it the Windy City because of its history of having many speakers who were considered to be full of hot air.

After the tour, I head back to my hotel still feeling like a tourist. I know that given time, I will find the more meaningful places known only to residents of the city.

I wonder about Jenson but don't bother to give him a call. We are done. I don't want to prolong what we had in any way. I made it clear that he has to be out of the apartment at the end of the month. He is not my problem anymore.

When I get back to my room, I remove the key card from my purse to open the door and something falls out. It drifts to the floor.

I open the door and pick up the item that has fallen to the floor. It's the photo that fell out of the book when I packed.

I enter the apartment and I place the photo on the dining table before I start packing away the groceries into the cupboards and fridge. After a small dinner I call my mother to let her know I arrived safely and am settling in.

My mother asks about Jenson. She never met him, but I tell her we're done. She does not express an opinion either way since she does not know him. I also don't go into the details. I don't think it has anything to do with her. The entire time I'm eating dinner and talking to my mother, I can see the photo on the dining table.

When I'm finished eating, I sit at the table, lost in the memories that the photo brings. It feels like yesterday, but it's been almost fifteen years.

Feelings stir within me as I remember the moment in the photo. I feel as if my memories and emotions are being dusted off. This is not the whole photo. I cut out the part that I have because it was the only important part to me. It was more or less where we began even though we didn't know it at the time.

Him and I.

Bryce and me.

As I slowly open the door to let the memories escape into the present day, it's the last memories of us that seem to come to the fore first.

Last in, first out, I think.

I smile as I remember his promise to me and think how sweetly innocent it was.

Young, blind love.

'I'll write to you. I'll always write to you. I'll never stop writing to you. But it won't be e-mail or by post. I'll write the way I have been doing for a few years now.'

'What way is that?' I remember asking and I can remember his smile and the far-off look in his eyes. The dreamer's look, I called it. He always had that look when he was about to suggest one of his wild or romantic ideas.

'On the back of pictures in hotels. I've left a message on the back of a picture in every hotel my dad's worked in since I can remember. Only now, when I write on the back of a picture, I'll be writing something for you instead.'

'That's so sweet Bryce but c'mon. You know that's not going to happen and if it does, it won't last. You'll find someone new and move on. Besides, how on earth am I supposed to find your writing? How will I know which hotels you've been to? How will I even know if it's you?'

'That's the beauty of destiny, isn't it? If you're supposed to find it, you will. I promise you I'll write.'

'What about when you go off to college or university? You're not going to come back and work for a hotel, are you?' I asked in disbelief.

'Just trust that I'll write. Know that I'll write. Even if I don't work for a hotel, I'm sure I will stay in a hotel occasionally and I will write. If you're meant to find it, you will.'

He looked at me with that look that told me he believed himself and because he believed himself, I should too. He was kind of crazy cute that way. Just crazy cute enough to do it too.

'Why don't you just write to me like a normal person would? E-mail or the post?'

'It wouldn't be the same. Life's tearing us apart now and we always said we'd be together forever. So, let's leave it to life to bring us back together if that's what's meant to be.'

'The world's cutest, most handsome fatalist,' I teased.

'You can laugh now but someday we'll see who has the last laugh, babydoll,' he said imitating some gangster from a movie. 'I'm gonna find ya and I'm gonna take ya away so we can live happily ever after.'

'You're full of shit,' I responded, laughing.

We both fell quiet then. We knew our time was nearly up. It was his last day, his last hours before they would leave.

He was supposed to be home packing, but he didn't want to go and it showed. He wanted to stay, wanted to be with me, forever and always.

I wasn't in a hurry for him to leave either and I did not want to chase him to get going. I wanted a decent, long goodbye with tears and not a rushed one with a kiss that was little more than a peck, that would be forgotten by tomorrow because he had to hurry.

I moved closer to him, and we took each other's hands. I looked up into his eyes and he looked into mine.

We didn't need to say anything.

My vision blurred at last as tears flooded my eyes and then spilled freely down my cheeks and the side of my face.

He released my left hand and wiped my tears away gently. Then he bent and kissed my tears tasting their saltiness.

'They say the saltier the tears, the greater the love,' he murmured.

'Nonsense,' I choked. 'Who on earth said that?'

'I just did,' he smiled, and I laughed despite my sadness.

'How salty are my tears?' I asked.

'The saltiest in the world,' he smiled as he tucked my hair behind my ear.

'I don't want you to go,' I whispered.

'You and me both. Tell that to the world's most selfish dad,' he said.

'It's not fair,' I whispered.

'I know,' he said sadly.

Then we kissed. My tears moistened his lips as they met mine. As we kissed, I felt his tears meet my lips too. I tasted the salt of his tears.

If what he said was true, he must have loved me very much.

We kissed and held each other for what seemed like forever. He wrapped me up in his arms and held me tightly. I felt so secure as I clung to him tightly.

When we finally parted, we knew our time was up. He knew he had to go.

'I'll write, I promise,' he said.

'Just write like any normal person, okay? Please?'

He smiled wistfully and shook his head. 'Look for me. You'll find me. Look for me in the corridors. A love like ours is special and needs special care.'

'How is making it hard to find your writing special care?' I asked.

'Don't think of it like that. You're special and you deserve only the best.'

He stepped close and we kissed deeply but quickly again, before he picked up his bike and pedalled away.

'I love you, Nora!' he shouted as he rode away into the night.

It was the last time I saw him.

Fifteen Years Earlier

Bryce

My first day at another new school. I wonder how long this one will last. It's already the second one this year.

My record is three in a year. Considering it's only October and this is my second school already, I might make it four if I'm unlucky.

I'm looking forward to the end of this year after which I'll go off to college and I won't have to move around with the family every time Dad gets shipped off somewhere new with his job.

He's not in the military. I know families in the military get moved around a lot too. No, my dad works for a hotel chain. They're on a major growth drive and he is responsible for putting the procedures in place, screening recruits, and a bunch of other things I don't understand, before a hotel opens. Every time one opens, we usually have to move. Sometimes he commutes but Mom doesn't like it and they fight a lot.

He always argues that he's the breadwinner and Mom says she can't get a job because we're never anywhere long enough for her to get a job and 'win some bread'. We move so much she can't build up a decent resume for anyone to consider her worth hiring.

I don't get to make any lasting friends. Easy come, easy go, I guess. I'm never anywhere long enough to make a lasting impression on anyone. I feel like I'm always just passing through.

I stand in front of the school building and watch the kids entering. I'm early. I always get to a new school early on my first day. I've learned that I need to get there early to find my way around. There's no worse way to draw unwanted attention to yourself as a newbie by getting to class late.

I sigh, shifting my rucksack on my shoulder, and head into the school. I follow other kids that have just entered. I'm guessing they are headed for their lockers too. The kids turn the corner and I see the lockers lining the hall. I pull out my locker key and check the number. I scan the numbers on the lockers and find mine. I unlock it and then lower my bag to the floor. I remove the books I won't be needing and put them in the locker.

I disturb a small cloud of dust as I fill my locker and sneeze.

It looks so bare. I think of decorating it but ask myself, *What's the point? Who knows how long I'll be here?*

I finish packing my books and close the locker. I pick up my rucksack and turn to go and find my class.

I close my eyes instinctively as I collide with someone. I smell perfume. The scent is soft, beautiful, and mesmerizing. I don't have time to savor it though. I hear a thump and a soft grunt accompanied by a thud of books as the person I collided with stumbles back and falls to the floor.

I open my eyes and I'm frozen for a moment. The most beautiful girl I have ever seen is sitting on the floor. Her shoulder-length blonde hair frames her pixie face and cute, freckled, button nose. Her blue eyes look right through me.

She throws up her arms and looks at me as if to say, 'Well, are you going to stand there all day or help me?'

I recover from the stupor her beauty has caused and kneel before her, feeling like an absolute klutz.

'God, I'm so sorry. I didn't see you. Here let me help you.' I help gather her books as she watches me, not saying a word.

I pull her bag closer to put her books in and see that it's torn.

Shit.

'Your bag's torn,' I say. *Great. I ruined her bag too. Can things get any worse?*

'It was on its last legs anyway,' she says.

'Yeah, but how are you going to carry your books around?' I ask as I meet her gaze again. I'm hypnotized instantly but not for long as a knee hits my shoulder and sends me flying.

I look at who collided with me and I know who it is immediately. I don't know his name, but I know his type.

The school bully.

I was hoping that I would only appear on the school bully's radar later. Or never. I have yet to go to a school where that miracle becomes a reality. It's not going to be this school.

'What are you doing hitting on my girl, noob?' he asks standing over me.

'What? I wasn't hitting on her,' I say glancing between the bully and the girl I knocked down.

'You don't call knocking my girl on her ass hitting on her?'

For the first time, I see the bully's coward buddies. He has two. They're flanking him and snicker at his pun.

It's always so predictable.

'I guess you get an "A" for English with a pun like that,' I say.

'I'm glad you know it, punk,' the bully says. 'Seems you're a bit more intelligent than some of the others.'

'Why? Because I know you're using a pun, or because I know an "A" when I see one?' I ask.

The girl smiles and looks away as she catches my meaning. Even the bully's buddies have to stifle their snickers. The bully is not impressed though and things are going to go from bad to worse.

He leans down and grabs the front of my shirt. He is strong and lifts me to my feet easily.

'Gee thanks . . .' I say sarcastically.

He thrusts me backward and I hit the lockers with a 'thud' that rings through the hall.

Anyone who wasn't aware the bully had found a new target, is aware now. They all stop in the hall and turn to see what is happening.

'Listen smart mouth. You get one chance and you've just had yours. Now stop standing around and give my girl your bag so she can carry her books. You don't think she's going to carry her books in her hands all day, do you?'

I kneel and remove my bag from my shoulder. I do it not because he told me to but because I would have done it anyway.

'Oh no,' she objects, 'It's not necessary.'

'Take it,' the bully orders her. Hesitantly she reaches out and takes my bag. I open it and remove my books and pencil case. I place them on the floor beside the bag and I pick up her belongings and put them in my bag. I close it and offer the straps to her.

'There you go,' I say, smiling at her.

She takes the straps. 'Thanks.'

'No problem,' I reply.

'I said give her your bag, not chat her up,' the bully says as he kicks my books. They scatter across the floor and down the hall. Some kids laugh and the bully's buddies howl.

I stand and help the girl get up. Then I turn to the bully. His hair is short, military-style. He is taller and broader than me. His face is fixed in a scowl as he looks at me and I notice he is clenching and unclenching his fists. He makes me think of a gorilla.

'What's your name?' I ask.

'Walt,' he replies then adds, 'and you better not forget it.'

'I don't forget "A"'s,' I tell him.

He steps forward reaching for me but the girl steps between us.

'Enough!' she cries, looking at both of us. 'Stop it!'

Walt backs down when she intercedes. The girl takes his arm and pulls him away from me. He goes with her reluctantly but looks over his shoulder and winks at me. It's not a friendly wink.

I start to gather my books, but Walt's buddies stand on them before they leave, laughing. I look around quickly. Many students are still standing in the hall. Some watch Walt leave with the girl while others look at me. No one offers to help. No one knows me and now that I am on the bully's radar I may as well be radioactive. Anyone seen with me now might become a target for sympathising with me.

After I gather my books, I carry them to my first class and every class after that. I just have to make it through the day until I get home. I have plenty of spare bags at home. Every new school I go to, my mom buys me a new bag. I don't know why. It's like it's just an unspoken rule. I collect them anyway because a few of my bags have torn or been destroyed by bullies in the past.

Walt has taken a personal interest in me after our meeting at the lockers. He finds me between every lesson and pushes me around. After my last lesson of the day, I hide until I think he is gone and then sneak out of school.

Thankfully it seems that Walt wasn't able to wait for me and has taken off. I have, however, missed the school bus and have to walk home but it's better than having to deal with Walt.

As I walk home, I am surprised when Walt's girlfriend comes running after me a few blocks from the school.

'Hey!'

Nora

I wait for the new boy, Bryce, after school. I wonder where he could be. He hasn't come to his locker as most kids do after school and I guess he is hiding. Bryce is in my class and while we haven't spoken much, I'm well aware that Walt has been bullying him or trying to.

I find Walt lurking in the hall and I know he's waiting for Bryce. 'What are you doing here?' I ask.

'Waiting,' he answers.

'For what?'

'The noob,' he says, smiling at me.

I know he's not smiling because I'm here. He's smiling because he's bragging about what he's up to.

'Will you just give it up already?' I snap at him, making my irritation clear.

'Why? He needs to know who's boss around here,' Walt says.

'You know, I don't understand you. Why is it so important to push other people around?'

'Because they need to have respect,' Walt answers, confident that his reply makes sense.

'Respect isn't demanded or beaten into someone through thuggery. It's earned and the only thing you're earning from anyone is their fear.'

Walt studies me but says nothing.

'Have you stopped to look at yourself?' I ask pointedly.

He looks down at his shirt, lifts his arms and checks under them before scanning his trousers. 'Why? What's wrong?' he asks.

'Nothing is wrong with your appearance,' I say, almost laughing as he checks himself to see if there's something wrong with his clothes. 'I mean, have you stopped to think that people are looking at you waiting like a bully for the new guy? Does it not trouble you what others think? That they know you're standing here waiting for the new guy, you *planned* to be here waiting for him.'

Walt shrugs. 'So?'

'So?' I reiterate. '*So?*'

He stares at me stupidly.

'So, I wish you would spend that time planning something for us, something we can do together. Honestly, I wish you'd stop treating me like a hobby.'

I turn and start walking away.

'Hey! That's not true!' he calls after me. He comes unstuck from the wall where he was leaning so confidently and I hear him walking quickly to catch up to me. Bryce is now forgotten.

'Really? When was the last time you did something for us?' I ask walking fast. He is beside me now and keeping up.

'I . . . I . . . we went to dinner last weekend.'

'I suggested it. I chose the place too and I told you what was good on the menu and what wasn't.'

'The night after that we went to the movies,' he says.

'I suggested that at dinner the night before,' I respond quickly. The fact that I've been keeping tabs on who is putting effort into the relationship should be telling me something as much as I am trying to prove something to him.

'What about when we had milkshakes after school that Friday . . .?'

I think about the time he is referring to and I can only come up with a time further back than I can even remember.

'That was ages ago!' I exclaim and stop. He stops and turns to face me. I can see worry on his face. 'Walt, I just want you to show you care for me. Remember how you were when we first started dating? I want to see that part of you again. That's why I started dating you. You cared then . . .'

'But I still care,' he interrupts defensively.

'If you think beating up other kids is caring for me, you're wrong. They don't threaten me. How is that caring for me? On the contrary, I want to see you show compassion for others and not just me.'

I'm tired and bored of the conversation and I add, 'I forgot to tell you, Miss Crawford said if I saw you, to ask if you can please help her. She needs to rearrange some furniture in her class and she can't find the janitor. If you go and help her, maybe I'll think you care about me.'

'Why me?' Walt protests.

'Because you're big and strong and you can use your strength for things like helping people instead of bullying others. And right now you have a chance to help Miss Crawford but you can't be bothered judging by your response. So how do you care for others?'

Walt sighs. He doesn't have an answer. I didn't expect one.

I push on. I feel like a mother scolding a child. 'And don't forget you have detention. If you're late for that you might have detention again next week.'

'Oh shit!' Walt says and takes off without even saying goodbye.

I watch him go. I won't be with him too much longer. I remember how different he was when we first started dating. He was more attentive and caring but now I feel like a possession. He only shows an interest when he feels another boy is showing interest. I feel like a trophy, as if Walt feels that his status will drop if I leave him. When I try to talk about us, he always skirts around the issue and avoids it or promises to try and do better. I've spoken about breaking up a few times, but he won't let me go. I know he can't stop me from breaking up with him but for some reason I always listen to him despite the fact that I'm not happy.

I watch Walt disappear down the hall and when I'm sure he's gone, I return to the lockers. There's no sign of Bryce.

I give up, guessing that I must have missed him while I spoke with Walt.

I head for the exit and leave the school. I've missed the bus and strike out on foot walking quickly to get home.

As I walk, I see a boy from school ahead of me. He's carrying something because I don't see his arms at his sides and I realize it must be Bryce without his schoolbag. I walk faster and then begin to run, calling his name as I do.

He turns and stops and watches as I approach him.

'Hey,' I say breathlessly.

'Hey,' he says with a slight smile. He looks at me as if he sees right through me. Then he looks around scanning the street for Walt.

'He's in detention,' I say.

'Oh,' he says as his gaze finds mine again.

'Do you live this way?' he asks.

I nod. 'I do actually.'

'Well let's walk then,' he says and begins walking. 'Can I carry your bag?'

'It's your bag actually,' I say, falling into step beside him.

'It's okay. You can keep it. I've got plenty, but I'll carry it for you.'

I wonder why he would have plenty of bags and ask him.

'I get a new bag every time I change schools,' he says.

'What do you mean every time you change schools? Do you get expelled a lot?'

He laughs. It's a nice laugh and reminds me of the sunshine that warms you on a cold or cloudy day.

'Oh heck, you don't even know me, and you already think I'm the worst kid you ever met,' he smiles.

I blush. 'Sorry. I didn't mean it that way.'

'It's okay. I didn't take it that way,' he smiles. 'Truth be told, we move around a lot. At least twice a year, but this is my second time this year already. It's shaping up to be a record beater.'

'What's your record?'

'Three,' he says. I think he would have held up three fingers but he is carrying his books and pencilcase because he gave his bag to me.

'Wow, I'm sorry to hear that,' I say.

He shrugs. 'So would you like me to carry your bag?'

'It's okay, I can carry my bag,' I say. 'Besides you might move while you're carrying it and then I'd be in trouble for not doing my homework.'

'Cute,' he says.

I smile. 'I couldn't resist it. But seriously, I can carry my bag.'

'Okay,' he says.

We reach the corner of the block and he stops. He's going to turn right. 'Which way are you?'

'I'm your way,' I reply.

'Well, I'm this way,' he says and moves off to the right.

I follow.

'This isn't the way to your home, is it?' he remarks.

'Why wouldn't it be? There's not only one way to someone's house is there?'

He laughs again. 'I gotta be careful around you.'

'Why?'

'You're sharp. Quick.'

'Don't be careful then. Be sharper,' I smile.

'Wow. Are you always on form like this?'

I shrug. 'Only when I'm enjoying myself.'

He slows a few steps further on and then stops. 'This is me.'

'You live here?' I ask.

He nods. 'Do you want to come in? My mom's at home.'

I don't know if he says it to put me at ease by letting me know we won't be alone or if he wants to warn me about his mother.

How bad can she be? I wonder. He might seem like a nice guy, but I still hardly know him and just maybe I'm here out of pity more than anything else because of Walt.

'If it's okay with you and your mom.'

'Of course,' he says.

I follow him up the path as I look around the garden. The weeds and grass are striving to become a jungle. There's a lot of work needed but then I'm guessing they just moved in and they're renting. The garden is an eyesore compared to the other houses around it.

We reach the front door and Bryce sees me assessing the garden. 'That's my job. It's always my job when we get somewhere new. I'll start on the weekend.'

He opens the door and steps in. He holds it open for me and I enter.

I can't say much for the interior. I can smell it's been freshly painted. There's nothing fancy about it. I guess the house must be old. It reminds me of the seventies-style houses I've seen in old television shows. The parquet floors have been polished but they're still dull and scratched from the years of use.

'Mom!' Bryce calls.

'Here!' comes a voice from somewhere in the house. A moment later I see his mother appear from what I expect is the main bedroom.

She looks like she belongs with the house and for a moment I wonder if she was rented with it.

Her hair is in curlers under one of those old transparent scarves that women from the seventies used to wear. A cigarette is in her mouth. She smiles as she sees Bryce has brought a friend home with him.

'Mom, this is . . .'

'Nora,' I reply. He probably heard my name at school during class but just then I realize that I haven't given him my name since we started speaking. I think again of the case for putting names on lockers instead of numbers. But the school doesn't allow it. They prefer us to be known as numbers, I guess.

'Hello, Nora. It's nice to see Bryce making friends so fast,' she smiles as she puts out her cigarette and blows the smoke away from us. 'Call me Sharon.'

'Okay, Mrs Sharon,' I say and shake her hand as she laughs.

'Well, if you insist on the "Mrs" then I suggest you call me Mrs Darston.'

'Okay, Mrs Darston. It's nice to meet you.'

Bryce's mother still looks young. I'm surprised she looks so good. She must be at least thirty-eight. I thought she would have looked older for some reason, but I obviously keep my opinion to myself.

She leaves us and Bryce leads me into the kitchen. More seventies-style décor. He opens the fridge, removes a carton of juice and pours us each a glass.

He shows me around the house which is spacious. There's a pool out back which has been maintained well and Bryce says I'm welcome to come over for a swim anytime.

We talk a bit longer and then I excuse myself. I say goodbye outside.

'You know, you're not the worst kid I've ever met,' I smile.

'Thanks. I hope not,' he smiles then adds, 'I wanted to ask you if I could borrow your maths book. I was lost during class today.'

'Sure,' I say. I open my bag and remove my maths book. I hand it to him.

'Thanks, I'll give it back to you on Monday,' he says.

'Okay,' I smile. A moment's awkward silence passes between us and I decide it's time to leave.

'Gotta go,' I say.

'Okay. See you Monday,' he says.

I turn and start walking down the path when he stops me.

'Nora?'

I turn. Too quickly. As if I hoped he would call me back. I did actually. 'Yes?'

'I think you're the nicest girl I've ever met,' he says.

I feel myself blush as I stand there in the afternoon sun. 'Um . . . thanks,' I manage to say at last.

'I'll try to be sharper,' he smiles.

'Okay,' I say and then I wave shyly and turn and head down the path to the sidewalk. I look back when I reach the sidewalk. He's gone back inside and closed the door.

What did you expect, I ask myself? It's not like he's going to stand there staring after you.

I glance back a few times until his house is out of sight. I can't stop thinking about him.

Nora

I get home and head for the kitchen first. I pour myself a glass of juice and drink it quickly. It's hot outside and I'm thirsty from the walk.

Then I dash upstairs to my room where I drop my bag. I'm eager to listen to the new playlist that I've created. Only my tablet's not where I left it.

Or at least where I thought I left it.

I hunt all over my room, head downstairs and look around before it hits me. Ashley. My little sister.

'Ash?' I call as I head upstairs to her room. I push her door open and am in time to see her hurriedly sitting down on her bed with her hands in her lap.

When will she learn?

I mean who just sits on their bed with their hands in their lap waiting for their big sister to come into the room while they look guilty as hell?

I don't even pretend she doesn't have it. 'Where is my tablet?' I demand.

'I . . . I don't know,' she shrugs. 'Why are you asking me?'

'Because I know you have it. It's mine. Not yours. Just give it to me.'

She stuns me then and answers like she's never answered before. 'No, Ra. I don't have it.'

'What?' I ask, irritated. 'Did you just call me No-Ra?'

She rolls her eyes. 'What are you six? I said "no". You know, the opposite of "yes"? I said "no, Ra," so I called you Ra.'

'Very funny,' I say. I would never have believed a fourteen-year-old could be so obnoxious. She's changed so much lately. I don't know if it's a phase she's going through or the kids she hangs with at school.

'My name's Nora, okay?' I step forward and reach for her pillow. She jumps on it and tries to stop me from reaching under it but she's too late.

I grasp my tablet and pull it. I feel something give way and the next moment my tablet comes out from under her pillow with the stub of an attachment to something that's broken off.

'My earphones!' Ashley cries as she holds up her earphones with their snapped wire.

'Is it my fault?' I ask.

'Yes! You yanked your tablet from under my pillow!'

'And you shouldn't have had my tablet in the first place!' I say angrily pulling out the stub of her earphones from my tablet.

'You're going to buy me new earphones!' she cries.

'No, I'm not.'

'Just you wait. Mom will take it from your pocket money,' Ashley says.

'And then you will never borrow anything of mine again. I'll keep my room locked so tight you'll never get in again. In fact, from now on, I'll always keep it locked so you can't get in. Ever.'

I turn and leave her room.

I hear Mom downstairs. Did she have to get here now?

'Kids?' she calls up the stairs. She's heard us arguing.

'Mom, mom!' Ashley cries and flies out of her room and down the stairs. 'Look what Ra did to my earphones!'

'Who's Ra?' I hear Mom say.

'Ra,' Ashley replies as if Mom should know better, 'No-Ra.'

'Nor,' I hear my mother call.

Here we go, I think as I roll my eyes and begin to wonder how many ways you can slice and dice my little four-letter name.

Mom always calls me Nor. I've never complained before, but I guess now that Ashley has started with Ra, being called Nor irritates me just as much.

I get downstairs. 'Hi, Mom.'

'Hi Nor,' Mom says. 'Did you do this?'

She holds up Ashley's broken earphone cable.

'No,' I say. 'It's not my fault. She took my tablet without asking and when I asked her if she had it, she lied. When I grabbed my tablet, she tried to stop me, and the cable snapped.'

Mom crosses one arm over her waist and supports the elbow of her other arm as she puts her head in her hand.

I know the position.

'I'm taking the cost for a new one from your pocket money,' Mom says to me.

'*What*? That's not *fair*, Mom. She had no right taking my tablet . . .'

'It's not open for discussion,' Mom says.

Ashley looks at me with an 'I won' smile on her face. 'I told you Ra.'

'Stop calling me Ra, brat!' I say angrily.

'Ra, Ra, Ra,' Ashley chants.

'Mom?' I say, pleading for Mom's support.

'Ashley, stop it.'

'Why? You call her Nor,' Ashley objects.

'If you want to call me Ra, you better bow down and worship me,' I say.

'What? No way,' Ashley says.

'Yes way. Ra was the sun god in ancient Egypt and the Egyptians worshipped him. So, you better show respect and bow down when you talk to me.'

'If Ra was the ancient sun god, then you must be older than Grandma! Granny Ra!' Ashley snickers.

'Shut up!' I shout and head back up the stairs.

'Granny Ra, Granny Ra,' Ashley begins to chant as I go upstairs. I hear Mom scold her and smile to myself before I close myself in my room.

Peace at last.

I'm glad it's the weekend. I listen to music as I do my homework. I've got nothing planned now or for this evening and decide to finish my homework so I'll have the weekend free.

Mom calls us for dinner just after I finish my homework. I hide my tablet where I know Ashley won't find it and head downstairs. I can smell dinner as I descend the stairs. It must be roast something. I love it when Mom makes a roast. She always seems to get it just right. I can almost feel the soft meat in my mouth before I get to the dining room and taste the gravy that I pour generously over my rice and potatoes. I greet Dad who is headed for the dining room and learn that Ashley has gone out with her friends. It's just Mom, Dad and me who'll enjoy dinner together. I help Mom finish setting the table and we sit down to dinner together.

The food is fabulous, and I compliment Mom on her cooking as always. During dinner I look at them both and think how lucky I am.

Dad notices me looking at them and eventually asks, 'What's up?'

I shrug. 'I'm just thinking how grateful I am for our family and our life.'

'That's pretty profound,' Dad says as he scoops more potatoes onto his plate. 'What's brought that on?'

'I made a new friend. He's just started at our school. His family moves around a lot and this is his second school this year. He's nice though.'

'That must be tough,' Mom remarks.

'Yes but he seems to deal with it okay.'

'Well, you should invite him around to play board games on a Friday,' Dad says. There is hope in his voice.

'That would be nice,' I smile, 'but I don't think Walt would like that.'

'Are you still with that thug?' Dad asks disappointedly.

It's the first time my dad has ever voiced his opinion of Walt. I brought him around a few times for game night after we first started dating but I sensed that my parents didn't like him much and we started going out on Fridays instead. This at last is confirmation of how my dad feels about him.

'Don't you usually go out on Friday evenings?' Dad adds. I begin to feel that he has the senses of a shark and must be smelling blood in the water as far as my relationship with Walt goes.

I know my relationship with Walt is on a crash and burn trajectory but I'm not quite ready to let Dad know that he is right.

'He had a big family dinner tonight,' I lie. 'I thought it would be better if he spent time with them rather than have me around as well.'

Dad just nods and continues eating. I have no idea what Walt is doing tonight. He usually contacts me and asks what we're doing but he hasn't done so tonight. *Just another indication of where we're at,* I think to myself.

Perhaps he's angry because he realized that Miss Crawford never wanted to see him, but I doubt it.

After dinner, I help clear away the dishes and and we bring out the board games. I realize I had forgotten how much fun it is spending time together as a family and how we all enjoy ourselves thoroughly. I've really missed this family tradition.

We have great fun playing Monopoly until my sister gets home. She's too late to play so sits next to me watching the game and making a nuisance of herself. She smells like cigarettes and I wonder if Mom and Dad can smell it too. For her to smell so strongly of smoke, I am sure she must be smoking too. That or she's been somewhere filled with smokers. Either way, I am concerned and angry that she can sit here and think that no one smells anything. I'm also concerned that she might be mixing with the wrong crowd. But this is not the time or the place to bring it up.

I eventually stop playing when she starts calling me 'Ra' again and head upstairs to my room. I wonder if Bryce will enjoy playing board games.

Bryce

The second week at my new school is over. The highlight of my week was walking home with Nora twice during the week like I did the first Friday.

Other kids are mostly keeping their distance from me. I guess being the centre of the school bully's attention is cause enough for people to stay away.

Dad's home and he and Mom have found something to argue about again. I was hoping to at least have a quiet evening watching television with them but it's beginning to seem, and sound, more and more like it won't happen.

I turn up the music to drown out their argument.

While I have some hobbies to amuse me like reading up about astronomy, writing and listening to music or reading books, they only go so far sometimes. It's times like these when I wish I had friends.

My thoughts turn to Nora but I obviously can't ask her to go out. She's probably with 'A' anyway. I remember how she smiled on my first day when I first called him 'A'. I thought it was quite clever and since then I've come to suspect that she might not be that happy with him anymore. Whenever Walt comes up in our conversations, she steers us in a different direction. Her loyalty is remarkable. You shouldn't badmouth your partner in front of others and she sticks to that like it's a golden rule. It's frustrating but I'm learning to just focus on being me when we're together and showing her the kind of person I am and could be with her. Maybe that will be enough without having to talk about Walt.

I want to write something for her but I don't know if I should. As I think of what I would write for her I find that words flow into my mind, and I write them down. When I'm finished, I read them again and again. I'll worry about giving it to her later.

In a new place you've become my go-to.
I'm glad I met you and now I always look for you.
Where I am, I hope there you'll be too.
I'm sure there's more love I can offer you.
Thanks for being you.

I read it again and I think it sounds cheesy but it's a start. I wonder if I should give it to her and if so how and when. It might be best to slip it into her bag or locker although she might not be able to guess who it's from. Then there's the possibility that 'A' might find it and claim he wrote it and left it to surprise her. These are possibilities I'm not willing to entertain.

I rewrite the note neater this time. Then I decorate it with some hearts and stars that I colour in. It looks a lot better.

I copy what I've written into a notebook. For some reason, I want to keep it as a memory. I don't know if I'll ever look back on it and remember it as the start of something special, but you never know.

I look at the original and then insert it under the plastic wrap of the inside back cover of her maths book. I don't think she'll find it there, at least not for a while, like until she gets to the end of the book. When she finds it, it'll be a surprise. I think how much fun it would be to see her reaction when she gets the note.

I wish I had taken her number. I could have texted her. I wonder what she's doing right now. She's probably out at some mall with friends or with Walt. Girls like her are popular. They don't sit around waiting for someone to notice them. They live their lives and they are noticed because of it. At least that's what I think.

I look out the window and suddenly find the room stifling. All is quiet downstairs so it seems the storm has passed and Dad and Mom have made peace. Thinking that I might be able to find where Nora lives, I decide to go for a ride on my bike. If I find her place, I can use returning her maths book as an excuse.

I often go out late at night. It's nice to get out in the cool night air and feel the wind in my face and blowing through my hair. I love listening to the hum of the tyres and the *krrrr* of the chain when I freewheel. It has a meditative quality to it, especially when the streets are so quiet and it's the loudest noise I can hear.

My motivation is different this time though. I get dressed in my sweatsuit and head downstairs.

Mom and Dad are in the living room watching television. It looks like they've made up. I catch their eye as I pass the entrance to the living room and Mom calls out.

'Where are you going?'

'Just for a ride,' I reply.

'Are you sure it's okay to go out this late?'

'Yes, Mom. I've got Google Maps. I won't get lost.'

'Well, we haven't been here very long . . .'

'And we might not stay very long either so best I explore while I can.' I immediately feel guilty after I've said it. It's a low blow, I know.

Mom doesn't say anything about my remark. She only says, 'Well, be careful, okay?'

'Sure, Mom. I will,' I say.

Outside, I mount my bike and am soon headed down the road. At the corner, I turn and head in the direction that I saw Nora go.

I know it's pointless but as I ride, I look left and right at the houses and wonder which one might be hers.

I pass some younger kids on the street and recognize them from school so I stop.

'Hey,' I say.

They look at me, and then answer 'Yes?'

'Do you by any chance know a girl called Nora? She's in twelfth grade.'

'Oh, Ashley's sister?' one asks. 'You mean No-Ra?'

I didn't know Nora has a sister and I don't know where No-Ra comes into it, but I nod. 'Yes. I borrowed her book and told her I'd return it but I can't remember the address she gave me. Do you know where they live?'

'You're the new kid, aren't you?' one of the kids asks.

I wonder why they're calling me kid when I'm older than them both.

I nod.

'You better watch out for Walt. He's told everyone he's going to crunch you like paper into a ball.'

'Thanks for the warning,' I say.

Satisfied that they've given me the warning they wanted to, one of them points across the street. 'There. Number sixty-eight.'

'Thanks,' I say, and I start pedalling towards the house. I stop on the sidewalk outside the yard. It's a beautifully maintained white double-storey house. Nothing fancy but the garden is beautiful. Lights cast shadows and light across the perfectly cropped lawn here and there. I study the windows upstairs and wonder which one is Nora's bedroom window. I settle on the window where a faint glow escapes. It must be a desk lamp. I expect that would be what Nora would be using.

I should just go up to the front door and ring the bell but who returns a maths book so late in the evening? I'd rather not disturb everyone and decide to take my chances by trying to attract the attention of whoever is in the room upstairs.

A white picket fence separates the front yard from the sidewalk. There's no gate. I cross to a flower bed and search for small stones to throw at the window. I inhale the scent of the roses in the flowerbed. Using my hand as a rake I run it through the soil and gather small stones before approaching the house as close as I dare.

I pause and scan the downstairs windows worried that someone might look out and see me on the lawn lurking like a burglar. Satisfied that there is no one to see me from the downstairs windows, I throw the first stone. It falls short of its target and softly rattles down the slope of the roof until it falls into the gutter.

Not enough weight and momentum.

The next stone almost hits the mark but doesn't quite get there. The third one makes it with nothing more than a slight tap but it's enough.

A moment later the curtain is pulled aside and a face is silhouetted against the light. I can't tell if it's her but I think it is.

The curtain falls back into place. I can't believe she didn't wave. Maybe she didn't recognize me and has gone to call the police or tell her parents there's a stranger in the yard.

I should run.

I should grab my bike and ride away as fast as I can.

Instead, I decide to try again. My last stone hits the mark a little bit harder.

The curtain is pulled aside again and at least I know that whoever it is, hasn't gone to call the cops. I still can't be sure it's Nora but I start to jump up and down on the lawn waving my arms.

I'm sure I look like an idiot.

A moment later the person rises higher in the window as they see me. I can't tell if they're excited or worried but they look at me for a few moments, wave and disappear as the curtain falls back into place.

My courage fails and I run to my bike, afraid that I'm at the wrong Nora's house after all. Maybe the kids that told me this was Nora's house were lying. *What bigger joke could you play on the new kid?* I ask myself.

But even as my mind screams at me to ride away, I find myself unable to do so. Heart pounding, breath coming fast and shallow, sweat prickling my skin, I find I cannot leave.

The front door opens at last and I tense my legs ready to push off and ride away into the night. I see her silhouetted in the doorway. She steps out and pulls the door closed behind her before she descends the porch steps and approaches me slowly. I step off my bike and lean against it as I wait for her to get closer. She steps out from the shade of the house into the light of the almost full moon.

Her short blonde hair lights up like a halo in the light of the moon. Her robe is open in front, and she seems oblivious to the fact that its sash is dragging on the ground behind her. Under it, she's wearing a nightshirt and matching pyjama shorts. The colours of her pyjamas and robe are all pastel or white making her glow like an angel as she approaches me.

She reaches me and stops. Her gaze has been fixed on mine since she left the porch. The moonlight lights her eyes brightly and I can see playfulness and perhaps appreciation in them.

Her skin looks soft, pale, and pure in the light.

'This is a surprise,' she says softly as she smiles.

'I know. I wasn't sure if this was your place or not. Some kids up the street told me No-Ra lives here when I asked if they knew you.'

'You asked for "No-Ra?"' she asks in disbelief.

'No, I asked for Nora, and they told me No-Ra lives here.'

She sighs, puts her face in her hand, and shakes her head as she looks at the ground.

'I'm going to kill her,' she murmurs.

Bryce

'Kill who?' I ask.

'My sister,' she says as she looks up at me.

'That's what the kids up the block asked. They wanted to know if you were Ashley's sister.'

'I am she,' Nora said. 'I am sister to a pain in the ass.'

I smile. 'It can't be that bad.'

'Well, you don't have any brothers or sisters, so you have no idea.'

'You're right. But sometimes I wish I did have a brother or sister.'

'You can have mine,' Nora volunteers quickly.

'I think I'll pass. I'm thinking of more of a genetic connection.'

'Okay, Professor. Since you put it that way . . .' she says and trails off as she looks at me.

Her mouth is slightly open and her face turned up to me. She is beautiful. I want to tell her but don't. The moon lights the freckles sprinkled on her cheeks and nose like little blossoms in a field of snow.

'Do your parents know you're outside?' I ask.

'Yeah. They know I'm outside. I told them a friend was coming over to talk. As long as I'm in the front yard it's okay.'

'You didn't go out with A?' I ask.

'You should stop calling him that. I know he doesn't like you, but retaliation isn't always the answer.'

'I'm sorry. I guess you're right,' I say, feeling scolded even though the tone of her voice is normal.

'I just thought you'd be out on a Friday evening,' I remark. I really did think she would be out and I'm interested to know why she isn't.

'Not tonight,' she replies. 'I'm usually out with Walt on Fridays but he had some big family dinner tonight,' she replies.

'And you weren't invited?' I ask unable to hide the surprise in my voice.

She shakes her head and shifts her weight to the other foot as if she's uncomfortable talking about Walt.

'No. I don't know why.'

'I stayed home and played board games with my parents and my pain-in-the-ass sister. It's kind of a tradition on Friday nights if we're at home. If you came around earlier, I would have invited you in to play with us but everyone's getting ready to go to bed.'

'I wish I had known. I would have come around earlier for sure. I wanted to send you a message, but I don't have your number.'

'True,' she says, and I can see the surprise on her face at the fact that we've known each other three weeks already and still haven't exchanged numbers. 'Do you have your phone?' she asks.

I remove it from my back pocket, unlock the screen and hand it to her. 'Here you go.'

'Wow! You trust me with it?' she asks pretending that she's about to take off with it. I tense myself and get ready to give chase.

She realizes I'm ready to chase her and takes off across the front lawn. She kicks off her slippers mid-step as she runs so she's running barefoot across the lawn. Her robe trails behind her, caught in her slipstream. She looks like a white caped superhero running in the moonlight. I give chase, and she squeals as I catch her robe. She shrugs it off, so I'm left holding it in my hands. I catch her scent from the robe. It's so . . . her. In that instant I know I'll never forget that scent. I breathe deeply taking in her scent as I continue to chase her. I finally catch her and she tries to twist away but trips over her foot and goes down on the grass squealing and giggling as she pulls me down with her.

I manage to stay my fall and prevent myself from landing on her.

I push myself up and then position myself on my hands and knees over her. The moonlight catches her full in the face again and I'm mesmerized by her beautiful eyes and her lips. Her short hair is messed up from running and the fall, but it looks so perfect right then. She smiles. I haven't known her long but I have seen her smile before. Only those smiles weren't this smile.

This smile is different. It's a happy smile, but a different happy to what I've seen before. It's a contented smile, a smile that believes in the best in life and great things still to come. It's a smile that I'm responsible for. I want to give her more smiles like that.

There's a silence between us as we look at each other. She bites her lower lip as her eyes travel over my face. I see them settle on my lips and mine settle on hers.

I decide to take a risk and move closer to her ever so slightly. My movement is not that obvious but maybe she senses it. In the next instant, she holds my cell phone between us facing her. Then she turns it to me.

'You need to unlock it again.'

I push back so I can balance as I unlock my phone's screen again. I hand the phone to her and she takes it, her face lit by the screen and the moonlight now.

She keys in her number and saves it.

'There you go,' she says handing my phone back to me.

'Thanks,' I say as I begin to scroll to 'Nora' on my contacts, only there isn't any 'Nora' saved.

I look at her confused.

'You have to find my name,' she smiles.

'Oh really?' I ask.

'Yes really,' she says.

'Okay, I'll be up all night trying to find it.'

'I don't think it's that hard,' she says.

'You didn't save Walt's number instead, did you?'

She laughs. It's the first time I've heard her laugh. It's a clear laugh, a happy laugh. It's husky but also a bit high pitched and I'm pretty sure we've woken up her family if they were already sleeping. I glance at the house nervously.

'Don't worry,' she says. 'They sleep like logs except for my pain-in-the-ass sister.'

'You should stop calling her that.' I mimic her admonishment when she told me to stop referring to Walt as an 'A'.

'Touché,' she smiles.

We fall silent then. It seems like an eternity but it's just a few moments. We're looking at each other again and I decide to take a chance. I lean down slowly. She watches me and her face gives nothing away. I lose my nerve at the last moment with my nose almost touching hers.

Finally, she whispers, 'What do you want?'

I want to tell her, I really do. Right then, right there but I'm gripped by the fear of rejection. I'm terrified that if I tell her and she doesn't feel the same, this is as close as I will ever get and it will all be over like a dream that will fade into a memory.

'I like you,' I whisper. It's something. Not everything I want to say, but I'm dipping my toes in the water. I hope she'll reciprocate with something. She does, but it's not what I want to hear.

'My sister's watching,' she whispers.

When you're with someone you like you want to know there's a chance of something. You want to say how you feel but can't help being afraid they don't feel the same. You want an affirmation no matter how small it is.

Telling me her sister's watching is not that. It's like a way not to answer.

'Okay,' I say and push back. I get up and hold my hand out to her. She takes it and I help her up. We brush ourselves off and look at each other again.

'I guess I better be going,' I say softly.

She seems disappointed but nods. 'Okay.'

'I brought your book,' I add as I remove it from my backpack and hold it out to her. She takes it, thanks me and then turns and heads for the stairs leading up to the porch and front door.

'I'll look for your number,' I call loud enough for her to hear.

She turns and smiles. 'I'll be waiting.'

I watch her go inside and close the door before I get on my bike and head home.

I'm disappointed that she didn't say she likes me too, but maybe she was simply being honest and I'm just trying to read too much into it. I still have hope after she said she'll be waiting for me to find her number.

I get home, park and lock my bike, and head inside. Mom and Dad have gone to bed and I make my way to my room quietly. I close the door and turn on my desk lamp before I collapse on my bed. I unlock my phone and begin to search for her number.

I check my contacts once, and then again. She did not save it under Nora. I scroll through my contacts again now looking for names I don't recognize. I don't have that many contacts because I haven't made many friends with all the moving we've done.

I find a name that stands out from the rest. I don't know it. It must be her.

Viviane.

There's only one way to find out.

Nora

I lie awake recalling the fun Bryce and I had in the garden.

I hope he sends me a message. I remember how close we were. I wonder if he wanted to kiss me. I wish he had. I thought he wanted to, but I had been afraid. I had been sure my sister was watching and if he had kissed me, it would have been all over school on Monday which meant Walt would find out and it would become hunting season with Bryce as the prey.

I won't let that happen. My feelings for Bryce and thoughts about Walt finally bring home the reality that it's time to move on from Walt. I decide to break the news to him as soon as I can. Then, as if he knows I am thinking of him, of us, Walt sends me a text. I guess that whatever he did tonight must be finished. I feel irritation when I see it's a text from him and not Bryce. It's just another point that confirms I am over him. I answer his message and wonder if I should simply break up by text message there and then.

But that's not me. That's cruel. I know people who have done it. They even bragged about it like it's a status symbol or something. I think it's just cruel and cold.

I sigh as my phone vibrates with another message.

'Go to sleep already,' I murmur, thinking it's another message from Walt.

I unlock my screen and smile. Then I sit up.

It's a message from Bryce.

'Hi Viviane. I don't know a Viviane so I'm guessing you're Nora. Am I right?'

I smile and answer. I'm so excited my hands fly over the letters and I have to correct my words a few times before sending my reply. *'You're right. It's me. Nora Viviane. It wasn't that hard, was it?'*

'No. Should I call you NV or Envy?'

'Neither,' I reply. *'I don't believe I'm a jealous person.'*

'Maybe you haven't met the right person yet,' Bryce sends back.

'Another go at A?' I send back and realize my mistake after sending my message.

'Just saying,' he responds and adds, *'since when did you start calling him A? Something I should know?'*

I clench my teeth at my slip and decide to ignore his question and tease him with my own. *'Do you think you're the right person?'* He doesn't answer immediately. I see him start typing then stop. He starts typing again and stops again. He eventually answers. *'Do you want me to be the right person? Isn't A the right person?'*

It seems we're both good at sparring by text message. I hoped for more from him. I hoped he would be daring and put his feelings out there but he hasn't. Instead, he's turned it around on me.

I don't want to give him insight into what's happening between A . . . I mean Walt and me. It's not his business despite the attraction I feel for him. Even if I break it off with Walt, it won't be right to talk about us to Bryce. If I say something, he might say something to someone and then it would get back to Walt too. No. I need to end it with Walt first. But my irritation has now become a little emotional tantrum and I'm upset that Bryce has not ventured more, taken a risk, and come clear on his feelings. Maybe it's better that way though. My little emotional tantrum stops me from answering him again. I see Walt has sent more messages. I read them quickly and reply with a simple, *'Good night. See you tomorrow.'*

I put my phone on the bedside table and am soon fast asleep.

The next morning, I have to face Ashley at breakfast. She begins singing as soon as I enter the kitchen.

'No-Ra and Who-is-He sitting in a tree, K-i-s-s-i-n-g . . .'

'I wasn't kissing anyone. Mind your own business,' I say.

Dad looks over his paper at me and so does Mom.

'What?' they ask together. 'The boy who visited last night?'

'I didn't kiss him,' I say defensively. 'I wish turd breath would shut up and mind her own business.'

'Who is he anyway?' Mom asks. I can tell her interest is piqued.

'He's the new kid in school. I told you about him the other day. He borrowed some of my books to catch up on work and he wanted to return them.'

'You should invite him around to play board games,' Dad says again.

'I told him if he he'd been here earlier, he could have played games with us.'

'I think Walt's going to play with him when he finds out,' Ashley says.

'Stay out of my business. All he wanted was to return my books. It's got nothing to do with Walt.'

'Why? You've got nothing to hide from Walt, have you? Especially if Bryce was "just returning books",' Ashley says, her voice dripping with sarcasm.

I sigh and get up. I pick up my bowl of cereal and my coffee and leave the kitchen. I am not in the mood to listen to Ashley's trash so early in the morning.

'I didn't see any books by the way,' Ashley shouts at my back as I leave the kitchen.

'Must be because you're stupid and blind,' I call back.

'We'll see what Walt says about it,' Ashley calls after me.

I won't dignify her words with another reply. Life is too short and I want to enjoy my day even though I think she's ruined it already.

It's Saturday and I laze on the sofa for most of the morning. Ashley's gone out and so have Mom and Dad. Sometimes there's nothing nicer than being able to laze around the house on your own on the weekend. The house is quiet and there's no one to call and ask you to help with anything. I hear the grandfather clock chime in the hallway and resume its ticking. Things like that are music when the house is so quiet. Outside I can hear birds chirping in the garden. They sound so happy and free and from where I lie on the sofa, I can see them frolicking in the birdbath enjoying the water immensely. Everything is just so peaceful and I could lie here all day.

I eventually tire of watching television and relaxing on the sofa. I head upstairs, shower, and get dressed. I'm still not over my little emotional tantrum with Bryce but I check my phone anyway hoping he has sent me a message.

Nothing.

Just a message from Walt. '*Movie tonight?*'

That's it. I mean, really? Not a 'good morning', no emojis, nothing.

As I look at his message it strikes me how quickly my feelings for Walt have changed. But then, perhaps they hadn't changed quickly at all. Perhaps they have been like this for a while and I just hadn't bothered to notice.

So why am I noticing only now, I wonder? I don't have to think about it too hard. The answer comes to me almost immediately from that wise little voice in my head that always seems to have the answers.

Because you have an incentive. I know I don't need to ask what the incentive is. It's Bryce.

I know it's right. I like Bryce. But, I have questions.

I don't like other boys at school. Not because of Walt. There just hasn't been anyone that I like. Not that way anyway.

But I do like Bryce. But I wonder, even though I like him, is he really just a 'get out of jail free card' as far as Walt is concerned? Would he be a rebound relationship? I don't think so. After all, leaving Walt isn't going to cause me any heartbreak.

But why has it taken Bryce to make me decide to leave Walt? Why didn't I do it sooner? I wonder.

I can't answer that. The best idea I can come up with is that I have settled into a comfort zone. I turn on the radio to drown my thoughts. I decide to end it with Walt and reply to his message.

'*Let's just be spontaneous,*' I send him. '*Let's do dinner and then we can decide what we feel like from there. Okay?*'

'*Sure. Where do you want to do dinner?*'

It's the kind of answer I expect from him. He never suggests anything romantic or chooses a restaurant anymore.

'*Harry's Diner,*' I reply. '*I'll see you there. 7 p.m.?*'

'*Sure,*' he replies.

And that's it. The entirety of our conversation for the day. It's disappointing and I scroll back over the last few weeks' messages which becomes scrolling into the last few months' messages. I can't believe how long it's been like this and how long I have tolerated it.

It's time for a change. I toss my phone aside, wishing Bryce would send me a message but he doesn't. I'm too stubborn to contact him so I put on my headphones and grab my book. I read as I listen to music.

Boys. Who needs them?

Nora

Dad and Mom drop me at Harry's diner before seven. I go inside and choose my favourite spot. It's a booth in the back. I like to come here when I want some privacy from the world. Whenever anyone asks if I know the place or if I come here often, I always lie. I don't want anyone to come looking for me when I want privacy.

We're all entitled to that one place where we can be alone. You might think I could be alone in my room but Ashley does her best to make that impossible.

I take in the decor of the diner while I wait for Walt. The sofas are white and the tables aluminium topped. The tables are bolted to the floor which makes me think I'm on a ship when I come here. The round windows are like ship portals. All that's needed is the to and fro swaying like a ship and the sound of the ocean to complete the experience. Or the tilted deck feeling I think, because this boat is about to sink faster than the Titanic. I settle down on the sofa in the booth. I can see the entrance clearly from where I am. Walt arrives late as usual. I wave to catch his attention and he heads over to the booth where I am.

Walt does not apologize. He tries to slide into the booth beside me but I motion to the opposite side of the table.

He hesitates a moment, guesses I must be upset with him, shrugs, and then slides in opposite me.

'Hey,' he says with the usual half-smile on his face when he knows he's in trouble but hoping the half-smile will make the problem go away.

Perhaps I sound like a whining, judgmental bitch by now. I don't think I am though. It's taken a while to get to this stage. Walt doesn't seem to care anymore. He cared in the early days when we first started dating but now, he seems to take everything for granted, including me.

He's never on time for our dates anymore.

He doesn't dress as well as he used to.

He never apologizes for anything.

He never asks me how I am.

He always pays as if that makes up for everything.

Just once in a while, it would be great if he showed a bit of care, if he surprised me with a flower, even if it was a bloom from a weed he found on the way to me, it would be enough. But he doesn't. The only thing that matters is that I am his. I belong to him. Or so he thinks.

'You're late.'

'Yeah. Shall we order something?' he asks, opening the menu.

And there it is. That. Right there. As if I hadn't said a word. I don't reply.

He looks up from the menu when I say nothing. I'm looking at him as if my gaze could look right through him.

'What?' he asks. His tone suggests I have said something to indicate I am upset. I am.

'No. I don't feel like having anything,' I say, at last. My words are cold.

He looks confused and then he looks around as if making sure we are in a restaurant. His actions drip with sarcasm, saying what I know he is thinking but is afraid to say. It's not hard to read someone when they are so shallow.

He is thinking, *Why the hell did you suggest we meet here then?*

I know he won't ask though. He shrugs at last and then looks at the menu again ignoring the fact that I am still looking at him. If my eyes were lasers, he'd have two holes burned through him.

'Suit yourself. I'm going to order something,' he says.

I simmer in silence and watch him. He decides what he wants and motions to the waitress who comes over as soon as she is finished taking another couple's order.

I watch him as he gives the waitress his order. He finishes and expects her to leave without double-checking with me again.

She turns to me and asks, 'Would you like to order something?'

I can see by her expression she is amazed that Walt did not ask me if I want to order anything. I shake my head. 'No, thank you.'

She nods and leaves. I think she thinks we're arguing. She's not wrong. We will be soon.

Walt looks at me. 'Where are we going after here?'

Right then, I am done. Finally, at last, I am done. I know I made the right decision when I decided to tell him we were over tonight.

'Home,' I say coldly.

He looks at me for a moment and then his face lights up. 'Really? Are your folks going out? And Ashley too?'

I know what he's thinking. He's been pressuring me to have sex with him for ages. I kept putting it off because

I don't want to have sex with him and I don't think I'm ready to take that step yet with any boy. He thinks that at last, this is the night.

'No,' I reply. 'I've been doing some thinking.'

'What about?' he asks.

I decide to make it quick. 'I wanted to meet here because I wanted to tell you that I'm breaking up with you, Walt. '

Suddenly I have all his attention.

'What? Why?' He sits forward and leans his elbows on the table. 'Because I don't love you. I'm not happy when I'm with you and I want to be alone right now.'

The way he looks at me tells me he's wondering if I'm being honest. He can't accept that I am simply breaking up with him. There must be another reason and he draws his conclusion quickly. 'It's the new boy, isn't it?'

'No!' I exclaim a little too loudly. People at the tables close to us glance our way.

'I'm gonna beat his ass past Christmas,' Walt says, his eyes narrowed.

I lean forward and lower my voice drastically. 'It has nothing to do with the new boy, Walt.'

'What then?' he asks.

'It has everything to do with you and your attitude,' I say.

'My attitude? What's that supposed to mean?'

'Oh c'mon. You never show me respect. You never ask me how I am anymore. You can't even be bothered to send me messages that suggest you care about me. I'm just some girl that you like to have around when it suits you . . .'

I pause and then correct myself. 'No. Not you. Your ego.'

'My ego?' Walt asks. He doesn't seem to agree but why would he?

'Whatever Walt. It's over. Leave the new kid alone. It's got nothing to do with him. Don't go beating him up because you think I've got something going with him. I don't. Okay?'

He says nothing but stares at me.

'In fact, why don't you just stop beating him and anyone else up? You don't need to prove yourself to me. You never had to and if you did, I assure you I would not expect you to beat up other kids. It's just mean.'

He begins to react at last as the truth of what I am telling him kicks in. It's over between us. I know he doesn't want it to be over. I can see it in his eyes but he's not the begging type. So he reacts the only way he knows how.

'Well, if you're not going out with me anymore, then I guess you don't have any right to tell me what I should or shouldn't do.'

I'm not going to argue. 'Sure. I know that.'

'Doesn't seem like it,' he says with a sneer.

'What's that supposed to mean?'

'It means . . .' he starts to say as the waitress arrives with his order. He waits for her to leave and then continues, 'It means that if I want to beat up the new kid or any other kid, you don't get to tell me not to.'

It's the typical small-minded response I've come to expect from him. I'm glad his food has just arrived.

'You should think about growing up,' I say. 'That comment is exactly the kind of attitude that has brought us to where we are right now.'

I don't give him a chance to reply as I slide out of the booth. He watches me get up but says nothing.

'Enjoy your meal. I'll see you at school,' I say and head for the door. I know he can't run after me. He's got food he has to pay for even if he doesn't eat it. I can almost feel his eyes burning into my back as I leave. I don't give him the pleasure of looking back. I want him to know we are done.

I step outside and I know I need to get away from here. I have not arranged for my parents to fetch me here. I knew I wouldn't be long, but I wasn't ready to tell my parents I was coming here to end it with Walt. They can fetch me later. Just not here. I don't want to be here when Walt finishes his meal. I turn and start walking to the nearest mall.

Bryce

I lay awake waiting for a reply from Nora but she doesn't answer.

After thirty minutes I type another message but don't send it. I wonder why she stopped replying and decide it would be better not to force anything.

I'm curious but I also don't want to seem desperate. I remind myself that I'm the new kid on the block. I'll always be the new kid on the block until some other new kid arrives at the school.

The new kid on the block is always the outcast. At least in the early days. I realize that I don't know Nora that well even though I thought we had a great time outside her house.

If I look desperate, she might tell her friends I started stalking her or harassing her. It has happened before. I always come off second best. It won't be the first time. I reread our messages up to the point that she stopped answering me and I can't see what I've said wrong. I wonder if she simply fell asleep but I doubt it.

I realize she was asking me if I was interested in her and that I knocked the question back to her for the same reason I restrained myself from making my feelings too obvious when I was at her house. I know that saying I like her in a text message would mean that she has the proof to show others. It happened before and things did not end well for me. Could it happen twice? Yes. I don't care much for Walt, and she doesn't seem to either, but I don't want to provoke his wrath unnecessarily.

I finally manage to push the mess I've made in my mind into a corner and drift off to sleep.

I wake late the next morning and the first thing I do is check my messages.

Nothing.

I'm disappointed but now I begin to think that I might have dodged a bullet after all. Maybe when I didn't answer, she decided that I was onto her. If she fell asleep the night before, she's had more than enough time to send me a message this morning, but she hasn't.

I eventually get up and head to the kitchen. My parents have left a note for me under a fridge magnet. I read it before I open the fridge and remove the milk for cereal.

Mom and Dad have gone out for breakfast which leaves me home alone. My excitement and anticipation of hearing from Nora wanes slowly and hope turns to disappointment. I know why I am not contacting her but why she isn't contacting me, I have no idea.

I finish my breakfast and decide to explore the town on my bike. I haven't taken the time to get to know my new hometown and it's a great day to do just that.

When you've moved around as much as I have, you don't make friends easily because you don't expect to stay around very long in your new home. I have instead found appreciation for other things.

The blue skies and beautiful cotton clouds on bright sunny days, and places where I can be close to nature and alone with my thoughts. I started a journal some time ago in which I record the different animals and insects I find in the forests around the places where we live. It amazes me how I can find the same species so far apart and, on the other hand, how there can be so many different creatures in the world.

It's become a hobby to photograph insects and animals and then identify them in the library or online. I have built up a wealth of knowledge so far and it keeps growing. I find it to be quite meditative as well.

A millipede tickles my skin as its feet work in perfect unison like a tiny well-trained army to march across my hand. I haven't seen one like this before and I photograph it so I can try to identify it later.

Being out in nature does the trick. I have soon forgotten about Nora and am lost in the magic of the tiny world of creatures in the forest.

After I have studied insects and explored the forest for two hours, I reach the top of what I think is a small rise. The treeline ends a short way ahead of me. The trees have thinned and from where I stand, I can see for miles.

It's not what I expected and I advance to the treeline where I stop in awe. The ground drops away a short distance ahead of me and I think it must be a cliff. I'm hesitant to go much closer to the edge because I don't know how safe it is. Even so, from where I stand, I can see for miles around. The view is nothing short of breathtaking and I take it in, lost in the beauty of the view. I feel like a bird looking down on the world from my perch above it.

Eventually, I tear my gaze away from the view, feeling that if I gaze at it too long, it will lose its breathtaking value.

I look around me and spot a large, round smooth concrete slab. It's been built up out of the ground. I don't understand what its purpose is or who might have built it. I quickly look around, searching for more signs of humanity as I wonder if I am trespassing on someone's property. There are no paths leading here and there is no sign of civilization here other than the platform. I cross to it and then step onto it.

I think it would be great for camping and decide immediately that I will make a point of camping out here some nights.

You better do it soon, I think to myself, *before you move on again*.

If I have learned one thing in my short life so far, it's to do what I want to do as soon as possible. Especially when what I want to do relates to the area where we live. Too often I have missed out on things I wanted to do because I always believed I had tomorrow. I now know, that even though tomorrow may come, it might not bring the same opportunities we have today. Here today and gone tomorrow is a saying that is all too applicable to my life. Because of that, I've learned to follow my heart and listen to my gut and do what I want to do as soon as I can.

I sit down on the concrete platform and take in the surroundings. A soft breeze caresses the branches and whispers through the leaves while birds sound like a choir in this peaceful, unspoiled place. I watch clouds gallop and dance across the sky.

I marvel at how secluded this place is even as I wonder who built the platform. It's dusty and it's clear no one's been here in ages. I think how nice it would be to be here with someone else. There's only one person that comes to mind at the moment and that's Nora.

I wonder if she likes nature at all. We never got round to talking about things like that and I realize there's a lot I still don't know about her. If I had another friend who was interested in nature I would have just as much fun I think. Two people can always see so much more than one. It would double the experience of what I could see out here in the woods. I decide that I will return for sure.

I try to push thoughts of Nora away as fast as they enter my mind but it's not that easy. I check my mobile. No message. I'm disappointed but try to shrug it off. I can picture Nora out here in sneakers and jeans. Probably an old t-shirt. I wonder if she's the tomboy type in this environment or if she will be squeamish when she sees the bugs that I occasionally pick up and handle. A millipede tickles my hand with its myriad legs as I let it cross the back of my hand. A butterfly lands on me and I let it rest there as long as it likes opening and closing its wings, as if trying to hypnotize me before it finally flutters off into the woods.

Shadows lengthen with the afternoon sun. The air becomes chilly quickly as the tall trees block the setting sun's rays and darkness approaches faster than usual. I decide it's time to head home. After retrieving my bike from where I hid it in the bushes, I cycle home. I consider it a productive day and look forward to identifying the creatures I found on my hike through the forest when I get home.

Mom and Dad are watching television when I arrive. I greet them and am glad to see they're getting along. I wonder how long it will last before Dad brings home the news that we're moving again. The last place was a new record for the shortest period that we spent in one place. I've recorded the places where we've stayed and I always compare the time we stay to see if it's shorter or longer than ever before.

I have a quick dinner and then head to the computer in my room to complete my study of the new creatures I found in the forest.

Nora

Monday arrives at last. I've been irritated most of the weekend. I don't know what happened with Bryce. He hasn't sent me another message all weekend. But it's not just that. Ashley's been a pain the whole weekend. She overheard me telling Mom and Dad that I ended it with Walt and hasn't stopped accusing me of breaking it off because of Bryce.

I arrive at my locker. Bryce is there but doesn't see me because his locker door is blocking his view. I hope I can get my stuff and leave before he sees me.

I don't know why he didn't send any messages, but I don't want to talk to him. The passage is filled with students in the hallway equivalent of rush hour traffic. I just begin to think that I can get my book and make a getaway when Ashley dashes all hope. We parted ways when we arrived at school, but now she arrives with her friends and begins singing.

'No-Ra and the new kid, lying on the grass, k-i-s-s-i-n-g . . .'

I feel myself turn red with anger and embarrassment. I grab the books I need and turn, slamming my locker shut.

'Will you grow up?' I say loudly. 'We never kissed.'

Time seems to stand still. Bryce has closed his locker and is now looking between Ashley and me. Our eyes meet for the briefest of moments before I look at Ashley again.

'Who the hell would want to kiss him anyway?' I ask vehemently as my eyes meet his again. If he's offended, he doesn't show it. I don't have time to see his reaction because someone else has emerged from the crowd in the passageway. He's looking from me to Bryce and back again.

'So that *is* why you broke up with me,' he says, his face dark with anger. A murmur runs through the students gathered in the hall. Some pull out their phones to capture the drama that is about to unfold.

'No . . .' I object and cut myself off as I look at Ashley. 'Look what you've done now.'

She sticks her tongue out at me, turns, and heads away down the corridor proudly.

Bryce stands his ground and closes his locker door.

'You gonna stand and take your beating like a man or a dweeb?' Walt says when he gets to Bryce.

'I haven't done anything,' Bryce says.

Walt lashes out and punches Bryce in the stomach. He doubles over as he clutches his stomach in pain. 'You're wrong, punk. Just being here means you've done something wrong. If I see you, it means you've done something wrong.'

Bryce says nothing as he slowly recovers from the blow. The passage has fallen silent as everyone watches what's happening.

I realize I can't just stand there and let Bryce take a beating. Before I know it, I'm between the two of them.

'Leave him alone!' I say angrily staring into Walt's face.

He looks at me as his eyes narrow. 'You're protecting him. So there *is* something between the two of you! I knew it!'

Walt steps forward and pushes me aside. I lose my balance and fall in the middle of the passage but Walt doesn't care as he moves in to strike Bryce again.

Bryce doesn't stand for it. He lashes out with his foot and catches Walt between the legs. Walt reaches down and grasps his crotch as he groans and tries to ease the pain. He's doubled over and breathing heavily. Bryce steps past him and offers me his hand.

'Are you okay?'

I look at his hand and then my eyes meet his.

'I don't need you to care about me. I can help myself,' I say angrily as I gather my things and stand up, ignoring his hand. 'You're both so childish!'

I turn and head down the hallway. I'm going the wrong way and I turn around and head the other way.

'Turn that off will you!' I shout at one kid who's capturing the scene on her phone. Bryce is about to say something to Walt who has barely recovered and is wiping tears of pain from his eyes, but when he sees me coming back, he stops and watches me.

He is probably hoping I have changed my mind and am coming back to say something to him.

'You're still childish,' I say and continue past without stopping and head to class.

Everyone in the hallway has watched the drama unfold. I know I looked stupid turning around and heading the other way but what was I supposed to do? What happened had nothing to do with anyone else in the hallway and they can make of it what they choose. I don't care.

I see Ashley as I near the end of the throng in the hallway.

'You're such an ass,' I tell her angrily. Her friends look at me in disbelief. They can't believe I would say such a thing to my sister in front of her friends, but I'm not finished.

'Don't come near me again. Ever. What happens in my life has nothing to do with you. You're just a wannabe me and it's all you'll ever be. It's about time you tried living your life instead of trying to live or be part of mine. I mean it when I say that I want you to stay away from me. Got it?'

Ashley is speechless. She stares at me in shock. She never imagined that I would be so angry or so brutal, especially in front of her friends.

'Got it?' I repeat, louder this time. The hallway behind me falls silent as everyone turns to see what the new commotion is about.

Ashley turns red. All the attention is on her now. She looks back at me, swallows guiltily, and nods. 'Sure, Nora. Got it,' she replies just loud enough for me to hear her.

I resume walking. At the end of the corridor, I turn the corner and leave everyone behind.

Bryce is in my class and to say awkward is how the rest of the day feels, is an understatement. I am thankful that I am seated in front of him, so I don't have to look at him. I don't want him to see me looking at him at all and get the wrong impression.

The day seems to drag by slower than ever and when school is finally finished, I feel like the weight of the world has been lifted off my shoulders. I breathe deeply taking in the smell of the fresh-cut grass in someone's yard, the scent of fresh flowers and trees that line the streets and I soon forget about the day. I've been in a dark mood all day but it's improving now.

My best friend, Christine, wasn't at school today. That made the day worse. I haven't contacted her to ask what's wrong, but I do so as I walk home.

'*Are you okay?*'

My phone vibrates with her reply moments later. '*I have food poisoning. I'll be out for a few days. What happened to you today?*'

'*What do you mean,*' I send back.

She sends me a video of the incident at school. I watch it and feel my face turn red. I can't believe it. *Is nothing sacred anymore?* I wonder.

'*I broke up with Walt,*' I send back.

'*That's obvious,*' Christine replies. '*What about the new guy? I had no idea . . .*'

'*There's nothing to have an idea about,*' I send back angrily. I immediately realize my tone is wrong and send another message. '*Sorry, it's been a bad day. I'll tell you later.*'

I put my phone away and focus on getting home. I'm not in the mood for any more irritation today. It seems as if Ashley finally gets the message too. I enter our house and she immediately comes running towards me from the living room.

'Nora, I'm sorry, I . . .'

Her voice trails off as the look in my eyes tells her I might just have contracted rabies and am about to go feral on her. I stop, glaring at her while saying nothing.

   She stops, hesitates for the briefest of moments, and then turns and heads back to the sofa where she takes her seat and resumes watching television. Satisfied that she got the hint, I head upstairs to my room where I close the world outside my door and fall onto the bed letting my thoughts wander.

Bryce

I can't change anything about the fact that I have classes with Nora. It's awkward, to say the least. After the scene in the hallway, Walt appears to have decided to leave me alone. At least for the time being.

I'm not worried about him though. He's not the first bully I've had to deal with.

A few times, Nora's eyes meet mine during school. It's not that we're looking at each other deliberately. It's just the nasty way the universe has of making two people who know each other but don't want to, feel even more awkward around each other.

I contemplate moving to another desk but decide against it. I refuse to give Nora the pleasure of feeling that she has driven me to feel that I need to move desks to get away from her. What promised to be a great friendship is now so frozen, I'm sure our classmates can feel the cold.

The worst is that I'm not sure what happened.

Weeks pass and Nora and I are like ships passing in the night. We don't talk to each other. I keep a low profile at school, say little and stay out of trouble. I begin to notice other girls but feel guilty when I do. I try to keep my distance from other girls, but life is a two-way street and some girls notice me. Even so, I feel as if I am betraying Nora even though we never got anything started.

I keep telling myself to bide my time. *We'll move soon enough. We always do*, I tell myself. I find it ironic how having hated moving so much in the past, I now find myself looking forward to it. The universe seems happy to deny me my wish and our stay soon becomes long enough that it will never be considered one of the shortest stays in any place.

Walt finally tires of me and starts to bully other kids from the school. He tries his luck occasionally, but the fight seems to have gone out of him where I am concerned. I'm grateful he's had a change of heart.

I make friends with other kids. I wouldn't call anyone a best friend but it's nice to have friends that you can pass the time with. I am closer to Grant than any of the others though and one day after school he asks me about Walt.

'Does Walt still bully you?'

'No,' I shake my head. 'That stopped the day I kicked him. He tried a few times after that and then just seemed to give up. It's like the fight went out of him.'

Grant nods. 'What about that girl he was with that broke up with him?'

'Nora?' I ask.

'That's her,' Grant says. 'Was there any truth that you were dating her? It would have taken guts to cheat on him with his girlfriend.'

I can't help but laugh. 'It would have. But I didn't.'

'We all thought you were so lucky man. She's beautiful.'

I don't say anything. I don't want to get into gossip about Nora.

'Besides she broke up with Walt that weekend. It all seemed to fit.'

'Why don't you ask her out?' I say. 'I never dated her.'

Grant laughs now. 'No. I already tried. She's cold man. I don't know how you got close to her.'

I shrug. 'It kinda just happened. We were friends and then we weren't. I don't know what I did wrong. I just don't want to press the issue.'

'Well, she's not dating anyone at the moment as far as I know. You should . . .'

'It's in the past,' I say shaking my head.

We walk in silence for a while and my thoughts stay on Nora. I reached the end of my maths exercise book a few days earlier and I wonder how far she is from reaching the end of her notebook and if she'll find my note. Even if she has, or does, I'm guessing I'm the last person she'll think might have written the note to her when she finds it or if she has already found it. It's so far in the past and I'm sure that she must have lent her notebook to a few other people by now.

When Grant and I part ways, I'm left thinking of Nora again. I wonder if I should contact her and ask to meet just to clear the air. If nothing else, I can apologize for whatever it is she thinks I did or didn't do.

I wonder what has got into Nora. As far as I know she is not dating anyone and just about any boy at school would give anything to go out with her. Grant is just the latest boy I have heard of who she has turned down.

I'm curious what happened and I can't help feeling it has to do with the weekend that she stopped texting me.

Ally joins our class two months later and becomes the new kid at school. Her red hair looks like it's on fire. Her eyes are emerald green and her cheeks are sprinkled with freckles. She is beautiful and cute but mostly keeps to herself.

I find myself drawn to her because she is new and I know what it's like having no friends in a new school. I catch her after school one day as she is just beginning her walk home. It's the same way as I go, so I hope we can walk and talk.

'Hey, Ally,' I call as I catch up to her.

She stops and turns. Her shoulder-length hair looks like it has never known a brush, but the look suits her. It flies around now as she turns to see who's calling her.

Her eyes meet mine. I see the flicker of recognition in them, but her expression gives nothing else away.

She says nothing but waits for me to catch my breath before she begins walking again. There's an awkward silence between us that goes on far too long. I decide I better break it since I called out to her.

'How are you settling in?' I ask.

She shrugs. 'Okay, I guess.'

'Where were you before?'

'Oklahoma. People are more friendly there,' she says, looking down at her feet as we walk.

'Why did you come here?' I ask.

'My mom got transferred. What about you?'

She looks up for the first time since we started walking and meets my gaze. Her emerald eyes are bright. I think they're more full of life than she knows.

'Same. My dad got transferred. I know what you mean by people being more friendly elsewhere.'

'Really? You've been here longer than me,' she says. Her tone tells me her comment is more of a question.

'People just don't seem to make friends easily around here. The only interest I've had since I got here was the school bully.'

She laughs briefly.

'At least it's more attention than I've had,' she says.

'Kinda sucks don't you think?' I ask.

She shrugs. 'Maybe. I haven't been worried about not making friends. When we moved out here, I had no idea what it was going to be like. I was sad to leave Oklahoma, but I told myself it's a good chance to start over.'

'What do you mean start over? You're just a kid. We're kids.'

She laughs again. 'Well, sometimes you just want a change. I felt like I wanted a change even though I had to leave my friends behind. I have an opportunity to see a new town, another part of our country and hopefully meet new people but I haven't done that here. Met new people I mean.'

She walks in silence a bit and then answers me. 'I don't make friends easily myself so even though the kids at school aren't that accepting of newcomers either you can't blame only them.'

'I had the same experience and I'm still finding my way. But hey, I'll be your friend if you're okay with that.'

Ally looks at me as she considers my words and then finally nods. She holds out her hand and I shake it.

'Okay then . . . friend,' she smiles. 'I'm willing to give our friendship a try.'

I smile and we start walking again.

We make small talk and are soon so engrossed that I follow her home. We arrive at her front gate. The house is plain. If anyone asked me if it stands out from the rest of the houses on the street I'd have to say yes. It's the smallest of all the houses I can see. Ally and her mom don't live extravagantly. Neither do we, but I think we're maybe better off than Ally and her mom. I feel guilty about the thought immediately. I'm not materialistic and I've never been one to judge others by their wealth.

Other things are more important than a fancy house, I scold myself.

'Do you want to come in?' Ally asks. I accept her invitation. I have nothing else to do just then so I shrug and agree.

Ally opens the gate and steps through. She holds it open for me and closes it when I'm through. Then she takes the lead up the pathway that is made of slabs of smooth stone spaced at reasonable intervals so one can walk comfortably along it. Weeds have sprouted in the spaces between the stones, just like our garden at home.

Ally unlocks the door and enters. I follow. I look around the entrance hall as she closes the door.

The house still has that not lived in for a while smell about it. It doesn't look like they have settled in yet. Pictures in frames stand on the floor resting against the walls here and there. Ally catches me looking at the pictures.

'Sorry 'bout those. We haven't quite settled in yet. Mom knows where she wants the pictures to hang but she hasn't gotten round to hanging them. I guess it gives her a chance to change her mind too. She's changed her mind about where a few of them should go and moved them around. Good thing she hasn't found someone to hang them yet.'

'Oh,' I reply. 'I could hang them if you want. I mean I'm no expert at hanging pictures but I'm sure if you need help hammering nails into the walls, I can do it for you.'

Ally looks at me for a moment, as if she is surprised that someone who she has just met would offer to help them. 'Would you do that?'

I nod. 'Sure. Why not? I'm sure I couldn't mess it up,' I reply. 'Worst I could do is miss the nails and hit my fingers.'

Ally laughs. 'That's exactly why mom hasn't tried to hang them herself. I'm not much good either I'm afraid.'

'Well, give me some nails and a hammer and I'll do it for you.'

'Thanks,' Ally says. 'I'll tell my mom you offered and let you know.'

Bryce

She begins making her way down the passage. I get the feeling that she's lost interest in the pictures and wants to do something else.

I wonder if I should follow. I guess she is headed for her bedroom and as she walks, she pulls her shirt out of her jeans.

'I'm just going to get changed,' she calls over her shoulder. 'Why don't you grab us each a soda from the fridge in the kitchen?'

'Okay,' I call back as I begin to wander through the house looking for the kitchen. I look at the furniture in the living room and I feel as if I have been transported back to the seventies.

I cross to the fridge and open it and try to look for the sodas. I hate going through other people's things. Even though Ally told me to get sodas for us I feel like a burglar.

'Top shelf, back right,' Ally says from behind me, and I jump and turn.

'Shit!' The curse escapes me before I can stop myself and she laughs again. Louder this time. Her smile is wider, she looks really happy.

'I didn't mean to scare you,' she says at last when she stops laughing.

'Could have fooled me,' I say managing a smile of my own as my heartbeat slows to less than a hundred miles an hour.

She reaches past me into the fridge and I catch the scent of her perfume as she does so. It's soft and reminds me of the flowers I loved in the garden of the house we lived in before. She hands me one bottle of soda and opens the other as I close the fridge. I'm studying her with interest and she notices.

'What?' she asks curiously but defensively.

I shake my head. 'Nothing.'

She takes a drink of her soda looking at me over the bottle as she does so. She swallows, lowers the bottle, and lets out a belch looking surprised immediately afterward.

It's my turn to laugh as she asks, 'Where did that come from?'

Then she bursts into laughter. It's contagious and I burst into laughter before I can swallow my soda. Instead, I spray it over her and all over the kitchen.

'Ew,' she says calmly as if getting sprayed by soda is something she experiences every day. She wipes her face and looks at her clothes. I recover from my laughter and apologize.

'I am so sorry,' I say. 'Give me a cloth or something and I'll clean it up.'

Ally grabs a rag and hands me a bottle of household cleaner, then proceeds to watch me wipe down everything.

'When I asked you to come in, it wasn't so that you could clean the kitchen,' she says smiling when I'm done at last.

'Yeah, let's just say it's a little gift to help you settle in,' I reply.

'I should have you round more often then,' Ally jokes.

'Did I add, I only do it the first time I visit?' I ask playfully.

'Ha, ha. You're not so slow,' she smiles. Then she turns and heads for the living room leaving me to catch up. When I do, she's opened the door to the garden and is outside already.

I follow her and catch her scent again. I like it. I like her too, I decide. As a friend at this point. Definitely not how I felt with Nora but it's not always the same with everyone anyway.

I push thoughts of Nora away as I watch Ally. Her red hair seems to shine even brighter in the bright afternoon sun. There is a pond in the back of the garden. Stones protrude above the water. Ally crosses them like a ballet dancer with her arms outstretched for balance. I look around the garden so that I am not staring at her all the time. I look back at her and notice she is balancing on one of the rocks in the pond now. She is looking at me curiously.

'Are you okay?' she asks.

I raise my hand to shield my eyes from the afternoon sun as much as hide my face from her if possible. 'Yeah, I'm fine. I just thought I saw something moving in the flower bed.'

She motions with her hand as if to say so what and then asks, 'Why don't you try and cross the pond like me?'

It sounds like a challenge, and I feel like I have to take her up on it.

'I can, I guess. Don't let me catch you,' I say as I start towards the pond.

'I doubt you could do that,' she calls back raising the stakes on her challenge.

I land on the first stone and start making my way across. I am moving quickly and want to slow down but am afraid doing so will cause me to lose my balance. I am catching up to her fast and how I do not slip and fall, I do not know.

I try to slow my pace but just as expected, I start to lose my balance before colliding with her.

She screams and we go down in a tangle of arms and legs landing in the pond.

When we get up, we are soaked through and covered in dirt and algae from the pond.

Ally looks at me and bursts out laughing, oblivious of how she looks. She is soaked through from head to foot.

'What?' I ask tearing my gaze away from her.

'You're a mess. You look like you have pond plants growing in your hair.'

'Gross,' I say as my hand finds the slimy plants and algae nesting on my head.

She laughs again as she watches my reaction.

'You're not exactly a picture of beauty yourself,' I tell her.

Her laughter trails off as she looks down at herself for the first time. She suddenly becomes self-conscious. She crosses her arms as she steps out of the pond and starts heading for the house.

'I need to change,' she says.

I follow but stop at the door when she goes inside. It's her home and she can drip on the carpets—I don't want to. She doesn't look back but disappears down the passage. I settle on one of the garden chairs letting myself dry in the afternoon sun until she returns.

She is gone longer than I expected. I consider leaving but suppose it might be rude, so I wait for her. When she finally reappears, she has showered and changed.

She's wearing another pair of shorts and a tank top covered by a plaid shirt knotted at the waist. Damp tendrils of hair hang down on either side of her face. With her hair a darker shade of colour because of its dampness, her eyes look illuminated and her skin a shade paler.

'What happened to you?' she asks.

'What do you mean, what happened to me?'

'I thought you were going to follow me inside,' she says.

'I didn't want to drip on the carpets,' I say. 'Besides, I don't expect you to have a change of clothes for me.'

'Oh, right,' she smiles as if it's the first time the thought crosses her mind.

'I have spare clothes, but I don't think they'd fit you and I don't think they're your style either,' she smiles as she jokes.

I smile back. 'You're a real card,' I say.

Then she starts laughing loudly. I watch her in confusion wondering what she has found so funny.

'What?' I say at last, hoping she'll share the joke with me.

She finally chokes off her laughter and gulps air. 'I was just thinking what you'd look like mincing down the street in high heels.'

We talk a while longer before I have to go home. I say goodbye and head down the pathway to the sidewalk.

Bryce

Our friendship develops quickly and there is no way to hide anything from Nora. We're in the same class and by now it's obvious that Ally and I are close. I move desks so that I am closer to Ally than Nora.

Aside from Ally, Grant is there too. He's been at school longer than I have but he's something of a misfit. We just sort of ran into each other a few times and started talking. He also plays guitar and we have found common ground in playing music after school. Ally joins us sometimes and sings. Her voice isn't bad but she's not interested in forming a band.

The three of us normally hang out together at break times as well.

Ally and Grant get along fine, though I have a feeling Grant has a bit of a crush on her. I like Ally too and I begin to realize that if I want to be with her, I need to tell her or else Grant will ask her out at some point.

Ally and I are already so close that everyone believes we're dating. Grant is the only one that knows different. We never speak about Ally and the possibility that she could be my girlfriend or his—like it's an off-limits topic and to say anything about it might affect our friendship.

Teenagers can be so fickle sometimes. Often it feels like the three of us have built minefields around our personal space and relationships with each other. It's like we're afraid of each other without ever saying as much. Thankfully, it's never blown up into an argument. At least not for a long time.

But, as they say, never say never.

One break time while lying side by side on the grass, reading books, I notice Ally lower the book that she was holding up to the sky to block out the sun as she read. At first, I thought her arms were tired, but I notice that she turns her head to look at someone. Then, shielding her eyes she turns her face to me and remarks, 'I think someone likes you.'

'What?' I ask, lowering my book and squinting as the sun hits my eyes. 'What are you talking about?'

'Pink sweater girl, two o'clock,' she says.

I looked in the direction Ally is referring to and spot Nora. She looks away quickly when I look at her and then moves away.

'Why do you say that?' I ask, trying to sound disinterested.

'She's always looking at you,' Ally remarks.

I say nothing and she adds, 'Did you have something with her before I arrived?'

'What? With her?' I ask, sounding irritated.

Ally sits up and looks at me. 'You did, didn't you?'

'What makes you think I had anything with her?' I ask defensively.

'Because when I asked you, you didn't answer.'

'What's that supposed to mean?' I ask incredulously.

'You answered a question with a question which means that you don't want to answer the question.'

I look at her, mouth agape.

'She can look all she wants, there's nothing between us.'

Ally gathers her things and packs them in her bag and then gets up to leave.

'Where are you going?' I ask.

'To find someone that doesn't feel like they have something to hide,' Ally says and stalks off.

Grant has overheard the entire conversation. As Ally stalks off, Grant sits up and gathers his things. 'You're in trouble now,' he says.

'How do you figure that?' I ask.

'She's pissed man. Didn't you get that?'

'What? It's not like we're dating,' I say defensively.

'You could have fooled me, bro,' Grant says.

'What's that supposed to mean?' I ask him.

He looks at me as if I'm stupid or as if I've lost my mind.

'You two are so close, you may as well be boyfriend and girlfriend. I don't know why the two of you don't just admit it already,' he says. 'I don't know any other boy and girl at school that are as close as you two and yet the two of you aren't *dating*? What's wrong with you?' he asks.

We're good friends but I can sense the irritation in his voice and I know he is right.

I look around but Ally is gone already.

I sigh and sit up. I cast a glance in the direction where I saw Nora last. She's gone too. 'I hope you're happy now,' I mutter as if she can hear me. Then I look around to where I think Ally would be but she's nowhere to be seen either. I pack my things and get up.

'I'll see you later,' I tell Grant as I take off to go find Ally.

I don't find Ally until we're in class after the break and then we can't talk because of the class. Between classes she ignores me and I pray for the rest of the day to pass quickly in the hope that I can speak to her after school.

When the final bell rings, Ally leaves school quickly and I have to run to catch her.

'Wait up!' I cry as I run to catch up to her. She finally stops and lets me catch up to her.

She watches me as I heave for breath and finally asks sarcastically, 'Wow, are you actually running after me?'

I catch her drift and smile despite myself. When I straighten up, I meet her gaze.

'Yes, I am, obviously. We need to talk.'

'About what?' she asks as she turns and starts walking again.

'About us.'

'I didn't know there was an us,' she says over her shoulder bluntly.

'I sure didn't get the memo about us, but it seems you did judging by your reaction today,' I say falling into step beside her.

'Nope, never did,' she says coldly.

I stop walking and the distance between us grows rapidly. 'Just stop, will you?' I say. Perhaps it's the irritation in my voice that makes her stop and turn.

I approach her slowly. 'I never knew you had feelings for me. I know we're close, but we've never spoken about dating.'

'Duh!' she exclaims. 'Well maybe it's about time we did. Everyone at school thinks we're a couple.'

'Well, why do I have to do the talking and asking?' I ask offended.

'Because that's what boys do!' she exclaims and throws her arms up. 'I've been waiting for you for ages to say something but maybe you don't feel the same way as I do . . .'

She trails off sounding disappointed.

I don't know what to say. I do like her. I like her a lot. Why I haven't asked her out, I can't really say. I struggle to find the truth in myself.

'Well?' she prompts.

'I . . . I don't know. Maybe I'm just insecure. We're such good friends and I don't want it ruined because I ask you out and you're not interested in me that way . . .'

She looks at a passing car and then looks back at me. 'Well if you don't try, you'll never know.'

'What? Right now?' I ask, looking around.

We're alone on the sidewalk. Aside from the odd vehicle passing by every so often there is no one around—unless there are some people with nothing better to do than watching us from inside the houses around us. If they are, we must look like we are fighting.

She crosses her arms. 'I'm waiting.'

I sigh and move closer to her. When I reach her, I look in her eyes and ask, 'Do you want to go out with me?'

'Go out with you? Once? On a date?' she asks.

I nod.

'Just *once*?' she emphasizes.

I shake my head. 'No . . . I mean as a couple. As boyfriend and girlfriend.'

Bryce

She doesn't hesitate and shakes her head. 'No.'

'What?' I ask astounded. 'What do you mean, no? I thought you were upset because I haven't asked you out!'

'Yes, but I don't want you just to ask me out because it's what I want. Is it what you want too?'

'Oh. Sure it is,' I reply. 'I just didn't ask because I wasn't sure what you'd say. I didn't want things to be awkward between us.'

'Okay . . . I guess that clears that up,' Ally says, then adds, 'but there is more.'

More, I wonder. *What more could there be?*

'Don't you see how she looks at you?' Ally asks.

For a moment I am lost. I don't know what she's talking about.

Then it dawns on me.

'No,' I say. 'I don't.'

'Really?' she asks and I nod. 'There is something there. Something did happen between you two, right?'

I sigh and shake my head. 'I met her when I first arrived. Walt was her boyfriend and took a liking to me.'

'What? Walt? The bully? He wanted to be your friend? I thought he hated you,' Ally says in disbelief.

I begin laughing despite myself. Ally can be naïve in the simplest ways. When she says things like that it belies her street-smart attitude.

'No. I mean he took a liking to me as his punching bag. I think she took a liking to me as well. We spoke a few times and then she just ghosted me. That's all there is to it.'

'Really?'

'Yes, really,' I say as irritation creeps into my voice again.

'Any fool can see she's into you.'

I'm taken aback by her remark. 'So that's why were you so upset then?'

She is quiet for a moment and then answers. 'Because I like you. I know boys are supposed to make the first move but I think that's rubbish. Sometimes we don't see what's right in front of us. Rather than wait for something that might never happen, we should help people who can't see what's right in front of them. But I didn't ask you because I wasn't sure what the deal was between you and her.'

'Well, now you know. We've never dated. We certainly haven't known each other as long as you and I have so there's nothing to feel threatened about.'

She holds my gaze, saying nothing, and then finally moves towards me. She stops before me and looks up into my eyes.

'Okay then,' she says at last. She rises onto her toes and places her hands on my shoulders to steady herself, and then kisses me. Her eyes are closed as she kisses me and I take in the soft skin over her eyelids. I don't respond at first but then I let go.

When our kiss ends, Ally steps back and meets my gaze. She has a smile I have never seen. It's beautiful. I know

I haven't been with many girls, let alone kissed many girls, but I know I've just had the best kiss ever.

'Wow,' I say at last.

Her smile grows a bit wider then takes my hand and indicates we should walk together. I don't object and we start walking. Before long we find ourselves in front of her house. We haven't said much since the kiss. It's like we've been stunned and don't know what to do.

'Do you want to come in?' she asks.

I have nothing else to do and it seems like going home would be the wrong thing to do right then.

'Sure,' I reply and then follow her up the path to the front door. She lets us in and closes the door behind us. We drop our bags in the entrance hall and she leads the way to the kitchen where she opens the fridge. The door blocks her from my view and I hear the hiss of two bottles being opened. I wonder what she's doing.

She closes the fridge and I see she's holding two beers in her hand. She hands one to me and I hesitate only briefly before taking it. I wonder who they belong to and if we're going to be in trouble for drinking them.

Ally doesn't seem to care as she takes her first drink from the bottle she's holding.

'Let's go outside,' she says.

I follow her outside and we sit down on the chairs on the patio in the shade of the house. We still haven't said much since our kiss. I look at her wondering what to say. Something needs to be said but I can't think of anything that won't sound lame.

Ally finishes her beer and puts the bottle on the table. She stands and crosses to me where I am slouching in the chair. She stops in front of me and looks down at me. Then she relieves me of my beer as I raise it to take another drink. She downs what's left and places the bottle on the table next to hers.

Then she lets out a belch that rips through the quiet neighbourhood like a gunshot and I can't help but laugh. She smiles proudly before she kisses me again.

'So, what does this make us?' I whisper.

'Boyfriend and girlfriend. Kissers, officially official,' she smiles.

'You're not upset anymore?'

'Do you think people kiss people they're upset with?' she scoffed.

'Just checking,' I say. 'So when is our first date?'

'What about tomorrow night?' she asks.

We agree that I'll pick her up at seven the next evening. We talk and joke a while longer before I leave to go home. I'm happy and I'm lost. I've gone from being single to being in a relationship in an afternoon. I haven't had many relationships and trepidation sets in almost immediately as I wonder when we're going to leave this town and when I'll have to end it with Ally. I'm ambivalent about our relationship. We've been great friends since we met and while we've been inseparable as friends, we never crossed the line until today. I wonder if we have done the wrong thing and are going to destroy our amazing friendship.

I try to analyse my feelings too. I like Ally but I've never thought of myself as being in love with her. I wonder if I am or if I'm just going with the flow because it's happened. Despite my confusion, I tell myself that I need to see where this is going.

Thoughts of Nora enter my mind and I feel disappointed for some reason. I feel as if I have disappointed her but then ask myself how that is possible when she and I are no longer talking.

Bryce

We've been dating for three weeks and it's like nothing has changed. We had such an amazing friendship before and we still do. There's romance added into the mix now but it doesn't make that much of a difference.

One thing has changed and that is Nora. Since it's become news that Ally and I are dating I feel she is even more distant, if that is even possible. Our eyes have met a few times in class and maybe it's just my guilt creating impressions in my mind, but I feel that she is disappointed.

There are times that I find myself thinking of Nora when I am with Ally and I naturally feel guilty. I try to push the thoughts away and sometimes I succeed while other times I find myself hopelessly distracted especially when I see Nora at school—and even more so now at the cinema.

Ally and I are seated in the back row and we see her enter with her friend. I'm not sure if she notices us. If she does she doesn't give any indication that she has.

She sits down a few rows in front of us. I point her out to Ally who has seen her anyway. The movie starts and I find myself watching Nora more than the movie. I lose the thread of the conversation many times and at the end of the day the movie is wasted on me.

I know Ally is watching me to see if I am watching Nora but there is no way she can tell. I find myself wondering about Nora. I know they talk about people needing closure but I am not sure that's what I need. It's not like we ever really dated. I think it's more a case of wondering what exactly happened and what could have been if things went differently.

It's stupid but that's who I am—an overthinker at heart.

When the movie is finished we wait until everyone else has left before we leave. Outside we glimpse Nora and her friend, and she sees us as well. There is no possibility of ignorig each other and the best we do is manage a nod at each other.

Ally and I leave the cinema and wander around the mall a bit before finally leaving. An uncomfortable silence has settled between us and I can't say why.

I'm not sure if it's me or Ally but I am sure it has to do with seeing Nora. We take a cab home to Ally's house. I pay the cab and we find ourselves on the sidewalk as the cab drives off. I'll call another cab from here when I decide to leave Ally's place.

'That was an interesting movie,' she says, not making a move towards her house.

'It was,' I agree.

'I especially liked the part where she lost the code . . .' Ally remarks.

I have to think about the part and I take too long to answer.

'You weren't really watching were you?' she says.

I struggle to respond and says nothing but simply nod. 'I thought so.'

'Why?' I ask.

She looks at me as if I should know the answer. And I do. She knows I do. She doesn't invite me in but turns to go.

'Goodnight,' she says.

'Hey!' I call after her but she doesn't turn back and closes the door behind her.

I wonder if I should try again and ask to speak to her but eventually decide against it. I don't want to argue with her if that's what might happen. Especially if her mother is home.

Instead I call a cab and give the driver my home address. I send her a text message on the way home but I never receive a reply.

The next day at school, I wait outside for her and when she arrives I stop her before she can enter.

'Ally, talk to me please. What's wrong?'

'We can talk after school,' she says coldly and that's it. She won't entertain anything else. During the day I try to talk to her and sit with her during break times but she tells me to go away. By the second break I stay away and I see her sitting with Grant. They are talking and laughing and I wonder what they are talking about.

After school I find her waiting outside for me. I approach her hesitantly not sure what to expect.

'Let's walk,' she says.

We leave the school and head home.

'Look I'm sorry for whatever I did but I really don't know what I did wrong.'

She looks down at the sidewalk. 'What happened yesterday?' she asks as we walk.

'We went to the movies,' I reply. 'Nothing happened there.'

'Really? You didn't focus on the movie. Your mind was somewhere else,' she says. 'Why?'

'I don't know,' I reply.

'Well I do,' she says.

'What . . .'

'When she walked in,' Ally says.

'She . . . ?' I ask dumbfounded. I have no idea what or who she is talking about for a moment and then I realize. 'You mean Nora?'

'Yes, her,' Ally replies.

'Oh c'mon!' is my first reaction. 'She just sat in front of us. We never talked.'

'No, but something changed,' Ally said. 'I felt it. You even missed some of the movie because your mind was somewhere else. You never get distracted. I know you. You love movies.'

'There's always a first time,' I say defensively.

'Conveniently when she shows up?' Ally throws back.

I sigh and stop walking. 'Hey. We can't do this. If we're going to go through this every time we see her on a date then we're going to have a problem.'

Ally stops and turns. 'You're right. We are going to have a problem. You told me that there was nothing between you and I believe you but I watched you today and I know you were looking at her.'

'She's in our class!' I say throwing my arms up even as I know that she is right.

Ally looks at me and then begins walking again as she shakes her head. I run to catch up to her.

We walk mostly in silence and when we get to her gate she blocks me from entering. 'I want you to go and think about something and then come back to me with an answer.'

I nod.

'Good. I want you to decide if you really, really want to be with me. If the answer is no, I won't be upset but I'd rather know you're committed to me before we go any further.'

'Where is this coming from?' I ask in exasperation.

She studies me a moment and then says, 'I've just never felt comfortable about you and Nora. Maybe you never actually dated but that doesn't mean there's nothing there. I think there is and maybe after you really do some soul searching you'll be able to tell me one way or the other.'

Then she turns and walks up the path and disappears into her house leaving me irritated, frustrated and feeling guilty.

I finally head home, lost in my thoughts.

Nora

At home, I head upstairs and fall on my bed. I'm bored and don't feel like doing anything. I decide that I should do my homework and cross to my desk. I knock over the bookend on my desk and a bunch of books follow it to the floor.

I bend and start gathering my books. My maths book has fallen open face down on the floor and I hook my thumb into the spine and pick it up. I turn it over. It landed open at the back cover. I begin to close it but then notice something that shouldn't be there. I set the book on the floor and place the rest of my books back on the desk.

Then I pick up my maths book and open it to the back cover. I see the note and pull it from the cover where it has been tucked in to stop it from falling out. It's been decorated with stars and hearts.

I read the note and then read it again.

And again.

I try to think who would have left the note for me. It's been ages since I lent my book to Bryce. I don't recall having lent it to someone else since then. I wonder if anyone would have slipped the note in when I wasn't looking. I doubt it.

That means . . .

My heart stops. No, it skips a beat . . . butterflies take flight in my stomach and my lips part in a smile as I think it must have been him. Bryce.

I read the note. Again, and again. I rub it between my fingers treasuring the smoothness.

> *In a new place, you've become my go-to.*
> *I'm glad I met you and now I always look for you,*
> *Where I am, I hope there you'll be too,*
> *I'm sure there's more love I can offer you.*
> *Thanks for being you.*

The words are kind of cheesy, I know, but it's not just about the words. It's about the thought, the gesture. It's about how he did something for me and hid it where he thought I would find it later when it would surprise me. And it had. I was surprised. And over the moon.

He had succeeded.

I pick up my phone and open his contact. I look at it so long I have to activate the screen again a few times before I finally type the message to him.

I realize I can't be sure it's him. I finally type a question.

'*Did you leave me a note in the back of my maths book when you returned it?*'

As my finger hovers over the send button my mother calls me from downstairs.

'Nor, Ash! Dinner!'

I quickly press the send button, or I think I do before I drop my phone on my desk and head downstairs.

The message hangs there, waiting to be sent, cursor blinking until the screen locks to save the battery.

After dinner, I rush back upstairs hoping there's an answer for me from Bryce. I unlock my phone and check the icons on the top left of the screen. Nothing.

My heart sinks even though I tell myself that maybe he hasn't seen my message and that he'll answer later. If I checked the messages, I would have realized that I hadn't sent the message at all. But I don't and disappointment gradually turns to despair and then anger.

To hell with him, I tell myself eventually. I keep his message though. I clip it in a notepeg that stands in my pencil holder on my desk and take a picture of it. My eyes are drawn to it repeatedly as I do my homework and I vacillate between disappointment and hope for the rest of the weekend. By the end of the weekend after having received no answer, I have settled on disappointment and head to school as I wonder what the day will be like after Bryce got my message and didn't bother to reply. That in itself is enough of an answer for me regarding where we're at. I guess I couldn't really expect more from him after the way I scolded him before we stopped speaking. Besides he is with Ally now. Do I really expect him to answer me when any answer he gives me might cause him trouble?

Bryce

When I arrive home, I send Ally a message but she does not reply and I am left alone with my thoughts about Ally and Nora.

I realize that I haven't been able to put Nora out of my mind after all this time. I remember the brief collection of moments that were so special before she stopped speaking to me. I remember how I felt about her then and while I can't be sure I still feel the same now, I know I am still wondering what went wrong and what Nora and I would look like as a couple.

I recall the note I wrote to her and how we seemed to get along. It's different with Ally. Of course it is. It always is. I can't expect things to be exactly the same.

Ally and I have been great since we got to know each other. We've never had an argument until now and it is not really an argument. I can tell she is not happy though. She seems to sense something and maybe she is right. I suppose some people are better off as friends than they ever will be as a couple. And if I am still wondering about Nora, then I know I am not being fair to Ally.

The more I think about it Friday evening the more doubtful I become. I try to push away my thoughts and watch a movie to distract myself but it's no use so I decide to leave the house with Mom's usual admonishment to be careful.

I ride around aimlessly just enjoying the night air and listening to the sounds of the neighbourhoods I pass through. One house has a huge party going on and people are standing in the garden eating and drinking. The scented BBQ smoke drifts across the road and I inhale it.

I eventually come to a stop across the road from Nora's house. I study the window upstairs which I know is hers. The lamp is on just as before and I wonder if she is in her room listening to music or doing homework. *Is she even home at all?* I wonder.

I recall what she said before about Friday nights being game night if they are home. I study the front yard and recall the night I chased her around it when I returned her maths book. A small smile appears on my face.

I wonder if it would be possible to have that again. I know there's only one way to find out and I know what it means.

I ride off back home and get into bed where I lie awake and scroll through the few messages I had from her the night I got her number and started texting her. It was also the night we stopped texting each other.

I finally reach a decision. It's a decision only a fool would make and anyone would tell me the same thing.

I send Ally a message and tell her I've made a decision and ask to meet on Sunday. She agrees.

We meet in a coffee shop and though the day is not too hot and the coffee shop has air-conditioning, I am breaking out in cold sweat.

After placing our order, Ally sits forward. She looks pretty. Her short hair is tied up into a little ponytail. She looks cute and right then I wonder if I am doing the right thing.

'So?' she asks.

I wonder if she is expecting good news. I am sure she is.

'Like you said, I should give us some thought . . .'

She nods expectantly. She has a slight smile on her face and her gaze is, I think, hopeful.

'Well, you seem to have some doubts about how I feel about you . . . about us . . .'

She nods again, saying nothing, waiting.

'Well, I think you're right to have your doubts. We get on so well but I think there's something there that's missing. I don't know what it is but I think even though we're such great friends, we're just not enough for each other to be a couple.'

The small smile she had falters and then disappears.

I reach for her hand across the table but she pulls it away as tears fill her eyes. The waiter chooses that moment to arrive with our order and Ally looks away, out the window so he won't see her tears. Then she digs in her purse looking for a tissue to dab at her eyes as soon as he is gone.

She looks up at last, her eyes still filled with tears. 'It's her isn't it? I was right to be upset.'

'I can't say it's Nora,' I admit honestly. 'I'm not with her and we don't even talk. You can't say that I'm choosing her over you. That's not fair to either of us.'

Ally looks at me and then finally nods.

'I'm not with her. I just think that you're right. I think we're better off as friends—and maybe we can just stay friends.'

Ally wipes away fresh tears and nods. 'Maybe. I don't know about right now though. I'll need time, so I think it's best if we try to keep away from each other for a while.'

'I can respect that,' I say. It's not what I wanted but it's for the best.

We don't say much after that. Ally is mostly quiet, dealing with her pain and disappointment and we finish our drinks, pay and leave. We go our separate ways and I'm left wondering what the next day will be like at school.

Nora

Monday comes and I see Bryce at school as usual. Ignoring him has become a habit I am extremely good at but today I cannot ignore him.

I look at him before class and just as we enter class. Our eyes meet but he doesn't hold my gaze long enough for me to capture his attention and he gives no acknowledgement when our eyes meet.

I resolve not to talk to him. If he can't be bothered to answer my message then to hell with him. I reached out to say thanks and hoped to start things again with him but he's just been plain rude. The day passes slowly and my resolve not to talk to him slowly crumbles until, by the final period of the day, I have decided I will try to speak to him after school. Murphy's law states though that something will go wrong if it can. And it does. But challenges are also meant to be turned into opportunities.

In the final period, Bryce is sent to the office for not having done his homework and it gives me an idea.

Our teacher, Ms Evans, asks me for an answer to one of our homework questions and I pretend to fumble.

I page back and forth in my book until the teacher loses her patience with me.

'You haven't done your homework either, have you?' she asks. I'm one of her best students and I can tell from the tone of her voice and the expression on her face she is disappointed. Maybe even hurt. I feel sorry for her and wish I could tell her the truth.

I have done it, but right now, I want to be sent to the office so I can meet Bryce.

I shake my head. 'I'm sorry ma'am,' I say.

'It seems we're developing a habit of skipping homework in this class. Is there anyone else who hasn't done the homework? Anyone else who decided I'm too easy-going and never check the homework to be bothered to do it?'

No one puts up their hand and Ms Evans looks at me.

'You can join Bryce at the principal's office, young lady.'

I've been waiting for her to tell me to go to the principal's office and now I pack up as fast as I can without making it obvious that I'm in a hurry. From the clock on the wall, the period's almost up and when the bell rings it will be home time.

The bell rings as I get to the door and Ms Evans says, 'You're not saved by the bell. I expect you to go to the principal's office. I will check.'

'Yes, Ms Evans,' I say as I exit the door and walk as fast as I can without being obvious.

I wonder what she would say if she knew that I could not be happier to be going to the principal's office.

When I get to the office I report to the principal's secretary.

'Well, he has someone with him right now so just have a seat and he'll see you when he's finished.'

'I'm here for the same reason, I think, so it might be better if I go in and Mr Brunswick can see us both at the same time,' I suggest in the interest of expediency.

'He will see you when he is finished,' Mr Brunswick's secretary says firmly as she peers at me over the tops of her glasses. Her tone suggests she is surprised at my insolence in suggesting that I should go into Mr Brunswick's office immediately. I decide not to push it.

Bryce exits moments later and sees me. He does a double take but then continues without a backward glance.

'I'm here for the same reason as Bryce, Mr Brunswick. I didn't do my homework. Is he going to have detention now?'

'Yes,' Mr Brunswick says.

'Can I join him then, sir? If I have to do detention, I'll do it today.'

Mr Brunswick studies me curiously. I guess he wonders why I seem so eager to do detention but agrees. It's the easy way out. That way he can save an afternoon by not having to run detention on another day. That's what he hopes anyway.

He makes a note for my file and says, 'Class Two C. Detention starts in ten minutes. That should give you time for lunch.'

'Thank you, sir,' I say and leave his office as fast as I can.

Bryce

It's a shitty end to the week but then whether I was going to spend time here or at home doing nothing much doesn't matter.

I'm seated at a desk when Nora enters.

Great, I think to myself. I'm not really in the mood to speak to anyone least of all the ice queen. I've caught her looking at me a few times today. I wonder if she's beginning to thaw or if she has another reason for what seems like renewed interest.

She makes her way to the desk beside me and sits down.

An awkward silence follows before she speaks.

'Hey,' she says.

I look at her and she meets my gaze.

'I sent you a message a while ago,' she says.

I frown as I wonder what she's talking about before I shake my head and reply, 'I didn't get any message.'

'I know I sent you a message. Maybe you just haven't checked for messages from me.'

'I didn't get a message from you,' I repeat firmly.

'You probably deleted it,' she says accusingly, challenging me with her gaze.

I roll my eyes, reach into my pocket and remove my phone. I unlock it and hand it to her. 'Check if you want.'

She hesitates a moment then takes it. She finds her name in my messaging app and scrolls through the messages. She reaches the end and finds no message. There's nothing that says I deleted a message either. She checks to see if I blocked her and finds I haven't. She asks anyway.

'Did you block me at any stage?'

'What?' I ask irritated as I hold out my hand for my phone. 'I didn't need to. You stopped contacting me remember?' She hands it back and then takes out her phone. She scrolls through her messages and then stops looking confused.

I want to ask what is wrong but don't. I don't want to encourage a conversation with Nora. She still seems set on the idea that I'm the one doing everything wrong here.

At last she turns to me looking embarrassed. 'I'm sorry. I typed a message to you but it was never sent. I could swear I sent it but it's not here. I waited the whole weekend for your reply and never got one.'

'Like last time?' I ask as the penny drops at last. 'You were upset because I never replied?'

'Well . . .' she replies uncomfortably. 'I thought I sent you a message, but it turns out it never got sent.'

I look at her wondering where this is going.

She reaches down and pulls one of her schoolbooks from her bag. She lays it on the desk but before she can open it, Mr Brunswick enters the classroom.

'Right,' he says as he gets to the front of the class. 'I have things to do so I think we'll just settle for lines on the board. You can each take a board and write, "*I will always do my homework so I don't get detention*", one hundred times.'

Neither of us is keen to write lines, especially on the board but we don't argue. We get up and walk to the blackboard. We pick up chalk and begin writing.

Mr Brunswick sits down at the desk with his back to us and opens his briefcase. He pulls out paperwork and, after a brief look at us to make sure we're doing as told, he turns around and focuses on his work.

We look at each other and get writing. We sneeze occasionally from the chalk dust and the chalk occasionally screeches on the board.

We're not competing against each other but we look at each other's progress every so often. At one point, I realize that Nora is not writing what she's supposed to.

She's written, '*As I was saying, I thought I sent you a message.*'

I read it and reread it before I write my answer on my side. '*What did your message say?*'

She realizes I have caught on and she answers me with her next line.

'*I was asking about a note I found in my book that you borrowed from me.*'

I realize what she's asking about and I reply. '*What did the note say?*'

She looks at me and her eyes narrow as if she wants to punch me. She knows it's me and she expects me to give her a simple yes or no to confirm that it was me. I don't.

I shrug feigning ignorance. She puts the chalk down and crosses to the desk where she sat before Mr Brunswick entered.

He looks up as her movement catches his eye.

'Is something wrong?' he asks Nora.

'No, sir,' she replies. 'I just wanted to check something.'

Mr Brunswick nods and goes back to his work. Nora has removed the note I left in the back of her book for her and now holds it out to me behind Mr Brunswick's back.

I shake my head and indicate she should write the message on the board. She glares at me and looks like she wants to stamp her foot.

Then she starts copying the message onto the board, word for word all the while glancing back at Mr Brunswick nervously.

I watch as she writes the message.

> *In a new place, you've become my go-to.*
> *I'm glad I met you and now I always look for you,*
> *Where I am, I hope there you'll be too,*
> *I'm sure there's more love I can offer you.*
> *Thanks for being you.*

She finishes and adds a question, '*did you write this?*'

I smile and write, '*it's kind of cheesy don't you think?*'

'*Did you?*' She scribbles quickly making more noise than usual. Mr Brunswick raises his head briefly and glances over his shoulder. She steps closer to the board trying to hide what she's written.

Mr Brunswick continues with his work.

'*I did,*' I write on the board. '*I hoped you'd find it someday. It was meant to be a surprise but then you cut me off and got so angry when I finally stood up to A.*'

Mr Brunswick's phone rings and he picks it up. We have no idea who he's speaking to but it quickly becomes clear that he's going to have to leave. He pinches the phone between his ear and his shoulder as he begins packing his things into his briefcase. When he's finished, he stands and then asks the person on the phone to hold on a moment.

He looks at us and then glances at the board. We don't know if he realizes we have not been writing the lines he told us to. If he does, he gives no indication of it.

'I have to go,' he says. 'Finish your lines and you can go home. I will check so don't think you can skip out on the task, understand?'

'Yes, sir,' we reply at the same time. He grasps the phone with his hand again and heads for the door. A moment later he is out and gone, leaving us in silence.

She finally breaks the silence first. 'What do you mean "*I cut you off*"?'

'You stopped answering me when we were messaging,' I say.

'I stopped . . .' she stops mid-sentence. Her lips continue moving but I can't hear what she's saying. Then she looks at me and says aloud. 'No. *You* stopped answering me.'

'What?' I ask surprised. 'I never stopped answering you. This isn't my fault.'

I cross to my bag and remove my phone. I unlock it, find her contact and the messages we sent. I start scrolling. There aren't many anyway.

'There,' I say and show her the screen.

'*Do you want me to be the right person? Do I make you jealous in some way?*'

She reads the message and her reply that followed where she'd said '*Goodnight*'.

'Do you remember that?' I ask.

At last, she nods slowly. 'I guess I do.'

I don't want to start lecturing her but I add, 'I thought I'd said something wrong. You just said "goodnight" and that was it. I didn't hear from you again.'

'Well, why didn't you try again? Why didn't you contact me?'

'Because I thought you were upset with me after that. I thought if I contacted you again, I might look pushy or like a stalker. As the new kid in town that wasn't something I wanted so I decided to stay away. I also had a bad experience in another place and I wasn't going to take the chance that something might go wrong again. It's hard enough trying to fit in without having to deal with other people spreading bad news about you that's not true.'

'Well, I didn't, did I?'

'I didn't know you wouldn't, did I?' I counter.

She sighs. 'I guess. I wanted to send you a message but I was afraid of looking like I was chasing you. I thought I might push you away or look desperate.'

I start to smile slowly.

'What's so funny?' she asks.

'Well, we've both been idiots,' I say at last.

'Speak for yourself,' she replies defensively.

'Well, we have, haven't we? Here we are both expecting the other to send a message and refusing to send our message because we want the other to send a message first. We could have done so much more if we hadn't let our fears and thoughts get in the way.'

She looks at me as she bites her lower lip.

Nora seems to be thinking. She looks at me and then glances towards the door. Then she crosses to the door, peers through the glass set in it before she opens the door and looks both ways down the passageway. I'm not sure what she's looking for but then, in the next instant, she closes the door and locks it.

She walks back to me and stops in front of me. She looks up at me as she bites her lower lip again. Her eyes are a clear blue I haven't had much of a chance to enjoy until now. Right then, I could lose myself in her eyes. They look into mine and they seem to say so much.

I've missed you.

We're alone and we can do whatever we want.

I have so much I want to tell you.

I lose myself in her beautiful blue eyes as she moves closer. She's almost closed the distance between us when I stop her. I have a question and I need it answered.

Bryce

'Why were you so angry with me the day that I kicked Walt?' I ask.

'Because I thought you ghosted me. I broke up with Walt because I realized we weren't working. I wanted to be with you. I realized that who I was with you was different to when I was with Walt. You made me happy, you made me smile. But you just stopped messaging me and I didn't know why.' Nora answers. Her tone suggests I should have known that.

'Well now you know that I didn't stop messaging you. But since we're talking again I'll tell you that I didn't want the time we had in your garden earlier that evening to end. I wanted more then and I didn't care who saw us. But I felt that you were holding back for some reason already and then you didn't text me, so I guessed that was it. I still offered to help you on the Monday after you fell but you were so angry, I decided to leave it. And that was it.'

Nora has listened to my long-winded recollection of what happened. She looks back at the door quickly and then closes the space between us.

'You talk too much,' she says. Her voice is almost a whisper, and she catches me off guard. It's as if she floats towards me. She closes the distance between us, rises to her toes, reaches her arm up behind my neck and pulls my face down towards hers. There's no hesitation this time. Her lips find mine, kiss me, and then part as her tongue pushes forward, demanding entry.

I grant it entry and my tongue finds hers. But it's over too quickly as she pulls away.

I look at her confused and am about to ask her what's wrong when she grabs my hand and runs towards the classroom door pulling me behind her. I follow quickly, not wanting her hand to break free from mine. We reach the door, and she kneels pulling me down with her. I hear footsteps approaching in the corridor outside and she presses her finger to her lips indicating I should stay quiet.

I look back to where we sat. Our bags are still at the desks where we were sitting. Then the light entering the window in the door fades as someone arrives at the door and peers into the class.

I hope they can't see us. I can't see them so I guess the same is true for them not being able to see us.

Nora takes my face in her hands and kisses me again even as whoever is outside tries the door. I hear the handle move as they press down and push against the door. They try again and Nora kisses me harder.

I kiss her back passionately even as the person tries the door again. I think, *Who cares if they see us? If we're going to be in trouble, then I'll make sure it's worthwhile.* I raise my hands to her face and feel her soft skin against the palms of my hands. One hand moves behind her neck and tangles in her soft, silken hair while my thumb gently rubs the soft skin of her face. We breathe through our noses. We can't be heard by whoever is outside but to us, we sound like two people who are running as hard as we can.

I remember all my feelings for Nora. I knew I had feelings for her before we went all cold on each other. After kissing her I know they were true, still are true. I hate to think of the months that have passed in between.

I have come to live with the concept that my time anywhere is limited. I am now all too aware of that fact again as I think of the time that's slipped away from us after we ignored each other because of a stupid misunderstanding.

Then the person outside is gone. We finally end our kiss and look at each other without speaking. Neither of us can think of anything to say.

I eventually move first. I stand and help Nora up. Then I cross to the blackboard, grab the duster and erase our lines.

'What are you doing?' Nora asks shocked as she sees all our hard work erased.

'Going home,' I reply.

'But we haven't finished and now we have to start over . . .'

'No, we don't. We'll tell Mr Brunswick that we finished our lines, and that the janitor must have wiped them off the board when he cleaned. I've seen him clean the boards before. He can't blame us.'

'Maybe that was Mr Brunswick coming back earlier . . .'

'So?' I smile. 'Our bags were still in the class. If it was him, he would have seen them. He can't say we left without finishing. We tell him we had to go to the bathroom, so we locked the door.'

'Really?' Nora asks raising her eyebrows. 'We went to the bathroom *together*?'

I nod. 'Why not? This big school gets kind of creepy on a Friday afternoon when everyone's gone home. You were afraid and asked me to walk with you. I waited outside the girls' room for you to finish and come back. After that, we finished our lines and left.'

She looks as if she's thinking my plan through and then slowly a smile crosses her face as she nods.

'Okay. That'll work. Let's get out of here before he does come back and we have to start writing our lines all over again.'

We grab our bags and head for the door. I unlock it, open it and hold it open for her. Then I close it and we head in the direction we are less likely to encounter someone. We exit the school and run down the path until we get to the street. Only then do we slow down and start walking.

'So, what happened to you and A?' I ask as we make our way home. This time she doesn't object to me calling him that.

'I just decided it was time to end it. That was the day after you came to my house.'

'Wow, so I was the incentive for you to end it with him?' I pretend to tease but she sees through me.

'Don't flatter yourself,' she replies. Then after a moment's silence, she says, 'You're right though. I think you were in part responsible for my decision to end it with Walt. I guess that's why when I thought you ghosted me, I was so angry.'

'You thought you ended it with Walt for nothing because I never sent you a message?'

'I guess,' Nora says bashfully. 'But it was time for it to end anyway. We just weren't working anymore. I couldn't even understand why we started dating in the first place. I don't think there was ever anything there to start with.'

'Wow,' I say. 'I never thought that you'd date anyone you don't care about. You can choose whoever you want.'

She blushes and looks away. Then she says, 'What's that famous saying? Something is blind? I forget what it is . . .'

'Love is blind?' I ask.

'That's it,' she says, looking at me.

'You mean you were blinded by your love for A?'

She shakes her head as if to say she gives up. 'No silly, I mean you are blind.'

'You're saying I'm in love with you?' I ask surprised.

'It sounds that way,' she says. 'You think I can date anyone I choose.'

'Well, I mean it. You're beautiful, down to earth, fun to be with . . .'

She takes my hand. 'That's your opinion. Not everyone share's your point of view.'

'Really? Name one person,' I challenge.

'Ashley, my sister.'

'That doesn't count,' I say. 'Of course, she's not into you.'

'She still has an opinion,' Nora says.

'Well, I don't care about her opinion. If you want to listen to her then you're selling yourself short. Look how upset A was when you broke up with him. Besides your sister's never going to date you. I hope.'

'How do you know he was upset?' she asks as she smiles at my remark about Ashley.

'Because he came to beat me up for it,' I say.

Nora laughs. Her laugh is so pure and crisp in the afternoon air. 'He was going to beat you up anyway, not just because of me,' she says at last. 'But yeah, he was upset when I broke up with him.'

'There you go, then,' I say.

She blushes again but says nothing. Instead, she brushes a strand of hair behind her ear.

'Why didn't you start seeing anyone else after A?'

She shrugs. 'I don't know. I just wasn't interested.'

I nod. 'Well, things didn't work out with Ally. She could see I still had feelings for you.'

Nora is silent for a moment and then says, 'I didn't want to get in the way of you both. I decided I'd rather keep my distance from you when you were with her.'

'And are you going to keep your distance now?' I ask.

Nora smiles and rises and kisses me.

'What do you think?' she says.

Nora

It's been a month since our detention together and now that we've cleared up our misunderstanding, I feel like we are inseparable.

I never imagined being with someone could be so easy, so fun and so exciting.

Bryce keeps me on my toes and always has a surprise for me. He leaves me messages or little cards or wildflowers he's picked in places where he knows I will find them. Everywhere, in my school bag, my locker, my schoolbooks, the mailbox. It's always somewhere new and I am always surprised by him. The messages are always so meaningful. I started to collect these little notes and pasted them into a notebook. He even wrote me letters and mailed them to me so they arrived in the mail. I'm astounded since we see each other every day now. What he writes in his letters is nothing we have spoken about before. It's always unique.

There is one thing that sits between us. It's unspoken. This is our senior year. I've been applying to universities to get a business degree. Bryce is applying too. The process reminds me that our time is limited.

I'm guessing the chances of us studying at the same university after school are very slim. We have a higher chance of studying at different universities in the same city but I doubt that's going to happen.

Couples in high school seldom stay together after school. It's part of growing up I guess but I'm not ready to let Bryce go when that time comes.

We seem to steer clear of discussing the cities and universities we're applying to. It's like it just makes reality a bit less harsh.

'Do you want to go camping with me?' Bryce asks one autumn afternoon.

'Camping?' I ask, feigning surprise. I'm trying to process his question. I want to but I don't think I'll be allowed to.

'Yeah, you know, pitch a tent in the wild, hope no bears are around, make a fire, tell scary stories . . .'

'I know,' I say. 'I just don't think I'll be allowed. Not if it's just you and me.'

'Well, your parents don't need to know. Just tell them it's a group of friends. Will they trust a group?'

'Is that what you're going to tell your parents?' I ask.

He nods.

'I want to,' I say. 'It's just that Ashley will smell a rat. She always does. She's like, worse than my parents. She doubts everything I do because she wants to catch me out and tell Mom.'

'How will she know?' Bryce asks.

'For one, she'll go and ask the friends who I say I am going with.'

'Well, then ask your friends to lie.'

'I could do that, but someone is sure to screw up. The more people you involve, the more chance there is that it's going to be a screw-up.'

'Then don't involve a lot of people. Tell them Chris is going and I'm going, and my parents are going. She's not going to ask my parents, is she?'

'No. She'll probably ask Chris.'

'Well, is that enough?'

I nod. 'It ought to be. They can only say yes or no. I'll ask close to the time, so Ashley doesn't have much time to check.'

'Okay. I was thinking about this Saturday,' he says. It's more of a question than a statement.

'Wow, that's two days away,' I say.

'That's short notice, if you're worried about Ashley, isn't it?' Bryce smiles.

'It is,' I say. I'm excited at the thought of going camping alone with Bryce and I hope I can convince my parents to allow it although I will need to lie to try and get them to agree. 'Where do you want to go?'

'Not far. There's a nice place up in the woods just outside town. I like to go there to be alone.'

'Okay, I'll ask my parents,' I tell Bryce.

I haven't been camping in forever and I think it will be great but cold too. It's autumn and the nights are getting colder. But if we don't go camping now, it'll be too late and we'll have to wait until after winter. I'm becoming all too aware of the time we have together until the end of the school year. There's no telling what will happen after that.

My parents say I can go and I quickly set about packing my things. I have a backpack, sleeping bag, hiking boots and, of course, warm clothes. I pack as much as I can but I keep my bag hidden in my closet so that if Ashley comes snooping, she won't find out about my plans.

Other than asking my parents for permission to go camping, I avoid the topic and I avoid my parents too, as far as possible for fear that they might say something to alert Ashley about my plans.

On Friday morning, I greet my parents and remind Mom that I won't be home that evening.

'Why not?' Ashley asks. It's the first she's heard of it.

'I'm going camping with Bryce and his parents. Chris is going too.'

Ashley looks at me as if she wants to say something and then shrugs. 'Cool, I'll have the house to myself.'

'I'm sure you'll make the most of it. Stay out of my stuff,' I reply, shifting the focus to her and as far away from me as possible. If I can keep her from getting ideas about my camping then she probably won't ask questions.

'It's not like you'll know if I do,' she says.

'That's what you think,' I say. 'Did it ever cross your mind that I might just leave things in a certain way so I'll know if they're moved?'

'What does that matter? Who says it's me that moved it if you find something's been moved? It might be Mom or Dad.'

'And the chances of that are . . . ?'

'Pretty good,' Ashley sneers. 'Don't forget that you have to leave your room unlocked in case Mom or Dad need something. Those are the rules.'

'You know, you really should get a hobby or learn to love your life,' I say. 'If my room is so interesting, then knock yourself out. You probably want to wear my underwear, not that it fits you.'

'Ew!!' Ashley exclaims, disgusted.

I smile at her and then pick up my bag and head for the door after kissing Dad and Mom goodbye and telling them

I'll see them tomorrow. I have to return home after school, get my rucksack and then head to Bryce's place. I'll do my best to be in and out before Ashley gets home.

After school, I arrive home with Bryce. I run upstairs and grab my backpack. I head downstairs and Bryce offers to carry it for me. I give it to him and we leave.

Great, we made it in and out of the house before Ashley got home. Surprisingly, she seems to have let the idea of me going camping with Bryce's family go.

I warned Chris that Ashley might ask her and told her what to say just in case Ashley asked. Chris would have let me know if she did but she hasn't yet so I'm guessing that she believes I am going camping and doesn't think there is anything to check on.

We make it to Bryce's house, get his backpack and then start cycling to the campsite. I've never been there and don't know where it is. Bryce loads my backpack on his bike and carries his own on his back.

He pedals slow enough for me to keep up and we finally make it to the forest. We leave the road and follow a dirt path through the trees. It's narrow and the path is uneven but we navigate it reasonably well and finally, the trees open up into a clearing around us.

Bryce stops beside a big round concrete platform and leans his bike against it. I stop behind him and lean my bike against his.

I am swept away by the view. I never knew this place existed. Someone does though considering that someone must have built the concrete platform.

Bryce leaves the bikes and moves to the edge of the clearing where the ground falls away steeply. We can see for miles as we look over the town.

'It's beautiful,' I say.

'I thought you'd like it,' Bryce smiles. He slips his hand into mine and then turns to look at me. I look at him and we hug.

The trees around us create a channel for the breeze and wind which becomes cooler very quickly as the sun sets. We set about putting up the tent and making sure it's secure. We lock our bicycles to a nearby tree for the night. One can never be too careful.

Bryce says he's never seen anyone else up here in all the times that he's been here, but that doesn't mean other people don't know about the place. The round concrete platform is evidence of that.

Once our camp is ready, we make a fire and sit next to each other as we cook our dinner.

Our conversation eventually drifts to the question I've never asked.

Nora

There is plenty of firewood up here and we gather more than enough for the night before the sun goes down.

We snuggle up beside each other and watch as the food cooks over the fire. I brought some chicken and Bryce brought some steak. He's also brought potatoes and I am quite impressed that he prepared everything he's brought to cook on his own.

I guess being an only child and having the experience of moving around as much as he has, has made him quite independent. I watch him as he prepares everything and gets the fire going. He's like a real boy scout. At least what I imagine a boy scout would be capable of doing.

'I wish we could stay here tomorrow night too,' I say.

Bryce is quiet. I think he feels the same and is considering my words. We could do it.

'That would be nice,' he says at last.

We stare into the fire and Bryce reaches forward. He pulls some meat off the stick over the fire and hands me some.

'Can I ask you something?' I ask at last. I can't keep my thoughts to myself anymore.

'Sure,' Bryce says and looks at me. The light from the fire catches his eyes and gives them a warm glow.

I hesitate for a moment, afraid that what I'm going to ask is going to ruin the rest of our time out here. Bryce looks at me patiently, wondering what I want to ask.

'I've never been happier than I am now,' I say. 'I know in the context of life I'm still young and I still have a lot to experience and learn about this thing we call life.'

Bryce smiles but says nothing as he waits for me to go on.

'I like to think you're happy too,' I say.

Bryce smiles and nods. 'Of course, I am. Why wouldn't I be?'

I look at him and my eyes search his, looking for that something that I feel sits between us, unspoken.

'Are you?' I ask holding his gaze. His face slowly creases in a frown as confusion sets in.

He doesn't know why I'm asking.

He shakes his head. 'Of course, Nora. I've never been happier. Why are you asking this?'

I stare into his eyes and he holds my gaze moment for moment. I finally sigh and then look away into the flames.

'I don't know. Maybe I'm scared is all,' I say.

'Scared of what?' Bryce asks, taking my hand.

'Scared of losing you,' I mumble, still looking into the flames.

'What makes you think you're going to lose me?' Bryce asks.

I continue staring into the flames as I try to put my words in order. The sun went down ages ago and the night sky is clear. If we step beyond the light of the flames, we can see the stars shining brightly up here away from the lights of the town.

I sigh. 'There's something between us. I mean, I've never felt like this about anyone but I still feel as if there's something between us. I don't know what it is but I don't think it's me. It's like a resistance, a barrier.'

Bryce looks at me and then looks away. He says nothing for a while and I begin to brace for the worst. I can tell he knows what I'm talking about and I'm sure he realizes he has to say something. He knows he can't deny it. It wouldn't be fair. *Is he going to end our relationship?* I wonder. The look on his face is melancholic, almost sad. He finally turns so his body is facing me. He reaches out and takes my hand.

'I'm sorry . . .' he says.

Here it comes, I think to myself.

'It's me. I know what you're feeling and I'm not going to deny that it's not there.'

'What do you mean? What is it?' I ask.

'I've never been happier . . .' Bryce says and then trails off.

'But . . . ?' I ask.

'Every evening when my dad gets home from work, I'm afraid. My stomach turns.'

'Why?'

'Because every day I wonder if today is the day.'

Bryce is driving me crazy with his little bits of information. I want to scream at him to tell me what he's thinking but I don't. I realize that he's dealing with something I don't understand. Not yet anyway.

'What do you mean?' I prompt eventually, softly.

'I wonder if today is going to be the day that he gets home and tells Mom and me that we're moving again. I don't want to move. I've got you and I never want to lose you.'

When I hear his last words, I should breathe a sigh of relief. Instead, I realize I'm dealing with the same anxiety but I haven't thought of it in the context of Bryce leaving because his dad gets posted somewhere else. I've only thought of it in the context of us going our separate ways at the end of the year.

I now understand what Bryce is carrying with him.

'I don't want to lose you either,' I say but now I can't help but think about what he has just said. 'You don't think you're going to move again soon, do you?'

He shrugs. 'I never know until Dad comes home and mentions it. It's always a surprise. And because it's always a surprise, I fear it every day. I don't want to look in your eyes and tell you that I have to leave. Even worse, I don't want to have to say goodbye.'

I don't like what I'm hearing. 'Stop it,' I tell him. 'Let's not talk about it. Let's not ruin this night.'

He looks at me. 'You're right.'

We're silent for a while again and then I tell him my fears. 'I think about us not being together all the time too. It's going to happen when the school year is over. We'll go our separate ways to study. How will we stay together? Can we do it?'

'I want to. I never want to be away from you. We can keep it together.'

'Do you really think so?' I ask.

He moves closer until he is right beside me.

'I love you, Nora,' Bryce says. 'I've never felt this way about anyone. Maybe it's because I've never been in any place long enough to get this close to anyone but I don't think that matters. There was just never anyone like you before. I don't think there will ever be anyone like you again. We have to stay together no matter how far apart we might be while we study. If we love each other, we can do it.'

'I don't want to lose you. We'll make it,' I say.

Somehow, I don't feel it though. I feel as if we're running out of time especially now that we've voiced our fears. It's as if speaking them aloud will make our fears reality sooner rather than later.

Bryce pulls me close and we kiss. I close my eyes as I feel our lips touch and melt together. Our tongues softly push forward, exploring, seeking permission. Our kiss deepens. It's a closeness we have hardly shared yet and there is no urgency. Our tongues dance slowly, enjoying, exploring, trying to go as deep as possible as if it will bring us closer to each other, sharing as much of us as possible with the other.

I don't want this to end. We've never been alone like this, with the world so far away leaving just us to be together. We've never spent a night together and I hope we can have tomorrow night too. We go to the cinema often or on a date to the roller rink or the ice rink and it's fun but this is the best night I've ever had with Bryce.

We're together. Alone. It's just us, our feelings and our honesty. It's just us talking with no distractions and there's still so much we talk about but now that fear is eating us. It's in the open and we both feel it. At least we both have the same fear and feel it, share it. It makes our time together more intense, more meaningful.

I don't want this to end. I can't imagine a future with anyone else or a future without Bryce.

We eventually end our kiss, reluctantly and gaze into each other's eyes. There's a longing in our gazes. A longing for more. A longing for forever. For eternity together.

When we eventually go to sleep, we join our sleeping bags to make one big sleeping bag. Bryce zips up the tent and we shut out the world with nothing but the faint glow of the fire's embers outside.

'What do you want to be when you finish studying?' I ask Bryce.

He's quiet and finally kisses me. 'Your husband,' he says.

'Oh, you're silly,' I laugh. 'You don't have to study for that.'

'I didn't say I'd study to be your husband. I'll study you as an extra course to be your husband while I study for my degree.'

'You're so full of it,' I say.

'Full of love for you,' he whispers. He's got an answer for everything tonight, but I don't mind.

Bryce raises himself on one arm and looks down at me as he strokes my hair softly with his free hand. He brushes my face with his hand softly, enjoying the softness of my skin. Then he leans down and kisses me. He kisses my lips, my cheeks, my forehead, my ears and whispers softly as he kisses me. I lay still, basking in his attention and love.

'I could kiss you forever,' he whispers.

'And I would gladly let you kiss me forever,' I whisper in reply. I want to reciprocate and kiss him as much as he is kissing me but I know that to do so will ruin the moment. I will have a chance later to return his love. Right now, I soak up his love and let him take joy in smothering me with kisses.

Nora

We finally go to sleep after kissing long into the night and whispering sweet words to each other. I drift off to sleep and when I wake up later Bryce is asleep next to me. His arm is draped over me and I lift it so as not to disturb him as I turn on my side to look at him, fast asleep. He looks so peaceful. I want to hold the memory of him at that moment in my mind forever. I wish I can wake up next to him in a few years and see him sleeping just as peacefully next to me then as he is now.

Could it be possible? I wonder. No one can see the future and there is no way to tell where we will be in a few years. I struggle to get back to sleep as my mind starts to race. I look at the time on my smartphone. It's just after three-thirty in the morning.

My mind is filled with all sorts of thoughts, and I can't close the door on them.

Will we be together in a few years?

Are our lives planned for us?

Do we have any say in making decisions about our life or do we think we can direct our lives?

Will we be together until the end of the school year?

How will we manage to be together after school ends?

Will we be one of the few successful couples that can stay together through a long-distance relationship?

I finally give up trying to go back to sleep. I want to wake Bryce and I'm sure he wouldn't mind if I did but I also know it would be selfish. Instead, I wriggle out of the sleeping bag and move to the zipper of the tent. I hesitate briefly as I wonder if it's safe outside but I can't hear anything that sounds like an animal scurrying around, so I undo the zip slowly. A cold breeze makes its way in and I grab my jacket before crawling out of the tent and zipping it up again.

I stand alone as the cool morning breeze teases my hair as if trying to coax me into following it in the direction it is blowing. I shrug my jacket on and follow the breeze which is blowing to the edge of the hill where we looked down on the town the night before.

Wisps of hair stray into my face when I stop at the edge. 'I'm not going any further,' I murmur to the breeze. The town still looks just as beautiful, the sky a little less black and a deeper blue. The moon is still high in the sky and will still be fairly high when morning arrives, fading away against the daylight as opposed to setting on the horizon.

I hug myself trying to keep warm against the chill. I feel a sense of sadness inside. Somehow, I know we won't have another night together. Not tonight anyway. I guess we can do it again another Friday or Saturday evening. We got away with this one after all. I guess we just can't do it too often or Ashley will get suspicious. It's a miracle this slipped by her in the first place.

Knowing that we won't have tonight as well makes me think I should be back in the tent holding Bryce close but it's just not as good as it would be if he was awake.

Does it matter? I ask myself. *Any time with him is better than no time.* I feel guilty for thinking it's not the same being with him if he isn't awake and know I'm being ungrateful. There's nothing I can do out here alone anyway. Even if I can't sleep again at least I'll have him next to me.

I walk back to the tent, shrug off my jacket and enter, zipping it up behind me. I wriggle back into the sleeping bag and try to cuddle up to Bryce whose back is turned to me now. He is bigger than me and I struggle to put my arm around him but it's enough. I press my face against his back and feel his warmth as I inhale his scent. I close my eyes and manage to drift off to sleep again.

When I wake up, Bryce is looking down at me. He smiles and kisses me. I realize he must have kissed me the same way he did the previous night, which is why I woke up. I smile, stretch slowly and wrap my arm around his neck as he leans in for another kiss.

'Good morning,' I manage to mumble just before our lips meet.

I worry about my morning breath for a moment but then decide, *what the hell.* I'm guessing he hasn't brushed his teeth either. One for one.

Our tongues meet and I pull him in deep this time. As deep as I can. I want this to be messy and I want it to be passionate. I want it to be the best kiss ever.

Our breathing gets deeper, faster as our passion builds. My fingers tangle in his hair and my fingernails gently scratch his head.

When we eventually part I look at Bryce.

'That was the best kiss ever,' I whisper.

'I agree,' Bryce smiles.

We get up and leave the tent. Together we walk to the edge of the hill where I stood a few hours earlier and look down at the town.

The lights are off now and the town looks more like a grey and white patch surrounded by brown and green with the blacktop stretching away in the distance. It seems so quiet and peaceful from up here. Not like the place we know it to be in reality.

'I wish we could stay another night,' I say as Bryce hugs me.

'Yeah, me too,' Bryce says. His tone says it's not going to happen. I understand. We didn't plan for it and our supplies are nearly finished. There's no way we'll last the day, never mind the night, without more supplies. Besides, we told our parents it was just one night. Something might seem off if we suddenly try to extend another night.

Master sleuth Ashley will probably check on Bryce's home if she hasn't already. I'm guessing she hasn't, otherwise I would have had a blackmail message by now. Trying to stretch it another night though might get me caught out.

'We should have planned better,' I say. 'Next time we'll plan for it.'

'Next time better be soon. This was one of the best nights I've ever had,' Bryce smiles as he pulls me close for another kiss.

His words remind me again of how little time we have and the fact that it might be even less if by some awful chance his dad gets transferred again.

We head back to the tent and sit down where we were seated the night before. I dig out the cereal we brought for this morning and two small cartons of milk. Enough for each of us to put milk over our cereal and drink what's left.

We eat breakfast and enjoy the cool morning air and the birds waking in the trees. When we've finished breakfast, restlessness sets in and we decide to pack up and head back to town.

We freewheel much of the way into town and stop at the first place where we can to dispose of our garbage before continuing on the rest of the way into town. We stop at a diner and order coffee and pancakes to fill the hole that the trip back to town has made.

When we're done, we head to Bryce's place. I message Mom and tell her we're back from camping but that I'll be home later. I'm in no hurry to get home and just want to spend as much time as I can with Bryce.

The day passes much too fast and I have to head home sooner than I would like to. I ride home as if in a daze as I think over our night together and the kisses we shared.

I push thoughts about the end of the year away. I am in heaven after last night and I want to stay there as long as possible before reality gets a grip on me again—which is all too soon.

It's as if the universe was listening when we spoke about possibilities and it's as if it decided to answer. But why is it that the answer the universe gives never seems to be the right answer?

Bryce

Despite how well things were going with Nora and me, I always knew there was the possibility that I would have to move. The thought of moving drifted further and further from my thoughts as time went on and our stay stretched into one of the longest in a place, ever. But it was always going to change. I had a feeling.

Maybe it was a premonition.

I felt as if something bad was going to happen. Like I was on a runaway train headed for disaster and there was no stopping it.

I tried to push the feeling away but it just wouldn't let go of me. It was my fear of having to move on and somehow, after we camped and spoke about it, it seemed to have intensified. Maybe the fact that we had spoken of it and Nora had admitted that she shared the same fear for a different reason, served to magnify it.

Every day that my dad did not come home and drop the 'moving' bomb on us was a blessing.

But it had to come sooner or later.

Two weeks after our camping trip. I'll always wonder if talking about it when we went camping opened the door to what happened.

Dad arrived home. We hear the car pull up outside. When he entered the house, I sense something was different immediately before he even entered the kitchen.

Maybe it was the door closing softer than usual, the way it does when a person gets home later than they should and hopes to quietly sneak into the house to avoid answering for being late or doing something wrong.

Maybe it was the fact that he seemed to take longer to enter the kitchen where I always waited for dinner as Mom prepared it. Maybe it was the way he entered the kitchen and offered a subdued greeting. Not the normal sprightly greeting he had every day when things were good or just okay even.

I think Mom knew it too then. She had been stirring gravy in the pot and I'm sure I saw her stirring stop for the briefest of moments. Dad crossed the kitchen, greeted me, and then puts his arms around Mom from behind. He kissed her.

He never did that. He was sucking up. He knew he was in trouble.

Mom stopped stirring and adjusted her head so he could kiss her better. When Dad stepped away from her, she stopped stirring and turned to look at him.

Her gaze said it all. It said she knew. I saw the look that passed between them. Mom's face was set determinedly. There was no happiness there despite the attention Dad had just given her.

'Is it what I think it is?' she asked coldly, in a low voice that I could have sworn trembles.

Dad did not answer. I wasn't initially sure what Mom was referring to but then the penny dropped. He didn't need to answer. His face must have been answer enough.

All the things that I sensed were wrong in Dad's homecoming came together to answer the question I didn't have to ask.

Mom untied her apron and hung it over the chair closest to her. It slid off and landed on the floor. She did not bother to pick it up.

'Dish up. The food's ready,' Mom said as she brushed past Dad and left the kitchen.

'What's wrong?' I asked.

Dad shrugged and pulled out a chair. 'I don't know. We have to move.'

The way he said it was as if it was just another everyday occurrence. Like ripping other people's lives apart was something that was okay to do every day.

My stomach turned as I felt my world coming apart. I felt as if I was on a huge ice floe that has just broken off the arctic shelf and I was adrift in the coldest ocean with no hope of rescue at all. I feel as if the floe was so large, to reach the end of it would take forever and even that would be pointless because I would forever be miles from anywhere else. If it ever struck land before it completely melted away, it would be the part farthest from me, and by the time I could get there, it would be too late. Always too late, always not enough.

Dad served us and I picked at my food. I had lost my appetite.

'What's the matter?' Dad said. He could tell I wasn't happy. I never picked at my food. I always had at least two helpings of food at the weekend lunch and dinner every day. I hardly touched the first helping.

'I'm not hungry,' I said.

'Aren't you feeling well?' he asked.

I realized then that he was asking because he felt guilty. He knew what he was doing.

'I'm fine. Just not happy,' I replied.

'Why not?' he asked.

'Because we're moving again,' I said and finally pushed my plate away as I stood up from the table.

'Where are you going?' my father demanded.

'Anywhere but here,' I said coldly.

'I haven't excused you,' he said, trying to assert his authority.

'And I didn't say you can rip me out of another school where I finally feel happier than I've felt in ages!'

'Don't you forget that it's my job that lets you go to school and puts a roof over our heads. It's my job that feeds and clothes us and gives you all the things you need.'

'Is that all you care about? Your job? That's more important than what it provides for us, isn't it? Do you even care about what I want? Do you *think* I want the things you get me more than having friends I can count on? Does it ever cross your mind that I don't have any friends? Do you know how hard it is to fit in every time I have to move to a new school?'

I stop my ranting and look at him for a moment in silence before I leave the kitchen and him. I go to my room, close the door and lock it and fall on my bed.

I stare at the ceiling. I'm upset and sad. I realize that I should have asked when we would be moving. I had plans to ask Nora to the prom but there's probably no point in it now.

I look at the closed door and I see a shadow pass in the hallway outside. It's headed for my parents' room.

A moment later I hear Dad's voice. I can't hear what's being said but he must be talking to Mom. I hear her respond. The conversation quickly escalates into an argument and soon they are shouting. I hear things start to crash and break.

I get up off my bed and open my door quietly enough that they won't hear me. It's not hard to do given the noise that they are making. I close my door quietly and head downstairs. I pass through the kitchen and leave the house via the backdoor. I mount my bike and am soon headed down the street away from the house.

It's one of the worst arguments Mom and Dad have had. It's not hard to understand what it's about. Mom is as upset as I am about having to move again. I can't blame her.

Since we arrived in the town, she seems to have been happier than she has been in a long time. She has made friends here and seems settled. Now she is expected to uproot everything again, leave her job, and move.

I realize that my start here was slow but now that I am with Nora, I am happier than I have been in a long time too.

Maybe we aren't fair on Dad. I know he hates his job and the job market isn't great right now. He didn't always have this job and I keep hoping he'll find another job that will mean we don't have to move around anymore. Somehow, I don't think it's going to happen because it's a crap job and no one else wants it. I've heard Dad saying he doesn't get on with his boss and I'm guessing that's why he's stuck with the job he has. If he wants to do something else, he'll probably have to quit and work for another company.

There are plenty of hotel companies and I am sure he can get a job with any of them. I don't know if he's trying or not. I guess not or else Mom wouldn't be so angry, and he would surely have had a new job by now.

I think of contacting Nora and seeing if I can meet her but it's a weeknight, and I doubt she'll be allowed out. It's late already and I don't want to burden her with this although I'm going to have to tell her sooner rather than later. It affects us. It's our fear finally become real.

I wonder if we'll be here long enough for me and Nora to make it to the prom. I doubt it. I wonder if I could come back for the prom. It's a possibility. As soon as I think it might be possible, I doubt it will happen. That's just the way it is. When Dad has to move, he usually has to move fast, and fast means we won't be here much longer, definitely not until prom.

Nora

It's a beautiful morning when I meet Bryce at school. It's chilly but the sun is shining. It's late autumn and winter is close. I wait just inside the entrance doors to the school where it's not so cold.

I watch Bryce arrive and walk up the path to the school doors. I can tell immediately that something's wrong. He is missing the spring in his step that he always has. His head is down as if he's trying to disappear into the scarf wrapped around his neck.

Maybe he's just feeling the cold because this morning is exceptionally chilly. I know it's not the case when he pushes through the entrance doors. He doesn't see me.

'Bryce,' I call.

He stops and turns to look at me. A smile appears on his face but it's weak. I know then that something is wrong for sure.

'Hey,' he says. He doesn't open his arms and hold them out for me the way he does every morning—as if he hasn't seen me in ages and is overjoyed to see me. I love how he wraps me up in his arms as if I am in a cocoon of his love. I feel so secure because of the way he pulls me close and squeezes me affectionately.

I love it that he does that. It makes me feel so special, so loved. Every morning. But not today.

I reach him and wrap my arms around him. He just puts his arm around me, and we start moving towards the lockers.

'Are you okay?' I ask, looking up at him.

'Yeah. I'm okay,' he replies. 'Just damn cold.'

'That's why we have each other,' I smile and squeeze him tighter. He responds and squeezes me a bit tighter too.

When we get to the lockers we separate and get what we need. Then we walk to class, comfortable with each other like an old couple. It's just that we don't say much this morning at all.

When school starts Bryce is in trouble. He hasn't done his maths homework again and is found out by the teacher. He gets sent to the principal's office and after he leaves the teacher says his attitude stinks. I don't know what she is talking about since I sit in front of him and couldn't see anything he might have done to give her that idea.

Bryce picks up his bag and leaves the classroom. I watch him as he walks past the windows outside hoping he'll glance my way, but he doesn't. It's not like him not to do his homework. I wonder if he just forgot but I doubt it. I suspect something happened last night. I cast my mind back to the text message he sent me before he went to sleep. I can't quite remember what it was and so I take out my mobile phone, unlock the screen and call up his messages.

It doesn't take long for the teacher to spot me using my phone.

'Nora, kindly remove yourself to the principal's office. You know the rule. No mobile phones in class.'

I lower my phone and glare at her. *Are you kidding me? The principal's office because of my mobile phone?*

Usually, Ms Jayor is easy-going. I guess she must have woken up on the wrong side of the bed. But then she never seemed to take a liking to Bryce either. He struggles with maths, and I help him a lot. He says I'm the best teacher he's had. I think it's just flattery, but I do seem to help him. Sometimes he doesn't do his maths homework and that doesn't help him as far as Ms Jayor goes. But somehow, I think she's just never liked him for some reason. The fact that he doesn't do his homework is beside the point. It merely exacerbates her dislike of him and gives her an opportunity to punish him. I guess he doesn't make it easy on himself.

I sigh audibly and Ms Jayor gives me a warning look as I start packing my things.

'What is it with you kids today?' Ms Jayor starts. 'No homework, mobile phones . . . not the slightest bit of respect.'

I pack my things in my bag and sling it over my shoulder. I begin to head for the door and my bag catches the corner of the desk knocking it askew. It's an accident but Ms Jayor seizes the opportunity to demonstrate her power and discourage anyone else who wants to break the rules.

'Do I detect a bad attitude from you as well?' Ms Jayor asks.

I don't answer but right the desk and head for the door.

'I asked you a question, young lady,' Ms Jayor says sternly.

I sigh again, slouch my shoulders and turn to face her. 'No, ma'am.'

I answer a bit too abruptly, so she continues. 'That's not the way it seems to me. Tell Mr Brunswick that I sent you for using your phone in class and a terrible attitude!'

I want to argue but decide to leave it. I won't win this fight and I can see another detention looming.

'Yes, ma'am,' I reply in a more polite tone than before.

'Good. You may go,' Ms. Jayor says, dismissing me. She turns to the class. 'Is there anyone else that wants to join Nora and Bryce?'

The class is silent.

I check my phone on the way to the principal's office. At least I have the freedom to do that now as I walk to the admin building. Bryce's message lacks something. I didn't think anything of it the night before but now I sense it.

I put my phone away and enter Mr Brunswick's outer office. His secretary, Ms Crane looks at me over the rims of her spectacles with disdain. I'm sure she despises children.

'May I help you?'

'I have been sent to see Mr Brunswick by Ms Jayor.'

'Another one?' she asks. 'The same class? What did you do?'

I resent her questions and tone. They imply that I must have done something wrong. I want to ask her why she can't believe that I might have sent here for praise, but I decide to leave it. I'll just be in more trouble.

'I used my phone in class and Ms Jayor said I have a bad attitude.'

Ms Crane shakes her head and tells me to take a seat. I look around quickly, but I can't see Bryce and guess he is already in the office with Mr Brunswick. I take the seat closest to the door hoping to hear what is said inside the office.

Bryce keeps his voice low, and I can't hear what he's saying but I can hear Mr Brunswick's voice and part of what he is saying.

'. . . that's no excuse. You always give your best . . .'

Bryce says something but Mr Brunswick interrupts him.

'I will not tolerate slacking is that understood?'

I hear a murmur which I assume is Bryce's agreement.

'Detention, Friday. And I hope this is the last time or I will be calling your parents next time.'

Bryce mumbles something and the door opens a few moments later. Bryce does not look happy at all, and he stops for a moment when he sees me. He looks guilty and confused all at the same time.

It's as if he is wondering why I am here and if I heard what he said. If he wants to stop and say something he can't. Mr Brunswick is behind him.

'Don't you have a class to get back to?' he asks Bryce.

'Yes, sir,' Bryce says and leaves the outer office as Mr Brunswick steps back to let me enter his office and closes the door behind me.

'You too?' he says as he circles his desk and sits down. He motions for me to be seated and I take a seat opposite him.

'Ms Jayor sent me because I used my mobile in class, and she said I have a bad attitude.'

He looks at me as if he is assessing me. He steeples his fingers on the desk in front of him as he studies me.

'You know Nora, you're quite highly thought of in the school. It worries me though that you are visiting my office again so soon. I imagine the fact that it is short on the heels of Bryce is no coincidence?'

'I had nothing to do with . . .'

Mr Brunswick interrupts me.

'I would hate for you to leave here with your reputation sullied. Stay away from kids that drift around. They don't have goals, and they're not a good influence.'

I can only imagine that he is referring to Bryce and I feel my face flush in anger. I realize he has deliberately not mentioned Bryce's name so he can't be held accountable if I tell anyone about our conversation.

I don't reply and I think he decides not to push it.

'Detention Friday. Don't be late. This better be the last time' he says sternly.

'Yes, sir,' I reply. I pick up my bag and leave his office. I want to get to Bryce and find out what's wrong.

Bryce doesn't open up during school. He's not himself and I begin to think whatever it is, he's going to break up with me. Maybe that's it. Maybe he wants to break up but doesn't know how so he thinks that being shitty to me will do the trick and make me break up with him.

I decide that the end of the day after school is make or break. That's when we'll finally be able to talk about what's troubling him.

Bryce

Nora gets caught up with someone after school. I don't know if I should feel happy or not. I know I've been avoiding her all day. I feel like I've been pretty shitty to her although I haven't intended to be.

I'm not ready to talk to her, to tell her, break her heart. I finish putting my books in my locker, get the books I need for my homework and head for the doors. I'm out and headed home before she catches up to me.

I hear her calling from way behind me and I stop, waiting for her to catch up.

'Hey!' she says when she finally catches up to me.

'Hey,' I reply.

'What the hell is with you?' she asks. I can tell she's not happy. She's not quite angry either, but she's getting there.

'What do you mean?' I ask.

That's all it takes to make her angry. 'Don't be coy with me. If you want to break up with me then do it properly. Don't think being shitty to me is going to do the trick. I deserve a hell of a lot more respect than that!'

I look at Nora not sure what to say. But she's not finished. 'Something's wrong and you better tell me. I checked your message from last night and I realize it wasn't the same

181

bubbly you. You didn't hold out your arms to hug me this morning as if you haven't seen me in a thousand years. You know I love that, and I missed it this morning. I've missed you all day even though you've been at school with me. You haven't been there and . . .'

I love the way she rattles on. She's losing some of her anger now as she carries on. I know she feels as if she is getting her point across. I can't help but smile then because she just looks so beautiful. She is so beautiful. All of her. Her voice, her eyes, her hair, her mannerisms, just her.

She shakes her head in frustration and her ponytail swings around behind her.

'What? It's not funny . . .'

I step forward, closing the distance between us and thinking what an idiot I have been today. We have limited time left and we can't make the most of it if I'm moping around and shutting her out.

I take her face in my hands and my kiss silences her.

When we part, she looks at me breathlessly and then kisses me again.

This time, when we part, she looks up at me and then pulls me close for a hug. I return her hug and squeeze her the way I always do. When I release her, she smiles up at me.

'That's better. That's the you I know.'

'Thanks. I know,' I reply. 'Let's go get a milkshake.'

'Okay,' Nora says and falls into step beside me.

'So, we scored ourselves another detention,' I say hoping to change the subject. I succeed for just a while.

'We did,' she says. 'What happened to you? Did you really forget to do your homework? I mean it's not like you not to do your homework.'

'I did forget. I was out late last night and got back too late to think of doing anything except fall into bed.'

'Wait, you were out late last night?' she asks me. It's a surprise to her and I know she's wondering if I was with someone. It's her next question. More or less. 'Were you alone?'

'Yes,' I reply.

'Well, why were you out so late?'

'Mom and Dad were at it again,' I tell her.

'Oh,' she says then adds, 'I'm sorry.'

'It's okay. I just needed to go somewhere to get away from it. I didn't think I could see you, so I didn't ask you.'

'You could have. I could have sneaked out of the house.'

'Really?' I smile.

'Maybe,' she says.

'I don't think so. We would have been caught and then we'd probably have been in more trouble. At least you would have, and your parents would have forbidden you from ever seeing me again, the bad influence and all that . . .'

She punches me on the arm. 'They're not ogres you know. They do have a modern view of things. They're hip.'

'Careful,' I tease.

'Why?' she asks, confused.

'It's hip to be square,' I reply, referring to the song.

'Maybe but that's not them, okay?'

I smile. 'Sure. I was just kidding.'

We arrive at the roadhouse and take a booth in the back. A waitress takes our order and brings our milkshakes and a waffle and ice cream to share.

We sip and eat alternately, and Nora gets back to the subject.

'What's up, dude? You haven't been yourself all day,' she asks.

I put my spoon down, look at her briefly and then study my fingers intensely. I don't want to tell her, but I know I have to. It's not fair not to and word will get to her anyway. She would want to hear it from me and not anyone else.

I finally look up.

Into her eyes.

I don't want to hurt her.

I don't want to give her the bad news.

She knows something's wrong, and I don't know what she thinks it is but her eyes become moist and I think she's thinking the worst.

'We're moving,' I say.

Silence falls between us and neither of us says a word before the first tear spills from her eyes. As if my words are the final push that's needed, the first tear spills over and then more follow. She leans back and looks away. I reach across the table, wondering why she is sitting opposite me instead of next to me. A stupid question I realize, as I remember that I'm the one who chose to sit opposite her. She ignores my hand and suddenly the table seems so wide.

I get up and slide in beside her. She is now looking away, out the window as I place my hand on her arm. She is covering her mouth with her small fist as the tears continue to run down her cheek.

I lean forward and wipe away a tear as I kiss her just in front of her ear.

'Hey,' I say, my voice is almost a whisper.

I feel her quiver as she sobs silently. She doesn't answer me for a while and when she does, she turns to me.

'Why?' she asks, and her eyes seem to dig deep into mine looking for an answer that she already knows.

'We always knew this was coming,' I say. 'It's just sooner than we expected.'

'Do you have to go?' she asks as her eyes beg for me to give her the answer I can't.

'You know I don't want to,' I tell her.

She nods and looks at our milkshakes. 'So, no prom then?'

'I thought I could come back for the prom. Maybe. I guess it depends on if it will be feasible or not. I don't even know where we're supposed to be going.'

'Really?' Nora says and laughs, finding that funny.

'Yeah. Dad broke the news, I got pissed at him and then he and Mom started arguing so I left. I guess I'll find out tonight.'

'Will you let me know?' she asks.

'Of course, I will,' I say.

'If it's close enough, will you come back?'

'For sure. I'll ride my bicycle if I have to,' I joke. I might be able to, I think to myself. 'Even if it's the other side of the country I'll want to come back.'

She smiles.

Nora

I slump against the back of the booth. I feel as if a hole has opened up and swallowed me. The bottom has fallen out of my world and I'm in freefall.

'Fuck,' I swear. I don't swear often but now I do. It feels good. A short, angry, bluntly shocking word. 'What about us?'

'We still have us,' Bryce says, reaching out his hand for mine on the table.

I slowly extend my hand until he can take it in his.

'How long do we have "us"?' I ask.

'Until I leave. Maybe longer.'

'What do you mean, "maybe longer"?' I'm getting irritated now because I am upset, and I need to let my unhappiness show. I know I am making him my target because he is the cause of my unhappiness too.

'I was thinking I could maybe come back for prom,' Bryce says. He looks out the window after he says it and I can tell he doesn't believe it'll happen. He's trying to convince me and himself otherwise though.

'If you leave before prom we'll know, won't we?'

'I guess. I mean if it's a plane flight away, I doubt my parents will pay for me to come back. Besides, I won't be at school anymore. They'll argue against the expense. If we're just an hour or two away they'll probably be okay with it. I can bus it.'

He pauses and then squeezes my hand.

'We always knew this might happen,' he says. 'We feared it but now it's real. It was always going to happen, regardless of whether it was going to be the end of the year or sooner.'

I start crying again as I look at him. 'I don't want you to go. Ever.'

He wipes away my tears. 'And I don't want to go, but what can I do?'

'Stay,' I insist.

'I've got nowhere to stay,' he says, his frustration clear. I wonder if my parents will let him stay with us, but I know it's a non-starter before I even voice the idea to him or decide to ask my parents later. I don't know what comes over me then, but I can't deal with the situation. I can't deal with losing him. I can't deal with seeing him every day knowing that our time is running out, slowly counting down to the end of us. And it will be.

The end of us, I mean.

We'll part ways and we'll never see each other again. I need to talk to someone, but no one will understand. *Young love.* That's what they'll say. *You'll get over it. You haven't met the man you'll marry yet.*

I feel as if the world is closing in on me and I'm beginning to panic. I pull my hand back from Bryce and grab my bag. He's in my way.

'I have to go,' I say as I look at him and wipe away more tears.

'Why?' he asks, confused by my sudden need to leave.

'I . . . just . . . need to go,' I say.

Bryce backs out of the booth and lets me out. I stand and turn to leave but he grabs my arm.

'Hey,' he says softly.

I turn to face him.

'I love you,' he says.

I don't say anything but turn and walk away. It's cruel, I know, but just then I'm not thinking clearly. It's hard enough when someone you love breaks up with you, but this is like a break up with a future date. I can't deal with seeing him and knowing that the last time we'll see each other is coming closer every time I see him, every time I say goodbye. I'm a fool I know. I should treasure the time we have left.

I get home and spend the afternoon doing my homework, ignoring Bryce's messages and calls, crying, listening to music, ignoring Bryce some more and trying to focus which is an impossibility. My heart is breaking more than ever now that I am trying to cut Bryce off.

He's not a quitter though and as I lay awake in my bed I hear the *tic, tic,* as small stones bounce off my window. I am unable to sleep anyway and my heart jumps with joy. It could only be Bryce. I sit up and look out the window. I can see him silhouetted in the moonlight on the front lawn. He waves to me.

I wave back and head downstairs. Everyone is sleeping already so I try to be as quiet as possible. I disarm the alarm and unlock the door.

I open it and then close it again as quietly as possible behind me.

I reach the top of the porch and look down at Bryce where he is standing in the garden.

I'm crying again. This time it's because I love him so much, because I'm hurting and because I'm glad he came.

I can't control myself then. I leave the porch. I'm wearing a white button-down pyjama top and matching shorts with socks. Bryce walks towards me, and we meet at the edge of the pathway. A car is driving somewhere in the neighbourhood.

I kiss him deeply and then pull away.

'Bring your bike,' I whisper.

Bryce goes and picks up his bike and heads back to me. I head to the side of the house where there are many bushes.

My white pyjamas are a giveaway in the dark. I'll stand out like a glow-in-the-dark bunny if anyone drives by or if my parents or, heaven forbid, Ashley looks out the window.

We reach the bushes and I pull him towards me. He lets go of his bike and it falls into a bush. I press my back against the wall of the house and pull him close to me.

'I'm sorry,' I say as my mouth closes on his before he can answer. My fingers tangle in his hair as we kiss. Our breathing is fast and deep. We are more passionate than we have ever been. I know it's my emotions and the pressure I feel of our time running out.

I'm sure he feels it too. His hands are tangled in my hair but then they move down my back. They stop briefly when he realizes I'm not wearing a bra. Maybe I'm mistaken. Right then I want more.

I drop one hand from his hair and start to unbutton my top from the lowest button upwards. When it's just the top button that's still done up, I stop. I pull his hand down and he finds my open top. His hand slips inside and finds my skin. I'm on fire with his touch and I want more. He lowers his other hand, and it pushes the bottom of my top open. His hands trace lines of sensuous fire across my skin. They're warm and soft and gentle. He runs his fingers over my skin softly as his hands circle round to my back and then up under my top. I arch my back and press myself into him.

'Your hands feel so good,' I whisper. I begin to pull on his shirt and lift it so my hands can find his naked skin underneath it. I want to feel his skin under my fingers too.

We kiss harder and deeper as our hands explore. His hands move around to the front of my chest and brush over the outer swell of my breasts before his thumbs brush over my already hard nipples.

I break his kiss and sigh with desire.

'That feels so good,' I whisper. His fingers brush over my nipples again and then his hands are gone. He removes them from under my top and places them on the outside of my top.

'What?' I ask him, surprised.

'I want you so bad, but I can't. Not like this,' he says.

'What do you mean, not like this?' I ask.

'I can't. It would be selfish and foolish. We don't have much time left and doing this now, is irrational. I don't want us to resent each other later for doing something silly. Even if we don't make love before I leave and we never end up making love, at least you can save yourself for someone who might be your husband. Besides, I don't have a condom, and do you *really* want to make love here in the bushes beside your house?'

I know he has a point. I take his hand and place it on my breast so he can feel my nipple through my top.

'Just enjoy it then,' I whisper as I kiss him again.

He slowly begins to massage my breast through my top and I pull him close again. His other hand moves around to my back, but this time slides south over my ass. My pyjama shorts are short and tight. His hand rests on the curve of my ass and then grabs it as we kiss.

I let him explore. If we're not going to make love, then at least I can enjoy having him touch me as I press myself against his hardness.

We explore a while longer, but finally we part, and he looks at me. His gaze tells me he wants to say something.

Nora

'Don't push me away, please,' he says. 'We don't have much time. At least let's enjoy it and enjoy being with each other.'

I look into his eyes. I know he's right and I'm already hurting but I know sticking with him will delay the pain until the end, until life finally rips him from me and my heart with him. But he is right. I want to make the most of what we have until we can't have it anymore.

'Okay,' I say softly. 'I won't push you away.'

We kiss a while longer and then decide it's time for Bryce to leave. He hauls his bike out of the bush and mounts it. He waits for me to go back inside and get to my room before he rides out of the yard. He stops in the street and waves at me before heading home.

A few days later everything is clear. The worst has come to pass. There is no chance that Bryce will be able to make it to the prom. They are moving too far away. To New Mexico this time. When he tells me, neither of us says anything more. There's no need to.

Bryce's Dad leaves the next day for the new place. That's how it is always. He leaves quickly when the instruction to move comes.

Bryce tells me his mother commented that the only reason she did not pack her bags and go to live with her sister is that someone has to stay and look after him until the move is finalized.

I realize it's a harsh thing for his mother to have said, especially when Bryce is there to hear it. He might be eighteen, but he is still their child and such things should be handled more delicately. I think so at least, although I've never experienced anything like it. I think it's the last thing Bryce needs to hear given his situation and what we're facing.

As it happens, the move is set up quite quickly and his dad is back in just a few days. He arrives midweek and the move is planned for a week from the next Monday. It just gives us this weekend and the next.

Some moves are easier and therefore faster than others. It all depends on how much support is provided for where they are going. I can't believe that of all the moves this turns out to be one of the faster ones.

It's as if the universe has decided that it wants to tear us apart as fast as possible.

My parents and Ashley have no idea that Bryce will be leaving, and I decide it's best that way. We decide to go camping for the weekend and this time arrange to go on Friday after school and return on Sunday morning. My parents say it will be cold, but I manage to persuade them that we'll be prepared. Of course, the fact that I tell them Christine is joining us gives them no cause to worry and makes it easier for them to agree. Amazingly, Ashley has no suspicions. Thank heavens for small mercies.

We pack our things and head off to camp immediately after school on Friday. We can't carry everything so we take the tent and some initial supplies and hide them in the trees at the site before we head back to town and buy enough groceries to last us while we are there.

The evenings are cold, but we dress warm and have blankets as well as our sleeping bags and pillows. It was quite a haul to get everything to the site, but we planned to make it as comfortable as possible.

The first night we huddle around the fire and reminisce about the times we've had. There are many good times we remember, and it hurts to think that we've made so many good memories in such a short time. I'm sad that it's coming to an end. When it's time for bed we crawl into the tent and into our sleeping bags which we have combined again to make one big sleeping bag. The only light we have are the embers from the fire. We have torches but don't use them.

The embers don't offer great light and I decide that since time is limited, I want to enjoy this night as much as I can. I strip off my clothes and climb into the sleeping bag naked.

I'm a bit shy but I'm also sure that Bryce won't mind.

He's already in the sleeping bag and when I cuddle up to him, he puts his arm around me. A moment later he sits up in shock.

'Whoa! What's this?' he asks, surprised.

'Don't be a nerd,' I reply. 'It's your girlfriend who wants to enjoy this time as much as possible. You can get naked too if you want. I want.'

He hesitates a moment and then pulls off his shirt and his boxers. Then he crawls back into the sleeping bag and pulls me close. We wrap our arms around each other and enjoy feeling our naked bodies against each other. There's something so special about being close together and naked.

I've never done it before, and it just feels so intimate. Our hands roam, exploring, caressing and tickling as we kiss and whisper to each other.

'You do realize if a bear comes now, we're in big trouble,' Bryce says.

'Well, I'm sure he'll get your bits first,' I say as I stroke his hardness.

'I think he'll find your bits better,' Bryce says as he massages my breasts and adds, 'If he's a boy. If it's a female bear, I would be more worried.'

'Very funny,' I say as we both giggle.

We don't make love. Bryce repeats what he told me before and we content ourselves knowing we want each other and just being close together and intimately naked.

As we hold each other in the dark he asks me what I'm thinking.

'I don't know what I'm going to do without you. No one will understand if we talk to them. Everyone thinks it's young love and we'll move on, but I don't know how I can, Bryce. I can't picture my life without you.'

'I can't picture mine without you either, but we have no choice. I don't know if I will move on. People say time heals all wounds, but does it? I think to me, you're always going to be the one who didn't get away but who I left behind.'

I know he's right and I couldn't have said it better. We finally fall asleep in each other's arms and do the same the next evening.

When Sunday arrives, we know we won't have two days like this ever again, and we are sad when we head home.

Time passes all too quickly the next week. Bryce packs whatever he has to so we can have the weekend to

ourselves again. He spends most of it at my place and sleeps
over on Friday and Saturday, but we can't get as close as we
were when we camped. Ashley is too nosy and won't give us
our space.

Monday arrives and Bryce lets me know their departure
has been delayed until Tuesday. Monday night is the last time
I see him.

He promises to write to me and while I'm grateful for the
messages he has written throughout our relationship I don't
want to think that he'll be leaving messages for me in hotels
that I might never find. It's like telling me that this is really it
and I won't hear from him again.

I have his e-mail address and I'll write to him if he doesn't
write to me. He's not getting off the hook that easy.

We do stay in touch for a while via text messages, but he
eventually stops replying and I eventually give up. I resort to
e-mails and send him a few.

I hope beyond hope for a message that he is coming
back for the prom. Other boys invite me to go with them
but I decline. I end up not going. Bryce does not turn up or
message me.

I guess time does heal all wounds. I begin to throw
myself into what is left of my life after Bryce leaves. I get
busier and am soon distracted. I am reminded of us when
I see other couples, but I continue to turn other guys down
feeling as if it would be a betrayal of us. I wonder if Bryce
does the same.

I like to believe that he does but it's foolish, and I wonder
if he has moved on already. I have no way of knowing.

I finally send him another e-mail telling him it'll be the
last time I'll write and that I haven't been near any hotels,
especially in New Mexico, so I can't read anything he might

have written for me anywhere. I tell him I love him, and I miss him, and I ask him to tell me if he's moved on or not and that I'll understand if he has.

I receive no reply.

Present Day

Bryce

Winter in New York. I exit the metro and walk into the freezing embrace of the winter wind as I make my way to the office. Snow is falling and the skies are deep grey as I walk. People around me are tucked deep inside their coats and pay little attention to others as they hasten to get to the warmth of their offices.

I'm back in town for a day or two and have been summoned by my boss. I wonder how my boss knows I exist. I'm always on the road and have been passed over for a few promotions already. I guess Lisa was right. Out of sight out of mind.

I'm not usually given to negative thinking but having been passed over for promotions, and even other roles I've applied for, doesn't instil confidence in me. I wonder if being summoned could mean one thing. I am no longer needed.

I take off my gloves and play with them nervously as I step on the escalator and head up to our department's floor.

My boss's secretary shows me into his office. She clearly knows that I am expected, and I am tempted to ask her if she knows what the meeting is about. Maybe I'm imagining things, but she seems a bit cold to me which probably means I'm getting fired today, or it could just be the effect of the cold from the weather outside. I doubt it's the latter since she appears to have been at her desk for a while already. In a way, I think being fired would be a blessing, to be honest. I could find another job that didn't require so much travel.

'Bryce!' my boss says cheerfully as he stands and rounds his desk to shake my hand.

'Graham,' I say, trying to match his mood as I shake his hand.

'Please have a seat,' Graham says, motioning to the chairs in front of his desk. I take a seat, and he returns to his chair. 'I'm glad you could make it.'

'Of course, sir,' I reply, feeling tense but a bit more relaxed. Unless he smiles and is cheerful when he fires people, Graham wants to see me about something else. I suddenly feel a bit calmer.

I glance around the office quickly. There is a distinct smell of polished wood. I notice the sideboard against the wall on which numerous ornaments, trophies, and other items are standing. The armrests of the chair I am sitting in are wood and the bookshelf behind me is also made of wood. The furniture contrasts well against the plush green carpet. The office is huge in my opinion. Maybe it just seems that way though seeing as I don't have an office. I have a cubicle which is shared with others whenever we come in off the road.

Graham's chair creaks as he sits down and leans back. He eyes me briefly, hands clasped in front of him before he gets down to business.

'I have good news for you,' he smiles. He wears round spectacles and his hair is thinning and grey. It's the last thing I should be noticing but we often think or notice the irrelevant at the most important times of our lives.

'That's great,' is all I can say.

Graham leans forward. 'I want you to take over the operations for the Northwest. Director of Operations will be your title. You'll have to move to Chicago though.'

I am stunned and have to stop myself from jumping out of the chair and doing a dance right there in Graham's office.

He is waiting for a reaction from me and before the silence between us becomes too uncomfortable I find my voice.

'Thank you, sir. That is wonderful news. Thank you for placing your trust in me.'

Graham shakes his head. 'Your recognition is long overdue. It's about time you got off the road and settled down.'

I want to tell him he has no idea how right he is, but I keep it to myself and thank him again.

'In your position, I am going to allow you to recruit your assistant.'

I nod and an idea strikes me almost immediately. 'Am I permitted to transfer someone from here?' I ask, thinking of Lisa.

'Assuming they are willing to move, I don't see why not. Leave their name with my assistant and we'll get in touch with their boss and them,' Graham says.

I nod. 'Excellent. I will do so.'

He pushes an envelope across the table to me. 'These are the details of your new role and increased salary. I need you to complete the document, sign and return it to Helen, my assistant outside, for your acceptance.'

I assure him I will do so, thank him again and after some small talk, I excuse myself.

When I leave Graham's office I am walking on air. I leave Lisa's name with Helen and wander over to my department's area and look for Lisa. A colleague tells me she's not in and

I can't believe my luck. It's beginning to feel as if we're not supposed to meet. I leave a message for her to call me and leave the office.

I take the rest of the week off to sort out what I need to before moving to Chicago.

Lisa calls me the next day.

'I believe congratulations are in order,' she says.

'Thank you,' I say.

'Perhaps I should be thanking you for thinking so highly of me that you would like me to move to Chicago as your assistant even though we've never met,' she says.

'You do deserve the promotion,' I say.

'Thank you. I'm not here for promotions though but perhaps the change of scenery is enough to tempt me. Can we meet for coffee before I give you my answer? I'd like to know who I'll be working for. I have an idea but there's nothing like talking face to face and I hope you won't mind if after we meet, I decide I'd rather stay here.'

'Well sure. Let's do coffee,' I tell her, trying to hide the disappointment in my voice at the thought that she might turn me down. On the other hand, I might just be dodging a bullet if she does turn me down. I suggest a coffee shop and she says she knows it, and we agree on a time to meet.

Before I end the call, I ask, 'What is it that you hope to glean by meeting with me?'

Without any hesitation she replies, 'I don't work for Jims. I don't date them either. There are plenty of people around whose names aren't Jim, but they should be. I want to be sure you're not a Jim.'

'You can explain that to me when we meet,' I say. and we end the call. I think I have an idea what she is talking about, but I want to be sure. Right then I wonder who would have said what she just said to someone who offered them a promotion. I like that she says what she thinks and am sure we will work great together. My last thought is, *What is it with her and men called Jim?* It might just be cause for concern.

It's awkward at first when we meet the next day. I arrive early and find a table by the window. I see her walk past as she heads for the entrance and recognize her immediately. I just know it's her. There's no way it could be a coincidence for this woman to be here when I arranged to meet the secretary from our department.

I wonder if I should run and hide but she's at the door, opens it and pauses just inside as she looks around for me. She spots me and makes the connection. I told her what I am wearing so she could recognize me but her hesitation at the door for just that moment longer tells me she remembers me too.

She puts her head down and then makes her way over to me. I stand as she arrives at my table.

'Lisa,' I say and offer my hand.

'Yes. You are Bryce,' she says.

'Please sit down,' I say, and she obliges.

'I want to apologize,' I say after I sit down. I'm not sure if she remembers me but I want to clear the air immediately just in case she does.

She looks at me quizzically and waits for me to continue.

'We collided in the office a while ago. I knocked you down and then helped you pick up the papers scattered all over the place. I'm sorry.'

Her face lights up as she remembers and blushes. 'Oh my God! That was you!' She buries her face in her hands for a moment and then looks up. '*I* should apologize. I was rude to you. I thought about it after I left. I must say I thought I would never see you again though.'

'Likewise,' I reply.

We order coffee and chat for a while. Sometimes when people have known each other from a distance the way we have, they don't get along as well when they finally meet in person. Thankfully, it's not like that with Lisa and me. We get along just great, and she tells me I am not a 'Jim' (though I still don't know what she means by that). By the end of our meeting, we're both convinced that we can work together and she agrees to be my assistant in Chicago. I couldn't be happier.

Lisa

When I arrive at the coffee shop I stop just inside the door and look around. Bryce told me what he was wearing. Then I see him, and I can't believe my eyes.

I remember the handsome man that I collided into a while back at the office. The same man I scolded and the same man who sat right there in the coffee shop.

I blush before I paste a smile on my face and begin walking towards him. I am sure he will remember me too and remember how I barked at him for knocking me off my feet. I imagine that my chances of getting this job now are slim.

I try to shrug it off. I mean, I'm not a corporate climber and I didn't ask for this opportunity. I'm happy where I am. So if he decides he doesn't want me because of that single meeting we had, if you can even call it that, I can live with it.

It would be a pity though.

I arrive at the table and he stands to greet me and I do the same before sitting down. He looks nervous, as nervous as I must be, before he confirms recalling our meeting and offers me an apology.

We talk for a while and he asks a number of questions which I answer and soon we ease into a more comfortable conversation, the initial awkwardness at the beginning of our meeting forgotten. I find out we have quite a few things in common and we've both been single for a while too. He asks if I don't think he is a 'Jim' and I tell him he isn't. Though I can tell he has no idea what I mean—maybe we will discuss it another time.

I eventually decide, as we are speaking, that I will take the job.

He seems happy which surprises me. It makes me glad too. I am sure I will enjoy working with him. I have so far, anyway.

'The company will pay for my move?' I ask.

'Yes, it will,' he replies. 'I just need to determine how soon they'll let you go.'

'I can sort that out,' I say. 'I'll keep you informed of my progress and we can play it by ear. I don't have much to move seeing as I am renting a furnished apartment.'

'Very well then, I am glad you are on board and I look forward to seeing you in Chicago,' he says.

We drink our coffee and mostly make small talk getting to know each other better. I am glad to see that the image I had of him before is only improved now that I have met him in person.

'I remember that day we ran into each other in the office. I told you the head of hospitality's replacement was going to be announced. I hoped you would get it but you didn't. I guess it's because there was something better for you which is this position. I think you deserve it.'

'Thank you,' he replies. 'I appreciate that. It came as a total surprise, and I am glad because I don't have to travel so much anymore.'

As we get more comfortable talking to each other, I take him in. He is handsome, kind, humble. I want to know him better and though I wonder if I should even be accepting this job when I already have a crush on my boss, I can't help myself.

If anything develops between us, you can leave your job. Problem solved. I tell myself.

'Do you have any ties to New York?' Bryce asks me.

I shake my head. 'No. I just have my mother and she's not in New York. If anything happens to her, I would have to travel to see her no matter where she is.' He nods his understanding and I have to stop myself from swooning yet again. I push my thoughts aside and try to stay professional. At the end of the day, Bryce is still someone I respect a lot and I know that we will have a great working relationship.

When we are finally done, Bryce tells me he will start the paperwork for my transfer with the human resources team who will contact me. He will be leaving within the next week. He only has his own things to worry about so the move would be a breeze.

For a moment I wonder how a man like him can be single and then I remember that he's been on the road almost twenty-four seven ever since I've known him. No one could maintain a relationship under those circumstances. I wonder how he managed to just do the job and be alone as long as he has. My feelings aside, I realize that I am truly happy for him and the fact that he has finally been promoted to a job that will let him travel less and be more settled. If anyone deserves it, he does.

We finish our coffee, and he gets the bill. We say goodbye and part ways. I have a spring in my step and I'm excited about the new adventure in Chicago. I'm excited about what the future holds and I can't wait to move.

Nora

I settle into my new role easily. Two months flash by and I'm buried in my work. There is so much that needs doing that I feel like I am constantly scaling a mountain. I can see the summit getting closer, albeit slowly. I know I am making progress and I am receiving positive feedback from my bosses.

Jenson is now a distant memory. I haven't heard from him since I ignored his last message about six weeks ago. I guess he got the message when I didn't reply to his.

I sometimes go out with work colleagues for a few drinks but never stay late and don't get too close to anyone. As a new member of management, I want to make sure I don't get too close to anyone that I may need to fire at a later stage.

It's the one aspect that makes my job difficult. I have no time to meet people outside of work and I need to keep my distance from the staff at work so I have no real friends or anyone with whom I have a deep connection that I can talk to.

I wonder if things would be any different if I had a boyfriend. Maybe. But then I'm so busy that I wonder if I would have time for him.

I get myself a cat and name him Jasper. He's black with green eyes and he keeps me company. He's loyal and always happy to see me when I get home. Partially because he's hungry and wants food, partially because he loves me. I don't mind. At least he does love me, and he provides some company on lonely nights and weekends.

I finally get to a point where the workload is beginning to ease off and I find myself with more time on my hands.

I decide to try speed dating. There is a regular speed dating evening held at a community centre close to the hotel where I stay.

I'm stunned when I read the advert.

Speed dating evenings are held every Monday, Wednesday, and Friday, two sessions per evening with a maximum of fifty participants.

I can't believe it. That's three hundred people per week! *Are there that many lonely people in this world?* I wonder. *How many of them go to every session? Do people have success finding a partner at a speed dating event?*

I have my answer soon enough. I sign up for Friday evening and arrive early. I register when I arrive and take a seat waiting for the evening to start. I notice some people looking around and a few catch my eye. I realize they're scoping out who they might like which I think is kind of shallow since they're only going on appearances.

I keep my hopes up. It is my first time after all. The least I can do is experience what it's like. If I don't find anyone this evening I can decide if I want to try again another evening. Maybe a different speed dating group.

The evening finally begins. The mediator explains the process and the bell rings. We have one minute with each person we meet and then we have to move on.

It's crazy and I struggle to resist the urge to laugh out loud. I wonder if all the people who attend speed dating evenings are like this. I know I'm being judgmental and immediately feel guilty for it.

The first person I meet is a man. He is in his early twenties.

'Hi. I'm Jack. You're really beautiful,' he smiles. His hair needs a cut and I wonder what he's doing here. He's quite handsome or he could be if he cut his hair and dressed a bit better.

'Hi. You're too young,' I tell him bluntly.

'Oh, c'mon. Age doesn't mean anything. Many guys date older women . . .'

Did he just call me an older woman? Technically I am but not in the sense that he means. I'm guessing there's not more than ten years between us.

'We've got time. We may as well use it to get to know each other,' he adds.

'Jack, what's the point? You and I are not going to date. Move on, okay?'

He looks disappointed but sighs. 'Whatever. A word of advice though, you're far too uptight for this to work for you. Relax a little and you might get a date tonight.'

'Oh, and I guess you're a speed dating pro?' I say.

'Actually yes,' he says. 'This is my seventy-eighth time.'

I'm shocked and hold my tongue as it hastens to deliver a sarcastic remark. The bell rings and we move on.

The next person is a woman. 'Hello there,' she says, showing obvious interest in me.

'Hi,' I say hesitantly.

'What's your name? I'm Angela and I know how to show a woman a good time.'

I cringe. Is the whole evening going to go like this, I wonder? I shake my head and tell her, 'Sorry, I'm not into women. We're just sitting opposite each other, okay?'

She looks disappointed, shrugs, and falls silent waiting for the bell.

The next person is also a woman.

'Hi,' she says.

'Hi,' I say hesitantly, then add quickly, 'I'm not into women.'

She leans forward and smiles. 'Neither am I.'

I heave a sigh of relief. 'In that case, I'm Viviane.'

'And I'm Lisa,' the woman replies. We chat quickly and exchange numbers. I think I've found a new friend at least if not a date. We can share our misery at the lack of having a partner over a few drinks some evening. I'm happy that I have made a friend.

We move around and the evening finally ends. I haven't met anyone I care to go out with. I look around for Lisa, but I don't see her anywhere.

At least I have her number, I think to myself.

I leave the centre and head back to my room. When I arrive home, I text Lisa.

'*It was nice to meet you,*' I say.

She doesn't answer but calls instead.

'Hey, it was good to meet you too. Did you get lucky?' she asks.

'No, did you?'

'Yeah, I met you,' she replies and giggles, then adds, 'I'm new in Chicago and I'm lonely so I figured I'd try speed dating.'

'Well, that makes two of us,' I tell her. 'I'm quite new as well and I haven't had a chance to meet anyone yet.'

'Maybe I'm getting old, but I don't know where to go to meet decent guys. You know this "no workplace dating" rule that most companies have sucks. It seems like all the nice guys work at my company. That or I don't get out enough.'

I laugh. 'Really?'

'Yes, it's just crazy.'

'Well, why don't we meet up for drinks tomorrow evening and share our troubles.'

'That sounds great,' Lisa says. I tell her I'll call her tomorrow and tell her where to meet. If nothing else, I have made a new friend and that will relieve some of the loneliness, I'm sure. I hope we can build a lasting friendship.

I remove my wallet from my bag and open it to put the piece of paper on which Lisa scribbled her number.

The photo of Bryce and me falls out again. I bend to pick it up and study it for a while. Then, I realize I am in a hotel, working for a hotel. I remember he said he would write to me.

In the spur of a moment, I cross to the door of my suite and open the door. I look out, left and right down the passage and see the framed pictures on the walls. The passage is empty and I'm grateful for that although I know that there is CCTV.

For the first time I really notice the pastel yellow walls of the passageway. The colour looks new, and I guess the walls were painted recently. I step out of my suite and cross to the nearest picture. I try to peer behind it where it's hanging but can't see anything. I turn on the torch on my handphone and shine it behind the picture.

Nothing.

I move to the next picture and check that one too. Nothing. And the next and the next.

Nothing.

I give up. I guess he never made it to this hotel.

I don't realize it at the time, but I've started a new habit. I travel occasionally and when I do, I start to check behind the pictures in the hotels I stay in just in case there is a message for me from him.

As time passes, I make a point of checking every picture on every floor in the hotel where I live.

Nothing.

Still, I keep checking.

Lisa

I wait for Viviane to arrive. I almost feel as if it's a date. In a way it is I guess. It's a date to make a new friend.

I have friends back home, but I have struggled to make new friends here and while I can Facetime and Zoom with my friends back home, nothing beats a face-to-face connection. I have dressed in a comfortable dress. It's not too loose and not too tight. I've paired it with a white button-down blouse and high heels. It's not too smart and not too casual and should get me in wherever we decide to go after drinks.

I see Viviane arrive and wave to her. She smiles and makes her way over to me.

'Hi. Am I late?' she asks.

'No. I was early,' I smile as she sits down. I've already ordered a drink and started drinking to calm my nerves. I wave the waiter over as I ask her what she wants to have. She orders the same drink as me, a gin and tonic, and the waiter leaves with an order for two.

We make small talk until our drinks arrive. Viviane seems to relax a bit once she has her drink, and we begin to delve into each other's lives.

'This is so much better than speed dating,' I tell her.

'It sure is. I'm glad I met you.'

'Me too,' I say. I learn that Viviane is working as the regional housekeeping trainer for a hotel group. She tells me that she left her boyfriend and moved in twenty-four hours after being offered the position.

'You must have been desperate to leave your boyfriend,' I joke.

She laughs. 'I never thought of it that way but that's the truth. What about you?'

'My move was quick too. It was quite an interesting way for it to happen though.'

Viviane asks for the details, and I tell her about working for the sales manager I had never met because he was always on the road and that he asked me to relocate with him when he was promoted to his position in Chicago.

Viviane nods, 'And?' she prompts. I continue and tell her we had met once before when we collided and he knocked me over.

'I was upset and told him he should look where he was going. After that though I thought I might have been a bit harsh on him. He was handsome and I never thought I'd see him again and then when he asked to meet me to offer me this job, I was surprised to discover it was him.'

Viviane is amazed at the story. It sounds like something from a novel. She thinks there's more to it and presses me for more details. 'So, are you seeing him?'

I laugh. 'If I was seeing him, I wouldn't have been at a speed dating evening. Besides, our company is very strict on workplace romances. They're not allowed.'

Viviane scrunches her face with disapproval. 'That just sucks doesn't it?'

I sip my drink and nod.

'Would you date him if you could?' she asks.

I think about it, shrug and then reply. 'We get along so well. I don't know if I would go that far. Sometimes when you get along so well at work it's best to leave it at that. You know if things don't work out, you lose a partner and work becomes awkward. It's like a double loss. Don't think I haven't thought of dating him though.'

'He sounds nice,' Viviane says with what appears to be a twinge of jealousy that at least I have a reason to go to work that isn't only work—despite not being able to date my boss.

'Perhaps I should meet him,' she jokes.

We both laugh. 'What about you?' I ask. 'I assume there's no man in your life unless you just like going to speed dating evenings for the suffering?'

Viviane laughs. 'You're right about that. That was my first speed dating evening ever. What an eye-opener. It reminded me of my ex, Jenson. He just wasn't interested in getting a job and would play computer games all day. I think if we were still together, I'd probably be trying speed dating anyway. He's got his perfect match. It's a game console.'

'Will you go back?' I ask.

'To Jenson or speed dating?' she quips.

I laugh and reply, 'Speed dating.'

'I don't know,' she shrugs. 'Was it your first time?'

'No, it's about my sixth. I don't know why I keep going back. Maybe I'm a speed dating masochist or something,' I joke.

Viviane laughs again. 'Sounds like you're a veteran. Do you always go back to the same speed dating event?'

'I do,' I reply. 'Maybe we should try a different one.'

'Maybe,' she agrees.

'Okay, we'll find one. What about the rest of the evening? Want to go clubbing?'

Viviane hesitates briefly and then shakes her head. 'I'm kind of enjoying just being here and talking to you. We won't get much talking done in a busy club.'

'I know but we might be luckier at a club than at speed dating,' I say.

'I guess you have a point,' Viviane agrees.

We finish our drinks, pay and go looking for a club. Neither of us has a clue where to go so we look up clubs on our mobile phones and agree on the closest one. It's disappointing and we call it a night after a few drinks and promise to meet up again soon.

Lisa

The following Friday we are having our weekly wrap-up meeting, and I am taking notes as Bryce makes points of things that need to be done or followed up.

I have noticed Bryce looking at me a few times, not just today, but since we have been working together. He tries to do it surreptitiously but doesn't quite succeed.

I have to admit I'm a little happy about it, but I know the consequences and remind myself that it's best to be professional. He's worked to be rewarded with this position and I would not want him to lose it.

After the meeting, I head back to my desk, but Bryce stops me with a question.

'How are you settling in?' he asks.

I stop and turn. 'Okay, I guess,' I smile.

'That doesn't sound very promising,' Bryce says, fishing for more.

'Well, I'm settled in my apartment but making friends is pretty hard. I've made one girlfriend who I get along with well so that helps. It would be nice to have more friends, but I guess Rome wasn't built in a day.'

Bryce nods. 'You're right about that.'

'What about you?' I ask.

'About the same, I guess. I have a place that I'm settled into, but I have no idea where to meet people and make friends. Where did you meet your friend?'

I smile and hesitate before blushing and answering, 'Speed dating.'

Bryce is speechless. He obviously did not expect to me say that. He looks at me curiously and I think he is wondering if I am joking. 'You're kidding right?'

I shake my head. 'Nope. I'm being dead serious. I didn't get a date but I got a friend.'

'What is someone like you doing going to speed dating? Surely you don't struggle to get dates?'

I blush and look down.

Bryce seems to realize what he's said and tries to fix it quickly. 'I'm sorry, I didn't mean to embarrass you or sound like I'm coming on to you,' he says.

I look up, smile and shake my head. 'Thank you for the compliment. I do appreciate it. If my circle of friends was bigger, I might have more chance of meeting someone. It's been an interesting experience though.'

Bryce looks relieved. 'Through my experience working with you, I think you're a great person all around. I'm sure anyone can see that. Surely, you don't need to go speed dating?'

'Why not?' I ask. 'Isn't it kind of how I agreed to join you here in Chicago?'

He blushes. 'Touché,' he responds before adding, 'I didn't know that was considered a date.'

I laugh. 'It wasn't but it was the quickest and least formal interview I've ever had.'

I have just thrown him a massive hint, but he seems to have missed it altogether. I press on. 'Why don't we go and have drinks after work today? It is Friday after all and it's not like we're dating, right?'

He thinks about it briefly and then agrees. 'Why not?'

Lisa

Even though we're not dating, we choose a bar quite a distance from the office. We don't want rumours getting started. Although choosing somewhere closer and frequented by other staff would be better to prove that we have nothing to hide.

Bryce orders our drinks and pays for them. We find a booth and sit down. It's not too busy in the bar and fairly quiet which is good. We can hear each other speak without having to shout or lean forward.

'Tell me more about the speed dating,' he says.

I smile and shake my head. 'Do not go there. I promise you do not find the kind of people you want to date there.'

'Okay. But if I wanted to? How would I find a speed dating service?'

'Internet. Look it up,' I say. 'There are so many, but at the end of the day I think if you've seen one you've seen them all.'

'That bad huh? How many times have you been?'

'Six or more. I lost count,' I reply.

'Wow. If you have such a low opinion of it, why do you keep going back?' he asks.

'Positive thinking,' I reply, tongue-in-cheek, before I burst out laughing. I laugh so hard that I attract looks from other patrons but I don't care. It feels good to laugh like that after so long. I finally get myself under control.

'That was a good one,' Bryce says. 'But seriously. Why?'

'I guess I do hope that someday I'll find someone there.'

'Surely you can find someone somewhere else?'

'Occasionally I go clubbing or to dinner if I am invited. I always keep my options open as far as events go. I even go to art gallery exhibitions and museum exhibitions, not to find someone, but to enjoy the art and history. If I happen to meet someone at one of those events, then so be it.'

Bryce seems impressed. 'Have you been to any exhibitions since you've arrived in Chicago?'

I shake my head. 'No. I haven't had the time. I did in New York, but I've only just about finished settling in. If I may ask, what about you? Why do you not have a significant other?'

'Well, you know how much I travelled. There was no way I could sustain any relationship in that job. I swore I would never do it to anyone. My dad did it to us. He also worked in the industry and every few months we were uprooted to go somewhere else.'

'Wow,' I say. 'That's unbelievable.'

'Yeah, I never really made friends, never really fit in anywhere. Mom eventually left. She'd had enough.'

'I'm sorry,' I say.

'It's okay. I learned from it.'

'But what about now? You must have met someone on your travels?' I feign nonchalance and hope he can't tell what I'm trying to do.

'That I did but you know, company policy.'

'Do you mean to tell me you've *never* bent the rules?' I ask, surprised.

'Never,' he confirms.

'Wow, that's something,' I say and tease him, 'You're a real company man. Isn't that like the equivalent of being a nerd back in school?'

'I've worked hard to get here,' he smiles, 'but in a way I guess you're right. Considering where I am now though, I guess being the equivalent of a nerd isn't all bad.'

'I know. You deserve it too,' I reply.

'Thanks,' he says, shifting in his seat as if he is becoming uncomfortable with the attention focused on him. He switches back to our previous topic of conversation. 'Let's talk more about the speed dating.'

'Okay . . .' I say hesitantly. 'If you're really interested, I can give you the contact and you can register to try it out.'

'Why not? I mean, if you've tried it six times it can't be all bad? Besides you said you keep hoping for something good. Maybe it just takes time. I'm interested to try it, at least once.'

'Don't say I didn't warn you.' I sigh as I smile and take out my mobile. I find the number for the speed dating service and forward it to Bryce. 'They meet weekly on Wednesdays.'

He thanks me and orders another round of drinks for us.

Our conversation takes a twist and we begin talking about dating colleagues.

'If the chance presented itself and you were sure you could get away with it, would you take it?' I ask.

'People never get away with anything,' Bryce replies bluntly. 'It always catches up to them.'

'Maybe, but . . . it's not like it's a crime to date a co-worker,' I argue.

'It's not a crime but the company doesn't allow it. They pay our salaries, so we have to toe the line. I mean, let's say hypothetically, you decide to date someone from the company. Later, the two of you break up but you feel wounded and want revenge. You go and tell human resources who fire your ex, and maybe you too. You might have promised each other you would never do that but when it ends, that is sadly what could happen.'

'That's what a bunny boiler would do,' I say disgustedly.

'A bunny boiler?' he asks, confused.

'Didn't you ever watch Fatal Attraction?' I ask.

'No, and I'm thinking it's just as well that I didn't,' he smiles then adds, 'When relationships end, often we can't see the wood for the trees. One of the people might decide to cross that bridge at a later stage if they feel that their ex abandoned them or cheated or whatever. Maybe you want him back and he did nothing, but you tell human resources anyway.'

'That's not me,' I say.

'Well, it's just an example. One can't say until the moment arrives. In a breakup, we often want to lay the blame somewhere.'

'I'm not that kind of person,' I insist.

'We all think it until the time comes . . .' Bryce says, unwilling to be moved.

I shift the focus of the topic we are on. 'If I may ask, when did you last have a relationship?'

Bryce sand shrugs. 'A long time ago.'

'Wow! You're a regular monk!' I tease him.

He smiles. 'Yes, one of these days they'll cart me off to become a priest in some monastery far away.'

Bryce

As the night continues, we talk more and order more drinks. I study Lisa as we drink and talk. I am amazed at how well we get along and I think if I were to date anyone, I would want to date her, or someone like her. She is confident and witty, and she knows it which makes her even more attractive. I still don't understand her fascination with speed dating and tell her it must be a hobby of hers which makes her laugh. I like her laugh. It's free and genuinely happy. I wonder why the first woman who I would like to get to know better in so long has to be untouchable because of company policy.

It reminds me of Nora who I left behind all those years ago. I've never heard from her or seen her in all this time. She sent some e-mails after I left but I never answered. I was a fool then. I tried to contact her since, but she has changed her e-mail and I simply refuse to do the social media stalk to try and find her.

As the night wears on, I find my resolve crumbling steadily. I drink slowly, and I am still thinking relatively clearly but at last, the evening must end and we call for the bill. I pay the bill and we find a cab outside. The cab stops outside my place first.

'Want to come in?' I ask her.

She looks at me as if I am some kind of alien for asking her. I guess after our discussion this evening, it's not something she expected at all. The truth is I've had a great evening and I'm not ready to let it end.

'Why not?' she says and grabs her bag and gets out of the cab. I pay the driver, get out and lead her up the path to the front door. I unlock the door and open it before I step aside to let her enter first.

I follow and close and lock the door behind us.

'Would you like a drink or some coffee or tea?' I ask as she wanders from the entrance hall to the living room.

'Coffee sounds like a good idea,' she says as she stops and admires the living room. 'I like what you've done in here,' she says.

'Great, I'll give you the owner's contact so you can tell him,' I joke.

'Oh, I thought that was you,' she says.

'No. I don't have that much considering that I was hardly ever home in my old role. I wasn't given to making my home as nice as this since I was never there. I didn't see the point. I also haven't been here that long so I haven't quite decided if I want to invest in making it more me. I like it the way it is actually and having travelled as much as I have, I guess it's taking me longer to put down my roots.'

'You have to put down roots sometime,' she says sounding concerned. 'I mean this role of yours isn't temporary, right?'

I realize why she would be concerned and try to put her at ease.

'I took this job because it's supposed to be long-term. You know how long I've been on the road. As a child, we were always moving and never put down roots. The experience is hard to let go of. I've wanted a job like this for ages. I haven't started a family because of my previous role. I always said I wouldn't do that to people I love.'

'Do what?' she asks.

'Drag my family all over the place or be an absent husband and father.'

After a beat of silence, I continue. 'I have not been here long and I'm hoping that moving and my days and days on the road are over. I might not have done much with the place but what I'm trying to say is that years of being on the road doesn't just go away like that. Plus, there's a lot at work that I need to focus on right now so that is taking priority.'

She nods seeming more at ease. Looking around my place again she seems to have something on her mind.

'What are you thinking?' I ask.

'Well . . .' she starts hesitantly. 'It's always been a dream of mine to be an interior decorator. If you're willing to let me have a go I'd like to redecorate the place after hours and on weekends.'

I hesitate and she notices.

'I'll discuss everything with you before I do it,' she assures me, 'and I think you'll need to check with the landlord what changes are permitted.'

It sounds reasonable to me and so I agree. I have to admit that I would like to have some changes made but don't have the time. If it's something that Lisa likes and wants to do then why not give her the chance to explore her dream? Besides, if she redecorates, I'll get to have her around more often and who knows where that might lead?

Lisa

I am concerned when Bryce says he hasn't quite settled yet. He hasn't made any real friends, has no girlfriend and hasn't settled properly. Is he happy here, I wonder. I moved here because I would be working for him. I know people say don't make a decision based on the boss you work with. When their next career opportunity comes along they won't make a decision that includes you. Sadly, many of us do make a decision on that basis because working for a great boss is better than working for a bad boss and you never really know a boss until you've worked for them right? I hope I have not made that mistake now and that Bryce will be around for a while

Bryce disappears into the kitchen to get the water boiling, get the cups ready and make coffee which he then carries into the living room. The aroma of the coffee reminds me of a coffee shop. Either the brand of coffee is great or he'd make a great barista. He sets the mugs down on the table behind me.

I am looking out into the backyard. The curtains are open. Lights set on a timer illuminate parts of the garden. The grass is short but a rich green in the light cast by the lamps spread around the garden. It looks soft and I long to feel it under my feet and between my toes. It looks so good it makes me think of the wide-open expanse of a golf course with well-manicured lawns.

The lights must have been set out by a landscaper. The pool light is also on, creating a contrast against the green grass.

'This place is really beautiful,' I say.

'Thanks,' Bryce replies from behind me. 'I fell in love with it the first time I saw it.'

'You have good taste,' I tell him.

'And so do you,' he compliments me. He is standing close to me and I catch the scent of his cologne. Now that we are here in his home there is little else to distract my senses and his cologne is striking. I inhale deeply, drinking it in. It is strong, masculine but not overpowering.

'I hope you're going to find a lady to share your home with,' I say. 'It is nice but now that you've told me it's the owner's decorating touch, I'm seeing a few changes that I would make.'

'Oh really? Care to elaborate?' he asks.

'We could make it a joint project and do it together,' I reply. I'm throwing out hints the entire time and hoping he's going to get them. Screw company policy. We can work around that, and I'll quit if I have to if something happens between us, but it's still too early to make that decision. Way too early. But the alcohol is talking, and I can't help myself.

He looks at me after my comment. I think he's finally caught the hint. I turn and meet his gaze and, plucking up all my courage, raise myself the rest of the way on my toes and kiss him softly. It's all it takes. His arms wrap around me, and he kisses me back.

'After I ran into you and knocked you over, I always wondered if you were her, the voice at the other end of the line. I hoped to meet you that day. I had made it to the office in time to meet you if only you had still been at your desk.'

I blush. 'You didn't recognize my voice when I scolded you?'

'No, I was too embarrassed and sorry for knocking you over to pay attention to whether your voice sounded like someone I knew.'

'You were embarrassed?' I ask surprised.

'Well, it's not like men like knocking women over.'

I smile. 'I guess you're right. I have to admit though that I wondered if you were you too. Although I was upset at what happened I couldn't stop thinking about you. Especially since I had a date with a Jim that evening.'

His hands are wrapped around me and holding me close. He kisses me softly but quickly and then asks, 'What is it with you and Jims?'

I smile, look into his eyes and then answer him. 'Take me to bed and I'll tell you.'

He looks at me for a moment as if trying to make certain I'm not kidding. Then he bends and lifts me over his shoulder. I squeal as he carries me to his bedroom where I make sure to tell him everything he needs to know.

Nora

I've had a bad day and I'm thankful that it's over. My presentation did not work properly, and I eventually ended up speaking purely from memory. All things considered, it went well, but when you're presenting to directors you don't want things going wrong.

My secretary handed in her resignation and gave twenty-four hours' notice. I wanted her to work a month's notice, but she refused. Her resignation was the last thing I needed. I am due to attend a conference next week and I need a secretary in the office. I have managed to arrange a temp which will have to do until I return.

My bad luck seems to follow me to the shops where I purchase some things for the weekend. My carry bag decides it is time to break and my shopping ends up all over the floor in the middle of the mall.

I stop and look at the broken bag which I still hold in my hand and glare at each item I bought that now lays sprawled on the floor. It is every item's fault that the bag broke.

Damn you all, I think at each item as if they conspired to break the bag. As I stand there wondering what I should do to get the items picked up and how I can carry them home, someone stops and begins picking them up.

I bend quickly and start picking the items up. There is a bench where people can sit and rest and I place the items on it. The woman who is helping follows suit.

'Thank you,' I say when the last item has been picked up.

'It's nothing,' she says. 'You looked like you needed help. I can't believe how so many people just walk by and don't help.'

'Each to their own,' I say. 'Would you mind waiting here while I quickly go get another bag to pack everything in?'

'Sure, no problem,' she says.

Trusting her because she helped me, I dash off to a small stationery shop that is still open. I quickly find reusable bags. I buy two and rush back to where the woman is watching my groceries.

'Your kids are well behaved,' she says when I reach her. I'm confused for a moment and then I start laughing. I realize she's referring to my groceries as kids.

'That's good,' I say at last. She helps me pack the groceries in the new bags and I thank her.

My mood is lifted as I head home to bathe and change for the evening out with Lisa. It's the second time that we'll be seeing each other since we met at the speed dating evening.

Lisa is waiting at the bar we've agreed to meet at when I arrive. She waves to me and I cross to the booth she has occupied. The waiter takes our order and we catch up where we left off last time.

'Have you made any new friends yet?'

Lisa shakes her head. 'I normally make friends quickly but I still haven't had much luck since I've been here. I guess it has in part to do with my late hours and the new project I've taken on.'

'What new project?' I ask, curious.

'My boss has agreed to let me redecorate his place. It's always been a dream of mine to be an interior designer and I'm so happy he's trusted me with the project.'

'Wow. Is redecorating all you're doing?' I tease.

The look on her face says it all.

'You didn't?' I ask in disbelief.

She nods, smiles and replies, 'Sure did.'

'You tart!' I tease her. 'You're in big trouble now. What if he doesn't like what you do with his place? What if you argue about what you want to do?'

Lisa shakes her head. 'I don't think that's going to happen. I've promised to discuss everything with him before I do anything, so he'll approve of it before it's done. He's even helping me with the redecoration. At least when we don't get distracted.'

I nod. 'Okay. Well good for you. I'm happy for you,' I say feeling genuinely happy and a touch envious.

'Before I talk any more about myself, tell me what's been happening in your life,' Lisa says. 'Have you made any new friends?'

'There was a lady who helped me at the mall this evening. My shopping bag broke and I had to get another one. She looked after my shopping while I went to get a new bag. I didn't get her number though. I should have. It's just been one of those days.'

Lisa nods. 'I'm sure things will get better. At least we have each other.'

'Agreed but I hope you're not going to disappear now that you have a handsome hunk keeping you busy after hours,' I say.

Lisa shakes her head, 'I think I can balance things,' she assures me.

We continue to talk and get to know each other better than before. I find that it's really easy talking to Lisa and that she seems to be very open and not guarded at all. I quickly build up trust in her and what little inhibitions we have fall away as the alcohol gives us more confidence.

'Why didn't you suggest a club this evening?' I ask.

'Last time we didn't find a nice club and besides, I enjoyed just talking.'

Our conversation moves to talking about other things such as our preferences in men and she tells me all about her experience with Jims and that her boyfriend had teased her and told her his second name was Jim.

'What is his name?' I ask, realising that she hasn't mentioned it yet.

'Bryce,' Lisa replies.

It's been fifteen years since I saw or heard from Bryce. For the briefest of moments, I wonder if it could be him before I tell myself no. Besides, there are thousands of Bryces in the world. I mean what are the odds that it could be the same Bryce? I have no idea where Bryce is today. He could be anywhere but from what Lisa's told me about her boss being part of a hotel group and having travelled as much as he did before he got the job here, I seriously doubt it would be him since I know how he hated moving around.

To me, there is simply no connection.

When we leave the bar which is on the third floor of a hotel, we wait for the elevator to take us to the lobby. It takes a long time and a picture on the wall catches my eye. I cross over to the picture and study it.

I wonder . . .

I step close to the wall and pull the bottom of the picture away from the wall carefully so I can look behind it. I want to see if there is any writing behind it. I suppose Lisa mentioning the name Bryce reminds me of his promise and now I'm checking to see if he might have been here.

Nothing.

I leave the picture and quickly move to the next one along. I do the same and Lisa is now following at a distance.

'What are you doing?' she asks curiously.

'Oh, it's um . . . just a curiosity I have.'

'What is?'

'I heard once that people write behind paintings in hotels and so I like to check if there is any writing behind the pictures whenever I get the chance.'

'Seriously?' Lisa asks. 'Is that a thing?'

'Absolutely,' I say. 'Check it on the internet.'

The elevator arrives and we get in. If it wasn't so full, I might have checked behind the picture on the back wall of the elevator too.

Bryce

It's Saturday morning and I wake up early. I asked Lisa to spend the weekend at my place because I have a proposal for her. Not to get married but that she moves in with me. I make breakfast, coffee and freshly squeezed juice which I place neatly on a tray, carry into the room. I set the tray down beside the bed on the floor and softly kiss her cheek. She stirs and then smiles as she realizes what has woken her up.

'I made breakfast for you,' I say softly as I brush her hair away from her face and tuck it behind her ear.

'Mmm, it smells so good,' she says.

I pick up the tray and place it over her legs.

'It's great!' she exclaims inhaling the aroma as her eyes drift from plate to plate taking in everything. 'I could get used to this hotel.'

She samples the food and hums her appreciation. 'I never knew you were such a good cook. We should stay in more often.'

'Well, we might do that,' I say mysteriously.

She casts me a wary glance, finishes chewing, and swallows. 'Let's see. It's not my birthday, it's not an anniversary, it's not your birthday or any other special occasion. What do you want?'

I laugh. 'Well . . . I wanted to ask you if you'll mind moving in with me.'

She stops chewing her food and looks at me. Then she continues chewing slowly until she swallows. 'Did I hear you right?' she asks.

'You did,' I say.

'What about company policy?' Lisa asks.

I sigh. 'We've managed to work around it so far. We can carry on doing it. It's not like anyone's going to audit my house and see who lives here.'

'What about my mail?'

'We'll rent a separate post office box. All taken care of.'

'Seems like you've given this some thought,' Lisa says looking at me.

'I have. If we want to get engaged later, then I guess one of us will have to change jobs but that's something for later.'

She hands the tray to me and I look at it. 'But you've hardly touched your food.'

'I know but this is more important. Don't get me wrong, it's delicious and I'll finish it in a little while but right now we need to finish discussing this.'

I place the tray on the floor beside the bed. As soon as I have released the tray she squeals and pulls me backward onto the bed.

'Of course, I'll move in with you!' She moves quickly and straddles me.

I'm so happy!' She peppers my face with kisses as we sink back into the bed. Breakfast could wait after all.

We get up later, shower, dress and spend a lazy Saturday at home. Lisa wanders through the house looking at all the rooms. She has already begun her redecorating planning. I enjoy just watching her move through the house and listening to her suggestions.

I can't fault her thinking and suggestions although I do add some of my ideas occasionally. By the afternoon, she has an idea all worked out of how she wants the place to look.

She drops onto the sofa beside me at last and puts her feet on my lap. It's her way of asking for a foot massage. I happily oblige.

'When should I move my things?' she asks.

'Wait,' I say, looking around as if searching for something, 'I thought you already did. Where is your stuff?'

She smiles. 'You mean I should have moved in already?'

'Absolutely,' I say.

'Tomorrow, I'll go home and pack my things. I don't have much to move. I also need to give notice on the apartment.'

'I'll come with you,' I say.

With our Sunday planned, we make love again and rest before we head out on our girls' and boys' night out.

Lisa is going out with her new friend, Viviane who she met last month. I am going to the club I have joined. They are having a gambling evening and although we don't play for real money it gets quite competitive and it's a lot of fun.

Bryce

I get home and pour myself a drink before I make my way to my study and sit down at my desk. Lisa still isn't back. I notice that her redecoration project has not reached the study yet and I have asked her to leave it till last. I eye the pile of notebooks on the shelf mounted on the wall.

I take one down and sit down at my desk again. I open it and begin to page through it randomly. I see all the messages I have left on the backs of pictures in hotels across the country over the years.

I feel a sense of melancholy set in as I ask myself what I thought I was doing and why I was such a fool. I realize that the odds of Nora ever finding the messages are slim. I ask myself why I never answered her e-mails all those years ago.

We might have been together today if I had answered her e-mails. I question why I left so many messages and think back to when I did. I can't say for sure if I still have the feelings that I had fifteen years ago. Why then did I leave the messages? Was it just because I needed to fulfil a promise I made? Was it just a habit? What would I do if I found her again? I realize that it might just be as simple as looking her up on social media. I'm sure I'll find her.

But what if she's married? What if she's changed her name? I wonder *You won't know if you don't try.*

I open my laptop and turn it on. I wait as it boots up and then open up the first social media platform that comes to mind. I type in her name and my finger hovers over the enter button.

I feel guilty. Why am I doing this? I promised myself I wouldn't do this. If I do this search and view her profile, I know she will get the notification that I looked at her profile. So what? Is that such a bad thing? Why do I want to do this? I've just asked Lisa to move in with me. Why would I go searching for Nora then?

Curiosity, I tell myself. *Still, there's no point.*

I hit delete and erase Nora's name from the search box. Then I type it again and hit enter before I can stop myself.

A few listings for Nora Halston appear. I scroll through them but don't see any that seem like they could be her from the brief descriptions. I finally close the platform and shut down the computer.

I have just shut down the computer when Lisa appears at the door of the study. She let herself in with the key I gave her and she leans against the door frame studying me in silence.

'Hey! You're back,' I smile as I close the notebook and push it aside as unobtrusively as possible. I know I need to decide what to do with the notebooks. They are a part of my life. They're also the reason I have asked Lisa to do the study last. They're a very personal part of my life and I imagine Lisa will wonder what they are and why there are so many of them. If she happens to look inside she'll see the writings and wonder who they were for or what they are. I don't really want to share the their history and so I know I need to move

them into a box out of the way but now that I have asked Lisa
to move in, I know I need to decide if I want to keep them
or give them up. The writing in them is poetic and beautiful.
Perhaps some day I'll write a book about them if I never find
Nora. *Maybe the book will find Nora for me*, I think and smile at
the thought. I can't help but feel that to throw them away
would be a waste. I doubt that Lisa would see it the same way
if she finds out what they are and who they were for.

Bryce

Lisa has taken the opportunity to do some more redecorating during the week while I've been away so she won't be in my way. I have asked her to leave redecorating the study until I can sort out my things. In the back of my mind, I know I am delaying the study because I still haven't decided what to do with the notebooks. I don't believe I can leave them there indefinitely. I will have to find some temporary storage for them but don't want to rent an entire storage unit since it's just the box of messages for Nora.

I know that if I decide to move them out of the house, I have to do it when she's not there. If I try to dispose of the notebooks while she is there, she will surely ask what they are. It's her nature. She is very open and has nothing to hide.

I think of the garbage bin that sits outside on the sidewalk. When I get home, I often feel as if it is calling to me and trying to tell me to get rid of the notebooks.

Hey, I'm over here. I'm hungry. I really like notebooks. They're my favourite food. What are you waiting for? You know you want to get rid of those notebooks. Just a few at a time won't be too obvious and they'll fill me up real good.

I smile and try to push the thoughts away. I know that my subconscious is telling me to act and I also know that I am procrastinating.

I started reading the messages I had written in the notebooks. I am amazed at the feeling, thoughts and emotions I put into the messages.

Why haven't you done the same for Lisa, I wonder? I tell myself that doing the same thing for her would be cheesy.

Couldn't you do something else equally romantic for Lisa? I wonder.

I tell myself I love her and that we are happy just the way we are. Sure, it would add something to the relationship if I did something like that but I do many little things—surprising her with lunches and dinners and little gifts and the occasional notes and flowers. Every relationship has its dimensions.

I realize though that I would not have these thoughts running through my mind if I simply got rid of the notebooks once and for all.

I never thought about them so much and I know that it is my guilt that is driving the thinking about the notebooks and creating my fear that Lisa will find out about them.

As with all things in life, when one struggles to make a decision about something, there is always something that happens that makes the decision for you or forces you to make a decision that moves you forward.

And so it was with the notebooks. I procrastinated because it is my place after all and I was confident Lisa would, indeed, leave the study alone. I fought my guilt, I fought my conscience and I fought the garbage bin. But the universe stepped in to balance things and move me forward in my decision-making process and when the universe steps in there are often consequences, and there were consequences this time too. Consequences that weren't as immediate perhaps, but created ripples that would only get bigger, not smaller, with time; ripples that would create an impact on some far-away shore, an impact that would force me to take a decision on what it was that I really wanted.

Nora

The conference I am attending is an annual hospitality industry conference in which leaders in the industry share their knowledge and genius on how to make the industry better, improve service and how to stop employee turn-over effective through management attitudes and principles.

It's my first conference and I am not a guest speaker which I am quite grateful for. I am however attending as many presentations as I can which are relevant to my role, as well as those pertaining to other areas of my interest, and soaking up as much knowledge as I can.

I meet people from other companies, swap contacts with them and start to build a network.

Some evenings are spent with people I have met at game nights organized by the conference organizer while other nights I go out to see the sights of the city.

Being in a different city in a different hotel, managed by a company other than the group I work for, also presents me with an opportunity to check pictures hanging in the corridors. The first evening I wait until it's late and then I leave my room and start checking behind pictures in the passage outside my room.

Nothing.

I am filled with doubt that Bryce ever followed through on his promise. What if he's never set foot in a hotel after he graduated? What if he was killed in an accident and never got to write anything at all?

I try to shrug off the negativity despite telling myself that I'm being silly. I think of it another way. If he had ever frequented hotels, where would he have written on the back of a picture? It depends on if he was a guest or an employee. I realize that either could apply. If he had been a guest, he would most likely have left a message on the back of a picture on the floor where his room was located. If he was an employee, he would most likely have left a message on the back of a picture in a more public area. I realize that I have to check both.

I check all the pictures on my floor, the next two floors and then do the next two floors below mine. Nothing.

All the while, I am waiting for hotel security to come and ask me what I am doing but surprisingly no one does. There are CCTV cameras on every floor and I know they can see me. I guess no one is watching or else they are waiting to see if I am going to try and steal one of the pictures before they act.

If I was them, I would already have dispatched someone since I would be concerned about hotel property. Anyway, that's their problem. I continue my search undisturbed and eventually give up for the night.

During the next few nights, I search behind pictures in other areas with no luck.

Time is running out and I realize that there might be nothing in this hotel at all. I widen my search on the last two nights to neighbouring hotels. I am stopped both times by security and I try to explain to them what I am doing. They don't care and ask me to leave.

I obey since I do not wish to be detained for something that will not be understood by anyone else. I am sure if I am detained, I will be fired.

I enter the lobby of the hotel where I am staying and stop and look around. I nod to a few people I recognize from the conference. I can't help but feel disappointed.

It all seems so silly but I had hoped that by some chance I might actually find a message. I look around and decide to try the first floor. I haven't checked that floor yet since it's a bit more public but it seems quiet now and I decide what the hell.

I head for the escalator that will take me to the first floor. I wonder why I am suddenly so obsessed with finding a message from Bryce. People make promises about the future in the spur of the moment but later, after they have time to think it through, they often renege on their promises.

I ask myself if I was Bryce and I had time to reflect on what I promised to do, would I go through with it? Probably not is the answer I'm leaning towards.

Even so, I reach the top of the escalator and step off. I pause as I look around the first floor. It is open in the centre looking down at the ground floor and the lobby. Anyone from there will be able to see me as I go from picture to picture.

So what, I tell myself. Most of them probably won't know me and besides, I can give them the explanation that I am searching for pictures where people have written on the back. Over the years since Bryce promised to leave messages for me like this, I have searched the internet for articles about it. It is a thing for some people. I must say I find it quite interesting.

I make my way around the floor from picture to picture, and picture after picture my disappointment grows. I am just over halfway around the floor with hope fading fast when a man speaks from behind me.

I did not hear anyone approaching given that the floor is carpeted. I jump and with a small squeal, I turn around.

I am looking at a man who is well dressed in a spotless white shirt that looks as if it's just been pressed and black trousers which fit him perfectly. He has a well-trimmed moustache and beard and is balding. His blue eyes are crystal clear but hold a kindness that calms me.

'May I help you, ma'am?' he asks.

'Um . . . no . . . Thank you. I was just looking at the pictures.'

'I noticed that but normally when someone looks at pictures, they study the picture itself not the backs of the pictures.'

I feel myself turn bright red with embarrassment.

The man continues. 'My security informed me that you were checking the backs of all the pictures in the hotel last night and now here you are doing it again. Are you looking for something in particular?'

I blush again. 'Forgive me. Please. I hope you won't arrest me. I'm not planning to steal any pictures. I am looking for a message.'

'A message?' the man asks. He seems curious. More so than being worried about me stealing pictures.

'Yes. It's hard to explain and it probably sounds crazy . . .'

He nods. 'I am the hospitality manager for this hotel. My name is Harry Kestle. Perhaps it is not so hard to explain. Why don't you elaborate?'

I hesitate and then sigh. I realize that as the hospitality manager this man has much power and can destroy my career if I am not careful.

'I had a boyfriend years ago. He moved away but he promised to write. His dad worked for a hotel group, and they were always moving. When we parted, he promised to write but not in the way people normally would. He said he would leave messages for me on the backs of pictures in hotels . . .'

Harry nods. 'You do realize if that is the case, this is one hotel out of thousands across the country?'

I nod sheepishly. 'Yes. I am aware of that and that there might be nothing in this hotel at all.'

'You realize there might be nothing at all anywhere. He might have reneged on his promise.'

I nod again. 'I know.'

Harry is silent looking at me for a while. Then he says, 'Come with me.'

He begins walking and I fall into step beside him thinking, *I'm really in trouble, now. This is the end of my career.* I realize how ridiculous my explanation must have sounded. I am sure he is going to call my employer. I decide to see what he is planning to do before I start begging for his mercy. Maybe I won't need mercy.

We reach a picture and Harry stops. I stop and look at him.

'May I ask why we have stopped here?'

A faint smile turns up the corners of his mouth.

'Look behind that picture,' he says motioning to the picture on the wall beside us. I look at him wondering if he is being serious or if he is setting me up.

He raises his eyebrows when I hesitate too long. I decide to do as he told me and I step towards the picture. I pull it away from the wall gently. I can see the writing on the back of the picture.

I release it and look at Harry.

'Can I remove it from the wall, sir?'

He nods and steps forward. 'Let me help you.'

Nora

Harry removes the picture from the wall and turns towards me so the back of the picture is facing me. I am speechless when I see the writing and read the message.

The hairs on my arms rise and a shiver runs down my spine. I can never explain quite how I feel. It's as if Bryce is talking to me across the miles and through the years.

I read the message and my eyes fill with tears as I am overcome with emotion. It means so much to me that he kept his promise.

The message is dated almost three years before.

'Is that what you are looking for?' Harry asks from behind the picture.

I realize I am being selfish leaving Harry to hold the picture up while I lose myself in my emotions.

'Yes! Please put it down. Can I take a picture of it?'

Harry sets it down gently. 'Be my guest,' he smiles.

I fish out my cell phone, unlock the screen and take a picture. My hands are trembling so much from the shock and emotion that I can't get a picture that isn't blurred. Harry realizes that I am struggling and reaches out his hand for my phone.

'May I help you?'

'Yes please,' I say and hand my phone to him. He snaps two images of the picture and returns the phone to me. I take it from him and check the pictures. They are perfect. 'Thank you, sir!'

Harry smiles. 'Please call me Harry. It is my pleasure to be of assistance.'

He lifts the picture and hangs it on the wall again.

'How did you know?' I ask.

Harry looks at me a moment. 'I know the man who did this. I did not see him do it. He did the same thing in another hotel. That's where I found out the first time. You see the address on the back?'

I nod. 'Yes.'

'That address points to another hotel where he has left another message behind a picture. Since I discovered the first message it's become a hobby of mine to find all the messages. I must say they are very romantic. I was always sure he left them for a woman and wondered who that lucky woman was.'

Harry's gaze settles on me. I know he is asking without asking if I am that woman.

'How did you know about this?' I ask amazed.

'I met him at another hotel when he took a picture off the wall. He did it when he thought no one was around but I knew he had been up to something when he took the picture down. After he left, I checked the picture and found the message. I haven't been able to find any writing after what he did there but I have been able to trace a lot of it back before then through the other addresses he leaves behind each picture.'

'Is his name Bryce?' I ask.

Harry nods. 'Indeed. That is his name. He was very good to me. I owe the fact that I am in this position today, to him.'

The goosebumps keep returning with the chills as I am amazed at how the universe works. I cannot believe how small the world is. 'Do you know where I can contact him?' I ask.

'Certainly,' Harry says. He removes his phone from his pocket, unlocks it and scrolls through the contacts until he finds Bryce's number. He recites it to me and I save it on my phone. We exchange numbers as well. I nod. 'You said you have traced the messages back as far as possible since you found the first one?'

Harry smiles. 'I have. I love it. It's become my new hobby.'

'Do you have the messages?'

Harry nods eagerly. 'I photograph each one, then print it and stick in a book. Would you like to see?'

'I would be so grateful if you would show me.'

'Give me a minute. Why don't you wait in the lounge while I go and fetch my notebook from my quarters.'

I agree and find a seat in the lounge. I can't believe that Bryce kept his promise. The message I have seen is from almost three years ago which means that up until that time he was still leaving messages for me. If that was only three years ago, he must still be doing it today I tell myself. I check his number on my phone and I want to call it but I hesitate. I'll wait for Harry first.

Harry returns after ten minutes carrying a book. He sits down opposite me and places the book on the table.

'That's it,' he says.

I lean forward and pick it up. The cover opens with a crack sound that books sometimes make after they've been pressed closed by a heavy object. The pages are slightly warped from the pictures and the glue stuck on them. I read through note after note that Harry has found, photographed and documented in the book.

The words are so beautiful. Each message touches my heart and I can't help the tears that start to flow. I move the book away so my tears don't spoil it. Harry asks a waitress to bring tissues which he sets on the table between us. I take a tissue and dry my eyes smudging my makeup as I do so.

I can't believe that for so many years Bryce has left messages for me. I think of how I thought that he forgot his promise as soon as he left my life all those years ago. And yet it seems that I am the one who never believed he would keep it. I never bothered to look.

I cry because of the dedication it has taken to keep doing something for so many years knowing that it might never be found. I cry because I remember the time that we spent apart because of our misunderstanding during high school. Time we could have spent together. It was only a few months then, but this is years! Years that we could have been together! Years wasted.

Harry waits patiently for me to finish paging through the book and when I am finally finished, I place it on the table.

'Thank you,' I smile as I blow my nose.

He doesn't take the book but looks at me and asks, 'Can I ask you something?'

Wiping away fresh tears I nod.

'Those messages . . . they were all written for you?'

I smile weakly and blush despite the fresh tears that spill from my eyes.

He hands me another tissue and waits for me to calm again. 'They are truly beautiful,' Harry says. He picks up the book and holds it out to me. 'Take it. A gift from me. They were meant for you anyway and I still have the digital photos. I can always make a new book.'

'Oh, I couldn't . . .' I begin to protest but he interrupts me and holds up his hand.

'Please. I insist.'

I take the notebook and thank him.

'Why don't you give him a call?' Harry asks. 'You have his number.'

I nod. 'I should.'

I'm such a mess though. I imagine if I get through to him, I will burst into tears as I think of his dedication and hold the notebook with all his messages.

Harry seems to sense my hesitation and tries to reassure me. 'Just calm down, take a deep breath and go wash your face in the bathroom if you want. I'll order you some tea to calm you.'

'Thank you so much, Harry,' I say. I take the notebook with me and place it in my bag. It feels like the greatest treasure I have ever had.

When I return from the restroom I feel better. Harry is gone but my tea is waiting for me on the table. He returns a short while later and explains he had to take care of something.

'You look better,' he smiles. 'I think I will leave you to make the call. I am sure you will want some privacy.'

I thank Harry again and promise I'll be in touch if I succeed in contacting Bryce. We part ways and I head back to my room. I decide to send Bryce a message instead of calling. I have no idea where he is in the world but he might be sleeping, in which case I don't want to wake him up.

I type a brief message to Bryce and send it. I stare at my screen. The notification shows that my message has not been delivered.

I realize that it's late, but I don't care. Why wouldn't Bryce be excited to hear from me? I dial the number and put the phone to my ear.

I'm nervous.

The number rings. Maybe there's a problem with the messaging service.

My call is is answered.

Butterflies take flight in my stomach as I wait for his voice.

They settle again very quickly.

My heart sinks.

'*The number you have dialled is not in service,*' a recorded voice says.

I end the call. *Did I get the number wrong when Harry gave it to me?* I wonder.

I can't believe it. The elation of the evening from finding that he kept his promise and left messages up until three years ago was encouraging. But now the trail is dead.

Why? Who the hell changes their number in this day and age, I wonder angrily.

Then I remember that Harry said there was another message in another hotel nearby. I call up the pictures he took for me and read the message again. There it is. The name of the hotel. I grab my bag and leave my room. I don't know if Harry is awake but I send him a message anyway.

'*The number is no longer in use. Is the message from the hotel nearby in the book you gave me? If not I want to go look for it. Please let me know if there is someone that can help. Thank you.*'

He answers almost immediately. '*Meet me in the lobby.*'

I head for the lobby where I find him waiting.

'Harry,' I say. 'I'm so sorry to bother you.'

'It doesn't matter,' he says. 'I am coming with you.'

'That's not necessary . . .'

'No, but it will help,' he says. He takes my hand, and we step out of the hotel. We wave at the first taxi and jump in. Harry gives the driver the address and we head out into the night.

'What is the story with the two of you?' Harry asks.

'We were high school sweethearts. We loved each other very much but he had to move away because of his dad's work. He promised to write and leave me messages on the backs of pictures. I did not believe it but only lately have started looking behind pictures even though I could have searched a lifetime before finding anything.'

'Absolutely, but he is a man that keeps his promises I believe.'

'I don't know if there is still a chance for us but now that I know he left these messages, I have to find out.'

'It's amazing, to say the least,' Harry says.

It's a short drive to the other hotel and we hop out of the taxi and hurry inside. The staff that see Harry greet him, and I'm grateful that he is with me since I will be able to check pictures easily as long as he is with me. I suggest the first floor again since that is where Bryce left the last message.

Harry agrees and we head to the first floor where we start checking the pictures. It doesn't take long before we find the message. This message is accompanied by a number. I check it and discover it's the same as the number Harry gave me.

I take a picture of the message but my heart sinks. That's it. It's a dead end.

Harry must see my disappointment. He puts his arm around me. 'All is not lost,' he says. 'He works for the same group, so I'll call the head office in the morning and get his new number. It's not something I should do but under the circumstances it should be okay. I can check with him first just to make sure. If all is okay, and I don't see why it shouldn't be, I'll leave a message in your room or I'll send you a message. How's that?'

I smile and nod. 'Thanks, Harry. I appreciate your help.'

We head back to the hotel and part ways. I get to my room and collapse on the bed as I look at the messages Bryce left. They are so romantic but I am disappointed that I haven't been able to get hold of him now and something tells me not to hold out hope for tomorrow although I won't give up until Harry sends me a message telling me if he has succeeded in getting Bryce's new number or not.

I muddle through breakfast, not paying attention to the other people's chatter about the conference. My mind is set on Bryce and getting in touch with him. My find is far away as the morning sessions of the conference pass with no word from Harry.

At lunchtime, as I exit the room where the session was held before lunch, I spot Harry. He is waiting for me. I can tell immediately from his face that he does not have good news for me.

We greet each other and he breaks the news to me.

'I managed to contact his department. He was promoted recently to another part of the group. It meant he had to resign and sign a new contract with the other company in the group. His number was terminated and he has been given a new number with the new company. They wouldn't give more information than that. The only way I can get hold of him is if he calls me or if I find him on social media.'

I sigh. 'Thanks, Harry. I appreciate all you've done.'

He sees how sad I am and tries to make things better. 'Why don't you look for him on LinkedIn or Facebook? I'm sure he's there.'

I shake my head. 'He didn't want that. He refused to do it and didn't want me to do it either. Thanks anyway, Harry. I can never repay your kindness.'

Harry looks after me thoroughly confused. He is wondering why on earth two people who seem to care for each other so much would do everything not to be together when they could simply connect on social media and get on with it.

'Don't you want to be together?' he asks.

I nod. 'Of course, but that was our agreement.'

'But times have changed. Circumstances have changed. He changed his number. What are you supposed to do?'

'Fate brought me this far. It can take me the rest of the way if we're meant to be,' I say. I thank him again and leave him behind. He thinks we are cheating ourselves out of something beautiful.

Lisa

The redecoration has almost been completed. It's just our room and the study left. I have worked one room ahead the entire time and now that I'm about to start on the main bedroom, it's time to start taking a look at the study and what needs to be done.

Bryce has been quite particular about leaving it till the last and assuring me that he will sort it out. I wonder if I should leave it as is. In all, the decoration isn't bad but it's not the tidiest place which is surprising.

Today, I arrive home before Bryce since he has to entertain his boss who is in town for the day. They are having dinner and drinks and he will only be home much later.

I sit down in his chair and relax. It's so comfortable. I look at the desk. His personal laptop is on the desktop that was clean a few nights ago when we made love.

I swivel around in his chair and the pile of notebooks on the shelf catches my eye. The pile seems smaller than I recall, and I wonder what's happened to the rest of them. They were the biggest eyesore when I first walked into the room and looked so out of place.

Wondering what's happened to the rest of the notebooks, I look around and spot a box on the floor. I wheel the chair over to the box and look inside. It's filled with the missing notebooks.

At least he's trying to tidy up, I think.

My curiosity gets the better of me and I push the chair back to its place by the desk. I reach up and take one of the notebooks from the shelf. Setting it on the desk, I open it and pull myself towards the desk in the chair.

I read what's written in the notebook. I don't know what to think of everything that's been written there. I cannot begin to imagine what it is or who it's written for except that I know it wasn't written for me. There are verses written with dates and places detailed under each verse.

The verses are romantic. Very romantic. I wonder if they are a hobby or verses that he has seen in places and has liked and written down along with the date and place where he saw the verse.

It doesn't add up though. I've never seen the verses anywhere. There are so many that there may be some I have seen if I go through every notebook page by page, assuming he did not write them all himself. But, as I page through the notebooks, I don't find a single verse that is familiar which leads me to believe that he wrote them all.

Sure, he has travelled a lot and maybe I'm wrong but I don't think he gathered the verses during the course of his travels.

An idea hits me then and I boot up his laptop. He has no security on it and I can access it easily. I open Google and type in one of the verses on the page and press enter. It should work the same and bring up the author of the verse.

Nothing.

Impossible.

I try a second verse and then a third and a fourth. Nothing.

I believe it then. These verses are not out in the public. And if they're not out in the public then . . . Bryce must have written them himself. But why? And for who?

I grab all the notebooks from the shelf and skim through them, checking the dates on the front and back pages. They seem to progress in date order and so I move to the book at the bottom of the pile. It's old, dusty and yellowed from age. I open it. The message dates back almost ten years. I put the notebooks back in the ordered pile they were when I removed them from the shelf, cross to the box and carefully remove the notebook from it. I finally find the most recent date. It was a little over a month ago. Casting my mind back, I realize it was when Bryce travelled on business. I check the date before that and discover it was when he was still working at the other company and was on the road. The place listed under the verse makes sense. It's the hotel where he stayed. I know because I arranged the booking for him.

Once I grasp the idea that the verses relate to when he travels, I skim through the notebooks again and check the place names listed below the verses. I recognize most of them as places that I booked for him while we worked at the previous company.

I don't know what to think. It doesn't add up for me. It's romantic and a man does romantic things for a woman, but he said he's not seeing anyone. If that's the case who is this for?

Is he seeing someone? I wonder *Is he seeing someone from the company? I don't think it's possible. He's travelled a lot and seems to have written a note for every place he's visited. If he saw someone in those places they would have to travel as much as he did. Unless he's seeing someone in every place he's travelled to* . . . I discard the thought almost immediately. It's impossible and he is not that kind of person.

I am confused and jealous. He has never done something this romantic for me. I'm wondering what I should do when I hear the front door close. Bryce is home. For a moment I think of hurriedly packing up the notebooks and pretending I know nothing but then I can't. I need to know the truth.

I listen to him moving through the place. He must know I am here because my shoes are in the entrance hall. He doesn't call out though, maybe because he thinks I am asleep. I hear his footsteps coming down the passage and feel myself growing tense with fear and anticipation.

He finally appears in the doorway of the study and leans against the frame as he spots me seated behind his desk.

'Hey, honey,' he says crossing his arms.

'Hey,' I reply barely audibly.

'What are you doing in here?' he asks curiously.

'I came to redecorate and spent the evening wondering about these notebooks of yours,' I reply and then add quickly, 'I hope you don't mind, I never meant to be nosy.'

His face turns red with embarrassment I think, and probably guilt, before he pushes away from the doorframe and advances into the room.

I watch him nervously and despite what I have discovered, I feel guilty as hell. I press on regardless. There can be no going back now regardless of the consequences. 'What is this? You've been writing these notes for years. Have you been seeing someone else all this time? Did you meet them and give them the messages at the places written with each message?'

'What makes you think I'm seeing someone else?' he asks, surprised that I would think such a thing.

'Because these messages are romantic, Bryce. They're full of love. How much thought do you put into these messages? You must be seeing someone else.' I repeat.

I am now standing by his desk. He looks like a schoolboy who has been scolded and sent to the principal's office. He looks upset too but not with me, I think. It's a look that says he was a fool, that he's been caught and that he could have avoided this.

He circles the desk trying to get to me, but I push away from it making it clear I don't want him coming closer. He stops and then rests against the side of the desk. 'I remember some of the dates,' I say. 'They are when you travelled. Are you seeing someone? These words are so beautiful.'

He interrupts me. 'It's a long story but it's not what it looks like.'

'Well, what does it look like to you because it looks like a collection of love letters to me,' I remark bluntly. 'Are you in love with someone else? Why would you keep whatever you wrote to them?'

He sighs loudly. 'I didn't want you to find that,' he says, motioning to the notebooks.

He seems to hesitate as he looks at me and I wonder if he is going to say anything.

'It goes back a long way . . .' he starts at last.

He pauses, gathering his thoughts, and then continues. 'I loved a girl in my last year of high school, but I had to move away because my dad got transferred. I loved her like no one else. I guess you could say she was my first true love. They say they are the hardest to get over or forget.'

I nod. I think I see where this is headed but I listen instead of jumping the gun.

'When I left, I promised her I would write to her but not in the normal way. I told her I would leave messages behind hotel pictures and if one day she found them and contacted me then it might mean we should be together.'

I shake my head. 'That's . . . that's stupid. Why on earth would you make it so hard to stay in touch?'

'Because we were always moving around. I couldn't offer her anything. We were just kids and sometimes as kids we have dreams, and some of them are romantic. That's what it was. But we had university ahead of us and we didn't end up in the same place to study anyway. She sent me e-mails but I never answered.'

I shake my head again. 'It's stupid. You did this all these *years*? Why the hell didn't you just look her up on social media? It would have been a lot easier. Surely you can find her now? What's her name?'

She opens my laptop and presses the power button.

'Don't,' he says.

I look at him, 'Why not?'

'Because I never wanted to find her like that or for her to find me that way. Besides, I'm with you now. I love you.'

'Do you?' I ask quickly, feeling anger rise in me. He says it so easily, I wonder if he really means it or if he's simply hoping it will calm the situation and I'll fall for his trite assurance.

'Yes,' he replies, holding my gaze.

I'm quiet for a moment wondering how or why I should believe him and why he thinks I will believe him. 'Do you love her?' I ask at last.

'Yes . . . no . . . I don't know!' he exclaims, frustration clear in his voice.

'Well, that sounds encouraging,' I say, sitting back. 'Is that really supposed to provide me with any reassurance?'

'I can explain everything to you,' he says resting against the desk. 'I made the promise to write years ago. I started doing it and I never stopped. I've never seen her or heard from her since I last saw her. I have no idea what she is doing or where she is. I really don't even know if I still have feelings for her. I have asked myself so many times why I do this after so many years. I can't explain it. Maybe it's like a force of habit now more than anything. I don't know anymore, but this has nothing to do with feelings for her.'

'You are aware that you left a message for her almost a month ago? That was after we started dating.'

He nods. 'I know. I've asked myself since we started dating why I am still keeping all this, why I am still doing it.'

I say nothing and wait for him to continue.

'I've asked myself if I love her. I ask myself every time I leave a message for her. I just . . . don't know. It's been fifteen years. People move on . . .'

'You haven't,' I remark bluntly.

'What? Why do you say that?'

'Because you're still writing to her.' I choke, the hurt evident in my voice. 'Passion tells me your love is still very much alive. I can't imagine anyone who could write that beautifully for someone unless they really love them.'

Bryce sits down opposite me. 'No, that's not true. Please, Lisa. I love you. This is part of my past. It's not part of us.'

'It is part of us,' I fire back as tears suddenly spring forth and run down my cheeks. 'You left a message almost a month ago. We were dating already. Didn't you feel guilty?'

He leans forward and reaches for me but I walk away around the other side of the desk.

'You kept me out of here because of this didn't you?' I ask as it suddenly dawns on me. 'You didn't want me to see this did you? You were buying time for what? To pack it up? You wanted to hide it from me?'

He hesitates and that is answer enough.

I shrug and reply sadly. 'I think it's beautiful, amazing and so unbelievably romantic. But it's also so stupid if you can't be bothered to just get on social media and find her. It's sad. One of the saddest things I've ever heard or seen. For more than ten years you've loved someone from afar and never bothered to find out if they feel the same way. I don't get it. I've often wondered what could be worse than speed dating. Now I know. This is.'

He looks at me saying nothing and I continue.

'So you didn't want to get rid of it and you didn't want me to find it. You aren't ready to let go. You haven't let her go after all this time.'

'That's not true. Please Lisa . . .' his voice trails off, and he tries once again to approach me.

I look at him, I hear the sincerity in his voice, I can see the pleading in his eyes. I can see he means well. He approaches me slowly and I let him. He eventually takes me in his arms and I let him.

'I'm sorry. I was going to tell you. I really was.'

I breathe deeply, wipe the tears from my eyes and look up at him. 'I know you didn't mean to hurt me. I believe it. Just . . . give me some time to think about things. Please.'

We leave his study and turn off the light. We have a drink together but there is still tension in the air between us. We finally go to bed and I lie awake long into the night after Bryce is sleeping.

Has it become more of a habit or a hobby? What would I do if he ran into her after all this time?

I am tempted to find this mystery woman and bring them together. To give them a second chance and to put me out of my misery. The only problem is I don't know who she is or where to find her—at least, not yet.

Lisa

It's our ladies night and I meet Viviane at our usual bar. We like coming here because the staff know us by now and treat us as regulars.

'How are you? We haven't spoken in far too long,' I tell Viviane.

'You can say that again,' Viviane says as she sips her drink. 'How was the conference?'

'It was great!' Viviane responds excitedly, eager to share the details of it with me. 'I've never been to a conference like that in my life. It was my first one and I met so many people from all over and from so many different companies.'

'I'm glad you enjoyed it,' I smile. 'Did you get lucky?'

Viviane blushes and smiles but shakes her head. 'Sadly, no. No one showed any interest. There were a couple of handsome guys there, but I was too shy to make a move. I didn't want to look like an opportunistic tart hoping to use the conference to get laid.'

'Lots of people do,' I smile. 'You're too naïve, I think. Wait until you become an old hand at it. You'll see. At the next conference you go to, your eyes will be wide open. You'll see who's jumping who and who's available.'

'Ew,' Viviane protests. 'I'm not into that.'

'When in Rome . . .' I say.

'I did almost get lucky though with something related to a guy,' Viviane says.

The waiter arrives and brings us more drinks. We chat with him awhile and Viviane's remark is forgotten temporarily.

The waiter leaves and I look at Viviane. 'So, you were saying?'

We settle into a brief silence. I came tonight planning to speak to Viviane about what happened between Bryce and myself with the messages. I'm not sure how to bring it up but I don't have to.

Viviane nods. 'I was. I didn't almost get lucky with a guy in the usual sense, but I very nearly got lucky finding an old boyfriend.'

I lean forward. 'This sounds like it's going to be interesting.'

'Oh, yes,' Viviane smiles. 'But it's kind of a long story.'

'We have time and there are plenty more drinks,' I coax.

'Okay then.' she says and starts to tell me about a boy she knew back in high school and how he had to leave because his dad moved around a lot. It all begins to sound very familiar very quickly to me but I say nothing as I listen. I can't believe what I'm hearing. There is no possibility that this story is a coincidence. There can only be one like it—and I immediately feel my heart breaking. So, this is the woman that Bryce has been leaving the messages for. Of all the people in the world, it had to be someone whose friendship I treasured so much.

'He said he would leave messages for me behind pictures in hotels. I thought it was madness at the time. I mean how many hotels are there in this country? What are the odds that I would ever find a message from him assuming that he kept his promise?'

I nod and sip my drink. My mind is spinning with questions as I listen and fight through the heartache. I am afraid I will miss important details.

'I found an old picture of him when I moved. I forgot about him until then but finding the picture brought back the memories and I eventually started looking behind pictures at the conference.'

'So that's why you were looking behind pictures when we met last time. Did you find any messages?' I will myself to smile.

'I did,' Viviane replies. She is excited and looks like a child that has found the treasure in a treasure hunt. 'Here I took pictures of the messages.'

What are the odds? I ask myself as Viviane unlocks her phone and scrolls through her gallery to the images she is looking for before holding her phone out to me. I recognize the handwriting from the notebooks I browsed through a few days before. It's the same. There is no doubt. I know then that I am sitting across the table from Bryce's ex-girlfriend. I force a smile and when she finally finishes, I ask, 'Why wouldn't you two just keep in touch like other people do? Social media, e-mail?'

'He didn't want to. He said if it was meant to be I would find his messages.'

'Was there a number? Did you call it?' I ask, my expression giving nothing away.

'There was a number, but it's disconnected. He changed jobs and I don't know where to find him now.'

'LinkedIn?' I suggest.

'I guess but that's not what he wanted.'

I suppress a sigh. I have one more question. 'If you find him, would you try to restart your relationship?'

Lisa

I have to excuse myself to the bathroom to take a breather. I try to sift through my thoughts. I know I can't take forever; Viviane is still waiting for me.

I cry silently. I can't believe this is happening. It's unbelievable. I am in the middle of two people who loved each other very much a long time ago. *Maybe they still do*, I think. I know I won't know, and neither will Bryce and her know, unless they meet each other again but I'm not sure if it's something I want to do.

What's the alternative? I can keep them apart but what good would it do?

I've always been a believer in the energy of the universe and God. If I keep them apart, I'm pretty sure the universe will find another way to put them together.

If I don't let them meet, I'll be riddled with guilt knowing that I denied them the opportunity to. Knowing that I was selfish, I will always be looking over my shoulder, wondering when karma will come for me. Because make no mistake, it will.

'Are you okay?' Viviane asks when I get back.

I nod. 'I think we should get going though. I'm not feeling so great. I haven't drunk too much but maybe something I ate didn't agree with me.'

I get the bill and settle the drinks. After assuring Viviane that I will be fine, we take two separate cabs.

On the ride home, I cry to myself once again and when I get out of the cab later on, I hesitate to go back to Bryce's place. I'm a mess and I don't want Bryce to see me this way. I don't want to explain what happened, which is why I am grateful when I enter and see that Bryce hasn't returned yet from his evening out.

I heave a sigh of relief and change into my pyjamas, wash my face and get into bed. Sleep eludes me and I lie awake with thoughts running through my mind before finally making my decision.

When I hear Bryce come in later on, I pretend to be asleep. He leaves the bedroom light off for fear of waking me. I hear him undress in the dark and then he crawls into bed beside me. He kisses me softly and then rolls away.

When I hear his snoring and I know he is asleep. I get out of bed and leave the room. I am drawn to the study where I seat myself at Bryce's desk. He has moved the notebooks. Where to I don't know. I don't want to know either.

I know that I cannot pretend I don't know what has happened. I love Bryce very much and he says he loves me. But I need to know if he and Viviane still feel the same about each other after all these years. They need to meet—only then will I be at ease. Only then will it be clear if I still have a place in Bryce's life.

Perhaps someone else would see things differently but then they wouldn't be standing in my shoes now, would they?

Lisa

I search for a romantic restaurant and take down the details. I will call and make a booking when they open later in the day.

I write a letter to Bryce which I print and seal in an envelope and place in my handbag. By now I am sufficiently tired, and I return to bed and sleep through until the morning.

Bryce wakes me and I tell him I'm not feeling well. I tell him that I was sick the night before. I also tell him that I need to take a few days off to go and see my mother because she is not well. It's a lie but so what. It can be forgiven later if we are still together.

Bryce is concerned and asks if he should come with me. I tell him not to worry and that I'll be back in a few days.

He leaves for work after I almost push him out of the house. Once he is gone, I pack a bag and leave the house. I have not yet managed to get out of my lease on my apartment, so I still have it available. Perhaps that was a blessing in disguise. When I arrive at the apartment, I call a courier service.

When the man arrives from the courier service, I hand him two envelopes. One is an invitation to dinner at the restaurant I have booked. The invitation will be delivered with a note from me asking him to meet me there at the specified date and time.

The other is a letter which I ask to be delivered to Bryce's address in the evening after he will have left for his dinner with me. My instructions are simply that it needs to be left in the mailbox and a text message is to be sent after it is delivered to Bryce.

To finalize my plan, I send a message to Viviane asking her to meet me at the restaurant I have given Bryce an invitation to. She tells me she will be there.

With everything arranged, I try to enjoy the time alone in my apartment. Bryce does not normally frequent this part of town, but I stay off the street as much as possible. Considering that life has shown me that all sorts of coincidences are possible, I'm not taking any chances.

I spend the days alone watching television to distract myself, but it doesn't help. If I am not calm, I am alternately angry or weeping uncontrollably. I am tempted to call Bryce and tell him that I have chosen to end our relationship, quit my job and head back to New York. I know doing so would all be decisions made in the wrong frame of mind and so I hold off on any of it.

In the next two days, Bryce calls to ask how my mother is. We talk a while and I try not to be off or distant. He has received the invitation and tries to ask me about it, but I won't tell him anything and he gives up trying to get more information. He promises he will be there though which is all that matters.

The day arrives and I feel worse than ever. I feel like a fraud, a liar, a cheat and so much more. And I feel that I am losing Bryce for sure.

I try to tell myself that I have to be comfortable with whatever happens. If he is drawn to Viviane again after all these years, I will have to accept it. I have arranged this and now I must live with the consequences. I had a chance to keep them apart, but I didn't take it.

Whatever happens now is out of my hands. I have booked a table on the sidewalk at a restaurant across the street where I will have dinner and watch them. Their table is at the window where I will have a clear picture of their whole time together.

I feel guilty knowing that I will be spying on them but I'm not going to take any chances with this. I want to know the truth. I don't want a lie or a watered-down truth that is supposed to let me down gently.

I know too that one meeting won't necessarily be enough for them to decide if they still have feelings for each other. For me, it is enough though. If they want a second meeting, I will walk away. It will mean they want to explore their relationship further, and that the possibility exists that they will get back together. I won't stand for it though. That will be my cue to leave. I am sick again before I head out to dinner and hope I can keep my dinner down for the rest of the evening.

Nora

I was worried about Lisa after our last night out. I hope she is feeling better. We don't usually get together during the week but I'm up for it anyway and I hope the evening will make up for the way our night out ended last time.

I'm dressed smarter than usual just as she told me in her message. The restaurant was going to be an upscale place after all. I expect that in some way it's a special occasion and I am bursting to find out what it is.

I arrive at the restaurant a little early and I tell the receptionist I have a reservation and give her the table number. She checks the reservation and then opens the drawer of her desk. She removes an envelope and hands it to me.

'This is for you. This way please.'

I take the envelope. I'm a little confused as to why there would be an envelope for me here.

'*Do not open this until you are going home,*' is printed on the front of the envelope. I flip it over and the words '*I mean it!*' are scribbled across the back where it is sealed.

I put it in my handbag as I follow the usher who takes over from the receptionist to show me to the table. I am seated at the table and marvel at the restaurant's décor. The lighting is not too bright. It is perfect for the romantic ambiance of the restaurant which makes me wonder why we would be meeting here.

A waitress arrives and hands me the menu and the drinks list. I order a martini and the waitress leaves. The furniture is made from dark wood. I think it's oak. The chairs match but are all old-style with cushions inset in the seats and the backs. They are heavy but very comfortable and high-backed.

I look out of the window. People pass by on the street outside, mostly oblivious to the people seated in the restaurant. They are lost in their world.

The waitress soon returns with my drink and I thank her. She leaves again and a short while later a man stops beside my table.

I look up. He looks vaguely familiar. He also looks surprised.

'I'm sorry, there must be some mistake . . .' he says and then he waves to the waitress.

'Yes, sir? May I help you?'

'I think there has been a mistake. I am meeting someone else here, but this lady is seated at my table.'

The waitress shakes her head and checks the reservation schedule. 'It seems to be correct, sir. I have you down for dinner with Viviane.'

The waitress looks at me and asks, 'Are you Viviane?'

I nod.

'And you are Bryce, sir?' the waitress asks, looking at the man again.

He nods and as he does so, the penny drops.

'Bryce?' I ask.

He looks at me uncertainly, not sure if he knows me. It is him. I can see it now. He is older but it is him. I stand up. 'It's me, Nora. Nora Viviane.'

He realizes who I am and then his face lights up. 'My God. It is you!'

As quick as his face lights up it becomes clouded by confusion. His reason prevails and he turns to the waitress and tells her everything is fine before he takes his seat opposite me.

He stares at me for a long moment. After our initial amazement at meeting each other we come to the realization at the same time, that this dinner has been scheduled on our behalf.

'Lisa,' we both say and then laugh nervously.

Bryce stops laughing first and asks how she could have known. He realizes the answer to his question as he recalls that Lisa mentioned that she had made a new friend called Viviane.

'God, I never realized. Lisa said she made a new friend called Viviane. When did you stop using Nora?'

'Pretty much after school. I hated the name. Everyone abused it. I like Viviane much better.'

Bryce holds up his hand. 'Wait a moment.'

He removes his cell phone and tries to call Lisa. She doesn't answer. He gives up and I try. No answer.

Bryce looks perplexed and frustrated. 'She arranged this. I have no idea how she found you or why she would even want us to be together.'

'You're a couple, aren't you?' I ask.

'We are. We've been together for a while now. She knows about you. She found out about you, and it caused no small amount of tension between us. I'm still not sure I'm in the clear because of it.'

'Tell me about how she found out about me,' I say.

Bryce begins to tell me about how they met and how she found out about me, when she found the notebooks with all the messages that he wrote to me. I understand then how she made the connection and I feel a chill as I realize that the odds are millions to one that the connection would ever be made.

'You kept a copy of every message you ever wrote to me in a notebook?'

Bryce nods. 'Every message. Dated and with the location recorded.'

'But . . . why?'

'I thought they were beautiful, for one. I guess I also believed that if I ever found you, I could share the messages with you. I doubted that you would find and track down every single message I ever left for you. If we ever found each other again, I wanted you to be able to read every message. They were so beautiful too, that even if I never saw you again, I wanted to have a record. When I was wondering what to do with the notebooks just before Lisa found them, I thought that publishing them might be an option. I could picture the book and the story about them becoming a bestseller and a movie. If anything, I was sure that would let you find me too and I guess in a way I maybe wasn't ready for that because I'm with Lisa now.'

When Bryce finishes, I nod and after a short silence between us, I tell my side of the story so he can understand how this has all come together.

'I never thought of looking behind pictures in hotels. After all, I was pretty much confined to one hotel. Then I got promoted and moved here to Chicago and when I moved, I found a picture of us. Somehow it kept falling out of my wallet until I remembered that you had promised to write to me by leaving messages on the back of pictures. I started checking the pictures in my accommodation provided by my company and had no luck. Occasionally if I was out and about, I would check but never had any luck. Then I went to a conference and for some reason, it became an obsession with me. I checked almost every picture in the hotel until the hospitality manager came to see me and asked me what I was doing.'

Bryce laughs. 'I bet that was embarrassing.'

'Actually no. I thought he would have me detained and that I would lose my job, but it turned out that he knew exactly what I was talking about. He led me straight to a picture you had left a message on. Then he took me across town to another hotel where he showed me another message. It had your cell number, but it was disconnected. The number he gave me didn't work either. It was a dead end. I was so near and yet so far. I thought that was it and the man, Harry Kestle thought we were crazy for not just looking each other up on LinkedIn.'

'Oh! I remember him. I got him promoted. He's a great guy.'

'Is that right? Well, he really is a great guy,' I agree. 'In the meantime, I had met Lisa and when I got back from the conference, I told her all about us . . .'

I stop speaking as I remember the night that I told her about Bryce. I realize she must have known then. I remember how bad she had looked when she had returned from the ladies' room, and I understand why.

She had realized that I was talking about Bryce, and she had already discovered the notebooks.

'What?' Bryce asks.

'This isn't good . . .' I say.

'What? Why? What do you mean?'

'Lisa must feel awful,' I say.

'But she arranged this,' Bryce says, confused at my sudden change in attitude.

'Don't be such a man, Bryce. Why would the woman you love, who loves you, be fine with us sitting and having dinner?'

Bryce shrugs. 'I don't know.'

'She's testing us, Bryce. Every moment we sit here talking we are driving the knife deeper and deeper. I can't do this to her. I'm sorry.'

I get up and grab my bag. As I turn to leave the envelope that the receptionist handed me falls out. I pick it up as Bryce calls after me. I do not turn around and head for the exit.

Nora

Outside I hail a cab and get in.

I open the letter in the back of the cab and begin reading. True enough, it's from Lisa.

Hi Viviane.

I'm sorry for the surprise this evening. I just had to let the two of you meet again and see if there is anything between you that can be rekindled.

I was amazed at how the universe drew the two of you together again through me. I don't know why these things happen, but they do happen for a reason. I can only wonder what the reason is, but I think I have an idea.

You know the saying, 'If you love something, set it free. If it comes back to you . . .'

I guess that's what I've done for both of you with your meeting tonight. I want you to understand that if you want to pursue a relationship with Bryce, the door is open for you. I will walk away because there is no point in me trying to have a relationship with someone who would rather be with someone else. It's just a recipe for disaster.

I know you might feel manipulated and angry because of what I did to bring you two together, but I think if you look at it, you'll realize that I did it for the best of all of us.

We'll talk soon again. Please understand that I have no hard feelings. Whatever happens, I wish you all the best.

Your friend,
Lisa.

I begin to cry as I read the letter. How can someone give up so easily I wonder? But I know she is right. It's one thing to fight for someone but if there's no love to keep them with you, the battle is lost from the beginning.

I try to call her again, but she doesn't answer. I look out the window as the cab carries me home over the rainswept streets. The tyres make a constant hiss as I look out the window at the passing neon lights blurred by the raindrops on the windows.

I wonder then if I should have left Bryce or spoken more. I left because I felt we were betraying Lisa and hurting her with every minute we spent together. Even if she arranged the dinner, was it the right thing to sit there and speak to each other knowing what our feelings were for each other before and knowing that she knew about us even though she was seeing Bryce?

I feel guilty and angry at the same time. I arrive at my apartment and drop onto the bed reading the letter again and again. I try calling her again but get no reply. I send her a message asking her to please call me.

As I lay on the bed in the dark, unable to sleep, I think of Bryce. He is still the same. He hasn't changed. He's only gotten older. I think that I could try to have a relationship with him again. Here we are, both living in Chicago with very little to come between us aside from the fact that he is in a relationship with such a good friend of mine. I can't betray her.

Besides, after all these years, as good as it was to see Bryce again, I have no idea how I feel about him. It is not enough to decide to betray my friend and try to have a relationship just because there might be a chance that we could get back together. Love can last through years and absence makes the heart grow fonder, but does it? I can't say. I have Bryce's number and I send him a message.

'Sorry, I left like that. It was silly. Where are you?'

It takes a while, but he answers me.

'At home. It's okay. I understand.'

I want to ask him if we should meet again. I feel guilty now for running out on him too. But to ask him if we can meet is probably the wrong thing to do. It might create the wrong impression and that's not what I want.

Bryce

After Nora runs out of the restaurant, I suffer through the stares of other patrons who think we argued. If they overheard anything they probably think I'm also having an affair.

I don't finish my dinner but get up instead and head to the reception where I settle the bill. I get a cab home and I open the letter on the way.

Dear Bryce,

I truly love you and I hope you will forgive me . . . or thank me, whichever way this goes.

You must understand that I truly love you but for some reason, I have been a conduit to bring the two of you together. There's a reason for that. I don't want to say much more because I don't want to influence your thinking.

You need to make your own choices. Either way, I will understand whatever you decide. I need to know what you decide before there will ever be peace in my heart.

I can understand and accept your explanation about the messages but when I realized that Viviane was the same person you left messages for, I had to act. I could have kept quiet and kept you apart, but I would have felt like an evil witch for the rest of my life. I would rather be honest and let life take its course wherever it may go.

Love,
Lisa.

Short and sweet. Mature. She was being an adult about it although I wasn't happy at feeling that I had been manipulated.

Nevertheless, I had to consider it from her viewpoint, and I knew she was right. She was a bigger person than I could have been if I had found myself in her shoes. I also wasn't happy with myself for the pain I had caused her. It had never been intentional but that was the way I would see it. Her viewpoint was obviously and understandably different.

I could respect that, and I knew I had a choice to make.

Mentally, I flipped a coin in my mind. Not to make a decision, but in my mind, one side of the coin was Lisa and the other was Nora.

I assessed and considered each side of the coin. Lisa first.

I love her. We are great together and things were damn near perfect until I created this speed bump. If I hadn't hung on to the notebooks so long, this would never have happened, and I would never have met Nora again. Well, maybe as a friend of Lisa, but that would have been a tale for another day, or not.

And now Nora. I tried to determine if she evoked feelings in me. We had not been together nearly long enough before she had left. It had been great to see her, and I felt like we had simply been picking up where we left off. But that might be how it felt. It would take time to determine how we feel and if what we had all those years ago is still there.

After all, people move on, life goes on. But if that was the case, why had I continued to write messages all these years?

If I had not entered the hospitality industry like my father, would I have gone to hotels and left messages for her? I didn't think so.

And that brought me to my next question. Had I done it because I had simply promised to do so and felt the need to fulfil that promise for some reason, knowing full well that not a single message might ever be discovered?

I recalled questioning myself more than once when I had scribbled the messages, asking myself why the hell I was doing it. I had believed she would never find the messages.

Then came the question about the quality of the messages. I had thought each one out carefully, written and rewritten it until I felt it was awesome. If I hadn't cared about it and her, would I have gone to the effort of making the messages so special?

Or was it just like the act of a child? Something I did for the sake of doing it, because I promised to do it?

I couldn't say. I dialled Lisa again and left a message for her telling her I would like to see her sooner rather than later to talk. I received no reply and finally, after a few more drinks I headed to bed wondering when and if I would see Lisa again.

Sleep was elusive but I eventually drifted off to sleep and woke up the next morning with a headache. I stumbled into the kitchen and the aroma of freshly brewed coffee and found Lisa seated at the breakfast table reading the newspaper.

'Thank God, you're home,' I said.

The look on her face tells me that I might not have much to be thankful for after all.

Bryce

I move closer and sit down opposite her. Her eyes follow me, but she says nothing. I reach out and take her hand. I cover hers with mine. She gives me no reaction.

'Why did you do that last night?' I ask softly.

She looks away out the window and then finally back to me.

'How is it that I found myself being the person between two fools who couldn't do things the normal way? Why couldn't you just have looked each other up after all this time the way normal people do?'

I shrug. I know it all seems foolish, but I never imagined it would come to this. It seemed like a romantic idea fifteen years ago, but when I question my dedication to leaving messages for a woman I haven't seen in fifteen years, I have no answer myself.

'If you cared about each other so much, why didn't you just look each other up? You've wasted fifteen years of your lives with nothing to show for it. At least as far as a relationship goes. You're both still single, or at least you were until I came along. She's still single. There's something so . . . so . . . fucked in all of this.'

'I'm sorry . . .' I begin to say. She pulls her hand away and shakes her head angrily.

'Sorry can't fix this. I gave you all of me, Bryce. All of me. I just never realized I was living with the ghost of someone else. You said you never wanted to do what your father did to you and your mother. Well, congratulations! You have done it. Maybe not the same thing but you've done it. Maybe you needed to keep her at a distance while you had that shitty job travelling nonstop. And now . . . now that you've finally got a job that allows you to settle, she comes into the picture. So you've never done that to her just as you promised her you would not. But you've hurt me.'

'Please Lisa. I never meant to . . .'

She holds her hands up signalling me to be silent. 'We never plan to do anything! It's always what someone says when they hurt someone. You knew what you were doing when you left that last message. Did you not feel guilty?'

I nod.

'You did? So why the fuck did you do it? Didn't you think about what those notebooks would do to me if I found them and discovered what they held? You've never, never done anything for me like that. That in itself says a lot. I mean I don't expect that from you. I don't expect that you would do the same for me as you did for someone else.'

I hold my hand up. 'Please! Give me a chance!'

She stops and lets me continue.

'I didn't do that because I thought it would be cheesy. Doing something for you that I did for someone else. You deserve better. I know you wouldn't have known any better if you'd never found the notebooks, but I would have known and it wasn't acceptable to me. It would have lowered the quality of what I give you.'

'And now? What have you given me?'

I take a deep breath and list several moments I have created especially for her.

'Just because they're not consistently the same doesn't mean they're not as special. Besides, it's not about what someone gives you or what you get. I know I love you. I never wanted to hurt you.'

Lisa looks at me. 'Maybe not. But you have.'

She looks out the window again and then back at me.

'I was there last night. I watched the two of you.'

'What?' I ask, shocked.

'From across the road,' she adds. 'You looked so happy together. Relaxed, enjoying meeting again after all these years. It looked to me like you just picked up where you left off.'

'Well, if you think it went so well, why did she leave?'

Lisa simply looks at me.

'Because she cares about you. Both of us do.'

'Why do you think I had to be the one that brought the two of you together? What are the odds that one person, me, would find you and Viviane, and realize that you two were looking for each other? The odds of that are millions to one. Don't you think the universe or God is trying to do something? Things like this don't happen for no reason.'

'Maybe they do,' I reply. 'Yes, the odds are millions to one but so what? It's still possible. This has proven it. Does it have to mean anything? Maybe. Maybe not. Isn't it up to us to decide that?'

Lisa looks at me for a long time as she considers what I have said.

'Look, I did what I did. I fucked up. I accept that. It's done a lot of damage. I see that, too. If you want, I'll go and burn those notebooks. All of them. Forget about the fact that I think they'll make a good book. Just get rid of them and you and I can start over.'

She says nothing but continues to gaze at me and then finally looks out the window again.

When she looks back, she seems calmer, and she shakes her head.

'No. Don't burn them. Don't get rid of them. I have to admit that what you wrote in them is beautiful and there may well be a book in them. It's not for me and that's fine. Don't destroy something because of me. That would be selfish of me to expect, and I won't let you do that. In fact, I will wish you all the best and I hope you can get it published.'

'Thank you,' I say. 'Where does that leave us?'

She looks down and studies her hands. When she finally looks up her eyes are filled with tears. She blinks and looks away out the window trying to get her emotions under control. I reach for her hand, but she pulls away and finally looks back at me.

She shakes her head. 'I'm sorry, Bryce. I can't . . . I can't go on. Let me go please. I'll pack my things today and I'll leave. I'll move back to my apartment and then back to New York eventually. I'll work my notice so you can find someone else but that's it.'

I feel as if she is ripping out my heart. I don't want her to leave. I don't want us to end but I was a fool, and these are the consequences. Sometimes you get a second chance and sometimes you don't. I still don't know why I couldn't give the notebooks up and why I wrote the last message to Nora when I travelled. I remember wondering what the point was, but I still did it. I'm sure it was habit more than anything else. After all this time I never believed I'd see Nora again.

But maybe there is something in that and the way it happened. I can't say for sure if there were any feelings when I met her the night before. I can only remember thinking about Lisa the whole time. Nora and I certainly never spoke about our romance and the possibility of rekindling it. With Lisa leaving I don't know if I could get back together with Nora.

'Don't do this, please,' I say.

'It's done already,' she replies. 'I can't go back. I'm sorry, Bryce.'

She pushes back from the table, gets up and walks away. The air stirs as she passes me, and I catch her scent. It's the last time I will catch her scent in my home. She packs her things while I remain in the kitchen feeling my life shattering into a million pieces.

When she finally leaves, I greet her at the door. We don't hug, we don't kiss. It's as if in doing so we would betray ourselves.

'There's no need to come to the office,' I say before she leaves. 'I'll see that you're paid in full okay. I think it will just be too painful, that's all. I will manage, okay?'

She nods. 'Okay then. Give Viviane my regards.'

'I don't know if I'll be seeing her again,' I say.

'I won't be in touch with her again. She's a nice person, Bryce. You should give yourselves a chance.'

I don't reply and she finally turns and leaves. I watch her walk down the drive to the waiting cab. I want to run after her and beg her to stay but I don't think it's the right thing to do. I don't think it would help either.

After she leaves, I sit alone in my study staring out the window. I start writing Nora a message many times and then delete it every time. I eventually decide she should at least know that Lisa won't contact her again.

'Lisa wishes you all the best. She doesn't hate you but she won't be in touch with you again,' I send.

Nora replies almost immediately. *'Ok. Are you together?'*

'No. She's gone. It's over.'

Nora

Bryce is still Bryce. He has just gotten older. We stay in touch for a while via text messages, neither wanting to suggest we meet. There were so many feelings involved in what happened that it seems for us to get together would be a slap in the face for Lisa and very disrespectful to the pain Bryce had caused her.

I know Bryce is in pain too and that he needs to sort his pain from the guilt he carries. He seems to have used his work as an escape mechanism from dealing with it all. When I contact him, he is always busy.

Lisa has been true to her word and not contacted me again, and I have honoured her wish not to be in touch with me. I feel guilty too although I never did anything wrong, but I can only imagine how Lisa must have felt when she made the connection between Bryce and me. I will never know for sure, but I am sure the night she went to the bathroom was when she realized.

I struggle to put Bryce out of my mind. In a way I feel as if we are both trying to honour the memory of Lisa and show respect by not getting together despite the fact that she will possibly never know if we do, and she left because she expected us to get together again.

On the other hand, I cannot stop thinking about Bryce. Despite the guilt, I know he is free now, and we should be free to explore what might have been and see if it could be anything. But I am not going to push Bryce to meet and in so doing push him away.

I decide to explore other options and reluctantly book to join the speed dating evening again. Who knows what it might bring?

I see some of the usual suspects at the speed dating event when I arrive. I wonder if they don't ever tire of not meeting someone. By now when it comes to my turn to meet them for a minute, we just converse socially or sit in silence knowing we've been here and done this before and there's no chance of getting together.

I don't see him enter just before the evening's session begins. As it happens, we are the last people we meet for the evening.

When I see him a few people away, my heart skips a beat. I close down any conversation with other people waiting for my turn to meet him again. I never imagined I would see him here.

He sees me as we get closer and smiles and nods at me. It seems to take forever before we are seated opposite each other.

'This is the last place I thought I would see you,' I say.

He smiles. 'I didn't imagine I would see you here either.'

'How are you?' I ask him.

'I'm good but I'd be much better off far away from here,' he replies.

'Do you want to leave?' I ask.

In answer he holds out his hand across the table to me. I take his hand and we stand together. He climbs over the table and everyone around us stops and stares as we start to leave.

I hear some people say, 'Hey . . .' in protest but we don't care. Participants are supposed to complete the evening and talk to all other participants before leaving. They can follow up with anyone they liked after the evening is finished.

But we don't care. It's another chance meeting that fate has brought us together. Why should we waste another moment after all the years we have wasted already?

Bryce holds my hand firmly as if to say he is not letting me go again. In fact, he is simply holding on firmly to make sure we get out together and reach a cab as soon as possible. There is no affection other than that. Not yet anyway.

We get a cab outside and Bryce gives the driver the name of a small coffee shop nearby, so we don't spend too long in the car.

We take a small table in the shop where we can see the passers-by out the window. We order coffee and something small to eat. After the waiter leaves, we are alone at last and study each other saying nothing for a few moments.

'If that's not a sign from the universe I don't know what is,' Bryce says at last.

I nod my agreement.

'Why speed dating?' I ask him eventually.

'Well, Lisa told me about it, and I always thought she was crazy. I thought I might try it at some point and tonight was that "some point" I guess. Turns out it was worth it. So far anyway,' he smiles. 'What about you?'

I shrug. 'After Lisa left and I left you at the restaurant, I haven't seen anyone else. I felt like we needed to honour Lisa's memory, I guess. I felt guilty for what happened and thought it would be wrong to get together with you. I felt like I would be a vulture picking over the remains of someone else's relationship.'

Bryce nodded his agreement. 'You're right. I struggled with what happened too. But seeing you tonight was just the thing that told me it's time to accept what happened and move on. I mean Lisa left because she believed we had to explore what was unfinished between us. We're not doing her a dishonour by not exploring if there is anything between us anymore. In fact, I think if she found us now and discovered we were still not together or had at least never explored a relationship, she'd be even more upset.'

'I think you're right,' I add. I move on and ask, 'Have you left any more messages anywhere?'

Bryce shakes his head. 'No. I stopped after Lisa left, and I didn't see you again. I realized that if I continued leaving messages, I might really be wasting my time. Did you keep looking?'

I nod. 'I did. Not because I thought you might still be writing but because I thought I might find some messages that Harry hadn't found yet. Of course, I could just have asked you, but we weren't in touch . . .'

'I suppose I would have had to be in touch with you sooner or later though regarding the messages,' Bryce says.

'Why?'

'Well, I think I mentioned that I wanted to submit them to a publisher to see if anyone might be interested to publish a book . . .' Bryce trailed off.

'And?' I ask, believing I already know the answer.

'I've had an offer from a publisher,' Bryce smiles. 'Of course, if it's successful there'll be a lot of people asking who the lucky woman is and who the romantic messages were written for. I didn't want you to be blindsided with a bunch of reporters descending on you out of the blue . . .'

'You're joking right?' I ask.

'I'm serious,' Bryce says, with no hint of a lie. 'I agonized over sending it out because I imagined that it might upset Lisa wherever she is, but we all have to move on.'

'I guess,' I nod, 'You do know there are a lot of men out there who are probably going to hate you?'

'Why?' Bryce asks.

'You haven't thought of it?' I ask incredulously.

'Thought of what?' he asks confused.

'I can't think of a woman who wouldn't think what you did wasn't romantic. How many men do something like that for the woman they love? There are other good men out there, but they are few and far between in my opinion. And then take what you did and compound it over fifteen years like bank interest and add to it that it was for a woman that you didn't know you would ever see again . . .'

Bryce considers my comments. He nods with some concern.

'Someone might set a hitman on you,' I joke.

He laughs. 'I may be really unpopular, but I don't think anyone's going to go that far. The way you say it makes it sound so romantic. Maybe you should become the publicist for the project.'

I laugh. 'No thanks. I think I'll pass given that there might be a lot of people that will hate you for this as much as romantics will love you.'

'I think I . . . no, *we* will be scorned by a lot of people. They'll tell us we were stupid just as Lisa told us. We could have found each other a long time ago by simply using social media.'

'Well, that is obviously the practical solution isn't it, but I think the bigger story is that, despite our foolishness, the universe still brought us together. That's where the true story is,' I say.

Bryce smiles. 'Are you sure you don't want to be the publicist for the project?'

I laugh again. 'No thanks. I just hope I won't be looking for a job when the news about the book breaks and the world finds out who you wrote it for.'

'Well, there is another question that will be raised when it's been published,' Bryce says.

'And that is?' I ask. I already know the answer, but I want to hear him say it.

'What happened to us?' Bryce says simply and leaves it there.

'What happened to us, indeed,' I reply.

'It's never too late to find out,' Bryce says, looking across the table at me intently.

Bryce

I never imagined I would find Nora at a speed dating evening.
I'm happy I did though.

We start dating and get to know each other again. It's
almost as if we pick up where we left off all those years ago.
It doesn't take long for us to feel comfortable with each other
again. We still feel Lisa's presence between us in the early
stages of getting to know each other again but we eventually
move past it.

My book is accepted by the publisher, and we start to
work out the marketing plan. I try to work around my existing
schedule and line up leave dates so that I can follow the
marketing plan for other cities by utilising leave due to me.

This looks like it's going to work out fine but sometimes
the universe, fate, whatever you want to call it, seems to be
fickle and changes its mind just like we do as humans.

Nora arrives home later than usual. She told me she would
be late as she had a conference call to attend so I have made
dinner and set the table, ready to eat when she arrives home.

I am putting the finishing touches to the dinner when
I hear her close the front door. She kicks off her shoes and
drops her bag in the entrance hall before following the scent

of the food to the kitchen where she finds me removing the dinner from the warming drawer.

She kisses me quickly and studies the dinner.

'Mmm, it smells delicious. I am starving and can't wait to eat.'

'What was the call about?' I ask but she's already left the kitchen to take a shower before dinner.

I finish setting the dinner on the table and wait for her. She returns a short while later, with towel-wrapped hair, wearing casual shorts and t-shirt. She looks fresh but tired as she sits down at the table.

I serve the food for us and after praying we begin to eat.

'How was your day?' Nora asks first.

'Just another day at the office,' I smile. 'Nothing new. How was your day?'

She nods and begins to eat. She avoids my gaze and I immediately feel there is something wrong, something she is not telling me.

'Is everything okay?' I ask as I rest my knife and fork on the sides of my plate.

She finishes chewing, swallows and looks at me. 'I've been offered a promotion.'

'That's great!' I say. I know she deserves it. She works hard and is good at what she does. She deserves it and I am proud of her and happy for her. She doesn't seem to share my happiness for her. She eats some more saying nothing, and I sense there is more she is not telling me. 'Why do you not seem so happy about this?'

'They want me to relocate,' she says, meeting my gaze.

I'm stunned.

I can't believe it and wonder why, having been brought together again after so long, and getting along as good as we ever did when we were teenagers, if not better, the universe suddenly seems to want to tear us apart.

My joy switches to selfishness immediately. 'And? You're not taking it are you? You told them no?'

She looks at me then shakes her head. 'I told them I will think about it.'

'What? Why?' I ask. The stress in my voice is clear and comes across as irritation, maybe even anger. 'You're not seriously considering it are you?'

My stress rubs off on her in the wrong way as is often the case between two people in situations like these.

'I can't just turn it down like that,' she replies indignantly. 'Besides it's a great opportunity.'

'Where do they want you to move to?' I ask.

'New York,' she replies.

'That's on the other side of the country,' I say, emphasizing the obvious.

'I don't need a lesson in geography,' Nora remarks coldly. She is not liking my tone and attitude.

'I'm sorry,' I say. 'I'm happy for you and proud of you. You work hard and you deserve it. It's just . . .'

'Just what?' she asks.

'I guess we never really considered that this might happen. I mean, I always wanted you to be promoted but if and when it happened, I guess I always imagined it would happen here, you know . . . You wouldn't have to move . . .'

'It's the first thing that crossed my mind too,' she sighs, still seeming irritated. 'Remember all those years ago? When you told me you never wanted to do to your family what your dad did to you? That was the first thing that crossed my mind when I was offered this promotion. I wondered if I am going to be the person to do it to us. I mean, I know we're not married yet but . . .'

My breath hitches and I try to regain my composure before responding.

'No, you don't have to be the person to do it to us,' I say.

'But that means I turn down the promotion and with that my career probably dies,' she responds.

'Not necessarily. If the company values you enough, they'll accept that you want to stay here and next time something better comes up here, maybe they'll offer it to you.'

'They might but something better might not suit me. What then?'

I bite the bullet and venture out on a limb. Since she's already brought it up, I say, 'Well . . . we can get married, and I can support you if you decide to leave the company to find something better.'

'I don't really want to leave the company,' Nora remarks as if she hasn't heard me mention marriage.

'Well, you don't have to leave the company. If you don't accept the promotion you stay in your position, right? Maybe later you'll want to move and maybe the time will be right for us to move.'

Nora shakes her head and sighs as she eats another spoonful of rice. I wait for her to finish.

'I could never ask you to give up your job and follow me,' she says. 'But maybe later you'll ask me to do it for you. That's why I feel like I have a dilemma. Is it fair?'

I shake my head. 'No. I guess not.'

'So, help me out here. What do I do?'

'I'm guessing you think it's a great position, otherwise you would not be thinking about it so hard,' I say.

'Absolutely,' Nora replies.

I don't think I could give you any advice that would not be biased. Obviously, I need to think of my position as well. I would suggest you turn it down, but that would be me being selfish. But . . . if we were married it would be a valid reason to turn it down.'

Nora's grip on her spoon suddenly falters.

'Is that a proposal,' Nora asks at last.

'As good as, I guess,' I smile teasingly.

'Well thank you,' Nora clears her throat. 'It doesn't mean though that I shouldn't consider the promotion because we're getting married.'

'Given, but we don't really want to live apart do we?'

Nora shakes her head.

I smile at her again before speaking more seriously. 'I learned from experience as a child. You know that. We moved around a lot. I don't want to do that again. Family is more important than a job or a promotion. My father did it all the time and he never got promoted every time either.'

Nora nods as she absorbs what I say. I know she is ambitious too, and I am not asking her to shelve her ambitions forever, but I do believe there will be something else for her in the future.

As it turns out, there is something else which neither of us expected.

Bryce

A publisher contacts me and tells me that they want to publish my book. They are offering a big advance and are also interested in making a film adaptation. With the publication of the book, they want to plan an extensive roadshow to promote it which will take much of my time. I initially try to work it into my work schedule by planning to utilize my leave days but I come up short on leave and I know the company will never accommodate the leave of absence that will be required. I have a decision to make.

The biggest decision is asking what will happen after the book and media attention dies down. I never saw myself as an author and I do not know if I will write any other books. I never planned for the messages to Nora to be a book in the first place. It was more of an afterthought.

While I lean towards giving up my job, I realize it will allow Nora to take her promotion and move to New York. I can make the move with her as I will be travelling a lot and if I give up my job I won't need to be based in Chicago. If I leave on good terms, I might well be able to return after the book tour and promotion. If it is very successful, I am sure I could find another role quiet easily.

I have not informed Nora yet of what has happened and as I ponder what to do myself while considering that Nora has a choice to make soon too, the publisher calls back with another surprise to add to the offer—a surprise that is both generous and a high-stakes decision.

Nora

Bryce tells me to meet him at one of our favourite coffee shops after work. I am stressed about the decision I need to make. I do not have much time left before my boss expects to have an answer from me.

He has been understanding in terms of me needing to work out logistics of a move and a relationship if I do accept the position, but business is business and at some point they need to move forward and appoint someone else if I do not take the role. Dragging my decision out is also not professional.

I am feeling tremendously stressed as I sit down opposite Bryce after work.

'How was your day?' he asks, smiling.

'Stressful,' I say, wishing I could be as happy as Bryce is just then.

'Well, I'm hoping I have something that can reduce the stress for you,' he smiles as he reaches into his jacket pocket and removes an envelope. He places it on the table and pushes it over to me.

There is nothing written on the envelope. I pick it up and turn it over. It's not sealed, and I lift the flap and remove the paper inside.

It's an e-mail addressed to Bryce. I read it quickly and realize that it's from a publisher informing him that his offer is attached. I scan through it quickly and notice that Bryce has highlighted some areas of the offer in colour.

I look at him. 'This is the offer from a publisher?'

He nods almost smiling from ear to ear.

'This is very generous,' I say. It's more than generous. It's a dream come true for Bryce.

'I thought so too. What do you think?' he asks.

'I haven't finished reading it,' I reply.

'Just read the highlighted parts,' he says.

I continue reading and stop on the third page. I reread the highlighted section and then lower the page to look at Bryce.

'Is this for real?' I ask.

'Is what for real?' Bryce asks, feigning ignorance.

'Them offering me money?' I say.

He smiles again and nods. 'As real as the sun shining outside,' he says.

'But it means that I have to quit my job . . .' I start and then trail off.

Bryce looks back at me and simply shrugs. 'I know. I've decided to quit mine as well so I'm not asking you to give anything up without giving something up myself.'

'You're going to quit your job?' I ask incredulously.

Bryce nods. 'I've thought it through. They are offering a lot of money. It won't last forever but we can save most of it and I am sure there will be more opportunities for us once the book tour is over. We will find jobs again or maybe we will have an idea of a business we want to start together. I am sure we will find something. While we promote the book, we will have a lot of time to be together, we'll see a lot of our country and maybe even the world before we have to get back to the nine to five grind if ever.'

I look at him. I see no hesitation. I am tempted and his positive attitude towards the offer is contagious.

Almost.

What could go wrong? I ask myself. I want to understand the risks if I do this. The biggest one is that we break up while we're on tour. Is it likely? I don't think so. But then we're not currently being subjected to the bright lights of the media. Would it make a difference? I can't say. It's not like we're going to become Hollywood stars overnight. I don't care about the media attention that much either. What is tempting is giving up the day job and travelling around the country and maybe even internationally experiencing and seeing places I might not otherwise see. If I had to do that with anyone, I have to admit it would be Bryce.

'You have doubts?' he asks.

'I'm trying to understand the risks,' I reply.

'Such as?'

'Well, the biggest one is if we were to break up,' I reply bluntly.

Bryce shakes his head. 'Do you see that happening?'

I shake my head. 'No, but I'm just trying to consider the possibilities. If it were to happen it would probably tank the book and our futures.'

Bryce thinks for a moment and nods. 'I guess you're right, but I think for someone who dropped marriage into the conversation the other night, that's not really going to happen.'

I blush as I remember what I did. I even surprised myself and I know Bryce has a point.

'Let's just be spontaneous,' Bryce says leaning forward and covering my hand with his. 'Right now, we're together but we're in the daily grind like everyone else. If we take this opportunity, we get to spend a lot of time together. Time that can make up for the fifteen years we foolishly let slip away . . .'

Bryce lets the thought hang in the air.

It takes just a moment for me to realize he's right. We are together but we spend our lives in a daily rut. And sure, we may need to return to that in a year or so, maybe sooner, but why shouldn't we take this opportunity presented to us? Why not make the most of this opportunity?

My mind is made up almost immediately. There is just one more thing that troubles me.

'You do know this will be painful for someone if it becomes a big success,' I say.

Bryce frowns, 'What do you mean? Who will it be painful for?'

'Lisa,' I say. 'If the book becomes a big success and we end up on national TV, I'm sure Lisa is bound to hear of us at some point. She'll know we got together, and it would be like rubbing it in her face. Is that what we want?'

Bryce shrugs. 'I don't know if it will be painful for her. She left to give us the chance to try again. She accepted that we might get together and effectively stepped out of the way so we could do just that. I haven't heard from her since she left. Have you?'

I shake my head. 'No. Not a word.'

'Well, there you go. If anything, I'd like to think she'd be happy for us.'

I sigh. 'I know. You're right. I just can't help feeling guilty.'

Bryce smiles. 'I'm no cold bastard. I feel guilt too, but life goes on. We have a second chance thanks to Lisa. If I know her, I think she'd be more disappointed if we don't do this together and if we ever break up.'

'What, so we can never go separate ways if we want?' I tease.

'Of course, we can,' Bryce laughs before enveloping me in his arms. 'I hope we don't though. We've come this far after all.'

Nora

Bryce dedicates the book to Lisa—to whom we owe being reintroduced.

She was right. We have been two fools who squandered away years of love stupidly and for some reason, we would never understand why she had been caught in the middle and had to decide whether to bring us together again or push us apart.

She did the right thing from our perspective and many other people would share that opinion. Many others would believe she had been a fool and should have made sure we never met again. Many would think she hadn't fought hard enough.

But if she had made sure we stayed apart, what would it have done to her? And, if there is such a thing as karma, would it have resulted in negative consequences for her?

We don't dwell on it.

We both quit our jobs and take to the road for Bryce's book tour. The response to Bryce's book is overwhelming and the number of interviews and appearances on live television and radio shows quickly escalates as word of the book spreads like fire across the nation.

As demand for interviews picks up, any thought of enjoying the countryside as a benefit of the book tour quickly fades as our schedule becomes tighter and tighter.

I don't just participate in interviews but now also accompany Bryce to book signings, as people have started to ask for my signature in the book as much as they do for Bryce's. I don't complain since I am happy to spend every waking moment with Bryce.

Bryce, too, is happy with every moment I spend with him and the people who visit the bookstores for book signings.

Before long we find ourselves writing a column for a newspaper about relationships. While we are no experts, we find that working on the column together lets us explore aspects of our own relationship which simply strengthens it.

All through the book tour, I cannot stop thinking of Lisa. I believe that there is no way that she has not heard of the book, and I am sure is following our progress across the country. I wonder how she feels and if she is happy for us. There have been many times I have called up her number on my screen and been very close to pressing the button to dial her, but I can't bring myself to do it. I feel that she will think that I am superficial and simply calling to make her jealous of the success and I would rather avoid that.

At one of Bryce's book signing events at a bookstore in New York, someone places a copy of the book they bought in front of him to sign.

He has been so busy signing that he does not look up immediately but simply asks, 'Who do I sign it for?'

A woman answers, 'The Lisa to whom this book is dedicated.'

Bryce looks up then and there she is. She stands before him smiling. She is with someone, and a ring sparkles on her finger.

'How are you?' Bryce asks. He stands, rounds the table and embraces her like an old friend.

'I'm great,' she smiles before she introduces her partner as her fiancée, Mark.

Bryce congratulates her and Mark and they shake hands, and I do the same when I arrive a little later after getting some coffee.

They make a wonderful couple and I congratulate them and thank her profusely for everything she has done.

She waves it away. It is in the past now and she is happier than ever. It is what we had always hoped would happen for her. She deserves it.

We get to catch up a little and she even shares that she's pregnant and we congratulate her and Mark again. We promise to keep in touch and look forward to our newfound friendship in these happier times.

The book tour ends, and we decide to settle in New York for a while. We can't say that things return to normal but we are closer than ever before and that in itself is a good thing.

We are still invited for public appearances, and we attend the events while we continue to write the column.

I never imagined that I would get to work with my partner but here I am doing just that. It's a dream come true.

We are not married yet and we do not really talk about it. We have returned to the level of comfort we had before the book tour, where just being together is enough for us—at least for me but, as I would find out later, it seems Bryce wanted to change that.

Even though we write the column for the newspaper, and we know exactly what we have written, I read the column in the newspaper every day. I am proud of it as well as the success it has had.

But this morning there is no column. There is just a question. I am sure that it must be a mistake since I know we worked on the column together. As I reread the question again, I realize that there must be something bigger at play here.

I lower the newspaper and look at Bryce. 'Since when do we let people use our column to advertise?' I ask.

Bryce frowns and asks, 'What do you mean?'

'Someone's published a marriage proposal in the newspaper where our column is supposed to be.'

'Really?' Bryce asks, holding out his hand for the paper.

I pass it to him and watch as he flips to the correct page. He finds it, opens the newspaper wide and nods. 'It's no ad,' he says.

'What is it then?' I ask.

'A question that begs for an answer,' he remarks.

'I'm not understanding you' I say.

'Well? Will you?' he asks seemingly oblivious to my remark.

'Will I what?' I ask as the meaning of the question dawns on me. I blush as I think of the thousands of readers who have seen the question. I feel embarrassed, to say the least.

It takes but a moment for me to hug Bryce. 'Yes, yes I will,' I exclaim as I am overtaken by joy. Bryce fishes a small jewellery box out of his pocket and opens it after I release him from my hug. Inside is a beautiful ring set with a diamond.

It's a simple design but perfect in my eyes. Bryce slides it on my finger, and I can hardly stop admiring it. It's almost Christmas and snowing outside. We stay indoors all day, and in the evening we make love and fall asleep in front of the fire. In the morning I wake feeling like a different person.

I cannot help but think of that moment all those years ago when Bryce promised to write before he rode away into the dark of the night. I doubted I would ever see or hear from him again and yet here we are, the two of us, engaged to be married.

In reality, we have simply grown older, but we are still the same and our love for one another is vintage like a good wine. It has only become better and stronger.

I never imagined there was any possibility of finding us again, but it happened, and we have started fifteen years later as if we have never been apart.

Acknowledgement

I started this message of gratitude intending to say thank you to the team at Penguin Random House for making the publication of *Finding Us Again* possible. Before I do so though, there is one who needs gratitude above all and I say thank you to my Lord and Saviour, Jesus Christ, for his unconditional love, forgiveness, compassion, and guidance in every day of my life. He is with me every day in every moment and without him, this book would never have been possible.

I would like to extend a big thank you to the team Penguin Random House SEA for believing in me and my book. I cannot begin to describe the feeling that an author has when they finally make the breakthrough to getting published with a publisher. It has been more than a decade of toiling away, writing, editing and self-publishing until now. I have learned many lessons along the way, some of them expensive, but good, nonetheless.

In particular, I would like to thank Amberdawn Manaois, Swadha Singh, Surina Jain and Adviata Vats for their excellent editing skills and guidance as well as their patience in working with me. Thank you also for the great cover for *Finding Us Again*. A good cover is imperative to support sales of any

337

book and I am sure that the cover of *Finding Us Again* will attract potential readers.

On a personal note, I would like to thank my family for always being there for me. It's been a long journey and it hasn't been easy but you have always been there, in whatever way you could, every step of the way.

I can never thank you enough and no words can ever communicate my love for each and every one of you. It's been too long since we have seen each other, and I pray to see you all again soon.

Thank you again and God Bless.